That Don't Hurt

James E. Evans' Wild Exploits in the 1950's Alaskan Territory

Carol Corrin Evans

TDH PRESS

THAT DON'T HURT

James E. Evans' Wild Exploits in the 1950's Alaskan Territory

Carol Corrin Evans

Paperback Edition ISBN:-13: 978-1-7357101-0-5

DEDICATION

To the Evans Family who knew and loved Jimmy as Dad & Grandpa:
Danny, Stacey, Craig, Michael, Cheryl, Melinda, Brian,
Caleb, Courtney, Sam, Jonathan, Ben and Kendra.
Know that he loved you dearly as I do also.

CONTENTS

PREFACE

The story I'm about to relate is a memoir as told to me by my husband, James Edwin Evans. So often over our years together, Jimmy would recall a tantalizing piece of his childhood and early adulthood that would be difficult to get into context, sometimes funny and sometimes shocking. But never the whole story. In our later years, I decided to unravel the strange doings of Jimmy's "before Carol" past. Thus began the two-year interview. The quest became a delightful mission as it cleared the mists of his half-told stories. The best experience was Jimmy's obvious joy at hearing segments of his own antics read back to him night after night. Of course, I have changed names to protect personal privacy, but most of the locations are accurate. Travel with me through Jimmy's wild exploits as he remembered them, and as I fleshed them out as a narrator.

1
TO ANCHORAGE

Jimmy was hungry as hell. Propping his work boots against his boardinghouse bunk rail, he cinched them up while the pungent aroma of frying bacon urged him on. July had brought long hours of daylight, and the seventeen year old was up early bursting with energy and rarin' to go. Fairbanks, Alaska! Man alive! It was in his blood.

A year earlier, in 1950, he had discovered the wild west territory where he could pit his curious mind and lanky, strong body against the elements. And he'd embraced it all: The challenge, the adventure, the freedom. Having lived on his own since age fourteen, he'd long since learned the rewards of hard physical labor and considered himself a grown man. In Fairbanks he'd found a wild place, a place where he could escape his intense grief.

***

It had been only a year since Jimmy had migrated north from Fresno, California to Fairbanks, Alaska with his parents and three younger siblings. Setting aside his need to distance himself from his family, Jimmy, then sixteen, had agreed to help them relocate. The trip was a three thousand mile marathon. Considering the sojourn an adventure would barely describe the hardships that met the travelers after they reached Dawson Creek, British

Columbia, the halfway point in their trek. That is where they joined the notoriously rugged Alcan Highway and travel became much more challenging.

With their belongings strapped on their van's roof rack and a small utility trailer attached, they took on the next fifteen hundred Alcan Highway miles. Jimmy's stepdad, Dan, had prepared for the rigors of the crude gravel road by stocking up with tools, spare tires, gas cans, food and a tent. They made their way through long desolate stretches of distressed roadway, camping along the road, digging out of daunting mud bogs, scaling steep inclines, managing ungraded curves, grinding along at a top speed of forty miles an hour. The entire trip had taken nearly a month.

Finally arriving in Fairbanks in mid-June of 1950, Jimmy had helped his family get a start on their homestead five miles outside of Fairbanks. Once the family had raised a makeshift dwelling consisting of a wood frame enclosed by a canvas tent, a wood stove and an outhouse, the family's resources had been exhausted. In the boomtown that Fairbanks had become in the 1950's, Dan had been able to find a job right away with his automotive skills.

Just two weeks after arriving in Fairbanks, Jimmy was off to town to find a job for himself. While he'd gone along with his parents' wild idea of moving to "hell and gone" Alaska, he was anxious to finally get on with exploring the place and making his own life again. Jimmy had always been able to find a job or two. As he looked for work, though, he realized that the good paying jobs were hired on through the union halls where he would need ID to show that he was eighteen. After picking up odd jobs, the then sixteen year old, shortly figured out a plan. The Korean War was raging, and the Army recruiters weren't particular about verifying a birth certificate. Registering for the draft had seemed a simple solution.

Once he had his fake ID, Jimmy landed a job that both fascinated him and paid well for unskilled work. As a grunt on a gold dredge, he learned fast and became a right-hand man to the engineers who kept the huge steam-driven barge running. Repairs were constant on the dredge as it dug its way through the swampy muskeg soil, floating on its own man-made pond. During his twelve hour shifts he was hauling tools and often a heavy welder around the craft for the mechanics and engineers. Not only was he eager to learn the workings of the gold extraction process, Jimmy had found good living conditions. Operating some distance from town, the mining company had built a bunkhouse where they served three hearty meals a day. He had loved the job, had looked with wonder at the northern lights, had helped shovel the gold into canvas bags when it was harvested from the sluice box. All of it had intrigued him. When winter arrived, the pond had frozen and the operation shut down.

Jimmy was back living in Fairbanks for the winter of 1950 and looking for another job. He had earned enough money to stay in a boardinghouse right in town. He liked boardinghouse living with freedom to come and go, a good breakfast, his laundry done at a small cost, and accommodating landlords who lived on-site in a small apartment on the main floor. He was good with the shared dorm space in the loft where he had his assigned bunk and a locker to keep his belongings safe. He was not so pleased when the draft notices began to arrive but dispensed with them into the trash.

He'd been surprised to see paved streets and sidewalks when he'd first arrived with his family. Once he was living downtown he was intrigued to witness the wild lawless atmosphere with surging groups of men who seemed to have no rules. There were drunken brawls in bars and on the streets, whorehouses located right off of one of the main streets, little cafes and restaurants, local people shopping for groceries and supplies, GIs from multiple military facilities, tradesmen, construction workers, and serious gamblers. It was a tumultuous mix that surged day and night. Always an uproar. So many interesting people from all over the country. Jimmy loved it.

During the frigid, dark winter Jimmy was often hired for the day as a grunt for City Electric. He showed up nearly every day at the Electrical Union Hall to get his name on the roster and had learned what real cold felt like as he worked outside assisting the linemen repairing downed power lines. It hadn't taken him long to invest in a heavy parka and multiple layers of warm clothing as winter closed in and he realized that repair crews worked unless temperatures dipped below minus twenty degrees.

While his family had moved into town for the winter, he usually avoided visits. Periodically he'd drop by to bring some money and see his younger brother and two younger sisters. Each visit left him angry and agitated. He couldn't put aside his anger toward Mama for long.

***

Now, on a promising July morning in 1951, with a year of Alaska-living under his belt, Jimmy was getting an early start to meet his friend Steve at the union hall. July had brought daylight that lasted around the clock and warm weather that called him to do some exploring. He thought he might even look for a car to buy after work. Showered and ready for his day, his stomach growled at the thought of bacon and eggs, biscuits and sausage gravy as he laced up his work boots realizing he was hungry as hell. Up in the loft of the boarding house, he hung his wet towel on the corner of his bunk and bounded down the stairs into the kitchen.

He grabbed a spot on one of the long wooden benches on each side of a rough cabin-style table that could accommodate ten of the usual dozen boarders. Some of the guys were still asleep in the loft likely hungover, while others visited over breakfast and lit up cigarettes as they lingered over morning coffee. Fairbanks was bursting at the seams with itinerant workers who came and went on their own schedules. Breakfast was the only meal served at his boarding house, but it was a hardy meal for working men.

Jimmy filled his plate with bacon, sausage and scrambled eggs from the serving platters in the middle of the table and saw that Mrs. Turner, his landlady, was bringing over warm biscuits and hot gravy that she had been stirring on the butane kitchen stove. He gave her a grateful smile.

Mrs. Turner and her husband ran a tight ship managing the rough workers, but Jimmy knew that she kept an eye out for him. He dug into his breakfast enjoying every bite as he listen to the other guys spinning yarns, swearing and jousting all in good humor.

"Hey! Are you James Edwin Evans?" a gruff voice barked.

"Yeah," he answered, glancing up to take in the bulk of a uniformed marshal framed in the kitchen doorway. "What do you want?" he snapped.

"Listen buddy, you've been drafted. These papers say you didn't report, but you're going with me right now. Get your stuff.'"

"The hell you say!" Jimmy bristled. "I aint fightin nobody's goddamn war. Look, I'm workin a good job here at City Electric. Don't mess me up. Can't you bastards just let me alone?"

"Sorry, son. Let's go. I'm putting you on the next flight to Anchorage."

Jimmy clenched his teeth as anger ignited in his gut. *No use giving this bozo any crap,* he thought as he jammed his few belongings into his duffel bag. *The hell with it! I'm sick of throwing out the damn draft notices, anyway. I'll go face them assholes myself and tell them to screw off.*

The little two-engine plane bucked and shuddered as it made its way over the Alaska Range. Slouched in his seat, Jimmy peered out the window as towering Mt. McKinley materialized above the clouds, but he was far too churned up to enjoy the view or his first plane ride for that matter. *The goddam military ain't gettin my ass.* He knew that one thing for sure.

He had no trouble spotting the military transport bus waiting beside the terminal as he left the plane. There was no need to ask its destination. He fell into line with the other young guys who had been on his flight and slid into an empty seat, dropping his duffel bag on the seat beside him. As the motor revved and the gears ground, a hush fell over the assembled greenhorns who had been noisily getting acquainted. *Chumps!* Jimmy thought, turning to stare out the window as the bus ground away the few miles to Fort Richardson Army Base.

Anger and resentment filled Jimmy's belly as he threw his duffel on a bunk in barracks and sat rigidly on the bunk. When the other recruits were herded off to the mess hall by a sergeant, he chose to bide his time until the induction session began at sixteen hundred. *Military time. What bullshit!* Jimmy thought. The hours passed at a crawl as new waves of draftees periodically flooded into the barracks. When the call came to assemble, Jimmy didn't budge.

"Hey recruit," the sergeant shouted from the doorway. "Get your ass down to the induction session, now."

When Jimmy sauntered into the auditorium, he took a seat in the far back just as the captain began to address the group.

"Greetings gentlemen. I'm Captain Eagleton. I'm in charge of this induction facility. I want to welcome you into the United States Army."

As Jimmy sized up the officer with a skeptical and wary eye, he noted a man of average height, yet one projecting a commanding presence. The captain seemed to be somewhere in his fifties, stood rock solid straight, his eyes forward, his steel gray hair cropped short, his bushy eyebrows drawn together in a serious frown.

"Many brave men have come forward to defend their country in this time of war," he intoned. "We will train you to be top-notch soldiers. Our first order of business this afternoon will be to enlist each of you. When your name is called come forward to sign your papers. Sergeant Weaver and Sergeant Miller are up here to help you out."

With some two hundred men to process, it took a while before Jimmy heard his name called by one of the two clerks seated at the front table.

"You James Edwin Evans?" the sergeant asked, indicating he should sit in the metal chair across the table.

Jimmy remained standing. "That's right. I'm Evans and I'm sure as hell not signin up."

For a moment the soldier looked dumbfounded. "Hey, buddy. You don't have a choice. You've been drafted."

"Well, you got it wrong. I'm not signin. No way I'm going to any goddamn Korea!" Making a quick turn, he walked out.

Sitting on his bunk, Jimmy thought about the day he'd signed up for the draft. Now he was still only seventeen. But had needed the ID. He tried to look cool and unconcerned as the new recruits filtered back into the barracks. Some of them were already horsing around like they knew each other, bragging and joking. He didn't bother with getting acquainted. He wasn't planning to be there long. *You suckers are doomed,* he thought. *Just go ahead and follow along like dumb sheep with your heads up your asses.*

"You Evans?" asked Sergeant Weaver.

"Yeah," Jimmy answered, fixing him with a defiant stare.

"Let's go! Captain Eagleton's waiting."

The sergeant, a balding wiry guy, set a brisk pace toward a compact building a few yards away. Indicating that Jimmy should wait in a small outer office, he disappeared though an inner door after a quick knock.

Momentarily alone in the sparse room, Jimmy stood rigid, fists clenched as he prepared himself, stirring the coals of his righteous anger.

"Evans!" the sergeant barked from the doorway, jerking his head toward the inner office.

Jimmy sprang forward driven by pent-up tension nearly mowing down the sergeant orderly. Captain Eagleton, sitting ramrod straight in his black leather chair, eyed him from behind a massive walnut desk. Stopping short, Jimmy rocked back on his heels, crossed his arms and returned the stare.

The faceoff lasted nearly a minute before the captain cleared his throat and spoke in an authoritative voice. "Sergeant Weaver here reports that you refused to sign your enlistment papers."

"Yup. Sure as hell."

"Now it's my duty to inform you that you are obligated by law to serve your country. You've been drafted."

"You assholes can beat your gums all day, but I aint signin up."

"Is that so!" said the captain stone-faced despite the flush of red spreading up his neck. "Dismissed," he barked, turning to his orderly.

"Listen you little prick," the captain boomed once the door had closed. "You better get your ass over there and sign those papers if you know what's good for you. I can bring you up on charges of wartime desertion from the United States Army. Think you're tough? Try spending your next twenty years in Leavenworth Penitentiary. And in the future, you'll address me as 'Sir'."

"That all you got?" Jimmy snorted, trying to hide the tremble in his voice. "You're a bloody murderer," he yelled. "Why the hell would I call you 'sir' sitting there behind your fancy goddamned desk like a fucking god while you send guys like my brother off to be slaughtered. He took a bullet in the head for your bullshit. Aint that enough for you? Now you think you're going to send me off to bloody Korea to die, too? No! I aint singin my own death warrant."

Captain Eagleton stared at him as the flush engulfed his face and the cords in his neck became rigid. He stabbed at the intercom switch, "Sergeant Weaver! In here!"

"Yes Sir?"

"Get him out of here," the captain hissed, his voice suddenly muted.

Jimmy made for the door in angry strides and was outside the building before the sergeant caught up.

"Christ, kid. What'd you say to the old man? You don't want this kind of trouble."

"Trouble? Shit! You fuckers already killed my brother." Jimmy was having trouble controlling the shake in his voice and the tight lock he'd kept on his rage was slipping. "Leave me the hell alone!" he shouted.

Sergeant Weaver, who had adopted an undignified lope to keep up with Jimmy's long, furious strides, turned back with a shrug. "Dumb kid," he muttered.

After that, Jimmy was indeed left alone. Over the next few days he fell into a routine as he waited out long hours of anticipated confrontation and endless troubled nights. When he got hungry, he went to the mess hall, but he often forgot to eat. He passed the time lying on his bunk or wandering around the base. Free to walk out the front gate, he chose not to. There was activity all around him with new recruits coming and going in waves, but he rebuffed any contact. He sorely missed the hard work and the companionship of his coworkers on the line crew. That's where he belonged.

Reporting for his physical brought a short break in his edgy, monotonous routine. Grizzled old Doc Forrest checked him out and nodded, "Well, son, you're in good shape. At one sixty you're a little underweight for a six-footer, but you're strong as an ox. I hear you're holding out."

"I don't give a goddamn. They aint using me for a target. And I sure as hell don't want to kill no one."

"Yeah. You know, the military can make it real tough on you. Someone's got to defend the country."

"You see somebody invadin us?"

"No, son. I don't," Doc said, giving him a kindly pat on the shoulder.

***

"Put it down!" Everett yelled.

"It keeps squealin," Billy complained.

"See, I told you we'd find them," Jimmy gloated holding up a little piglet. "Jeez, but he's a noisy little sucker."

"Holy cow! You hear that?" Everett shouted; his eyes wide with alarm as he peered into the dark shadows cast by the tall pine trees.

The three brothers froze, their blood running cold as the crashing sounds coming from the brush ahead grew louder.

"Run!" Everett yelled. "The razorback's coming. She'll tear us up."

Dropping his piglet, Jimmy sprinted back toward the path, overtaking Billy who hugged his squealing hostage to his chest. "Drop it, drop it," he yelled, finally stripping the piglet from his little brother's grasp. Frantically, he glanced around for a tree with branches low enough to climb. Nothing. He could hear the plunging, snorting pursuer rapidly closing, but he dared not look back. He hoped desperately that the piglets would divert the enraged razorback.

"Hurry! Run!" Everett urged. He was jumping up and down beside a sturdy split rail fence fifty feet ahead. "Come on!"

Gripping four-year-old Billy's hand, Jimmy dragged him along with a strength fueled by terror. He hit the top rail in one leap while Everett boosted Billy and then scrambled up. Clinging to the rough rail and each other, the brothers gasped for breath. Seconds later the narrow-bodied mass of muscle attacked the post they were perched atop. She rooted and sliced at it with her razor-sharp tusks. With frenzied guttural screams, she fixed her beady black eyes on the boys and leaped at them, finally succeeding in planting her front legs on the lower rail which bought her snout within inches of their drawn-up feet.

Jimmy stared with horrified fascination at the menacing razorback frothing at the mouth as she whipped her head back and forth as if slicing him to bits with her stained tusks. The beast gave off a stench like rotten onions and her god-awful screams chilled him to the bone.

The boys were nearly paralyzed by the time the wild pig retreated to round up her brood. What must have been ten minutes of terror had seemed like hours.

Jimmy listened closely for the sound of her return, wanting to make sure she wasn't going to circle back. He found it hard to hear over the pounding of his own heart.

"I told you not to touch them pigs," Everett said, glaring at Jimmy as he put a tentative foot on the ground.

"Shit your britches, did you?" Jimmy retorted with false bravado.

"No. But I thought she had you for sure," Everett said, reaching up to help Billy down. "Come on Billy. Don't cry. You're okay now."

As they hurried down the path toward home, the older boys, aged nine and seven, made furtive glances over their shoulders. Newly arrived in the Louisiana bayou, the fearless adventurers were a bit daunted for the moment but not eager to admit it.

"Hey, Everett. Never saw you run so fast," Jimmy teased, then exploded into laughter born of giddy relief.

"Jeez, I saw that sucker gainin on you and you looked like you was stuck in quicksand," Everett choked out, catching the contagious hilarity.

"Did you smell it? What a stink!" Jimmy croaked, once again busting up.

"I didn't like it," Billy whined.

"But you ran like hell," Everett soothed.

"Yeah. I ran like hell."

"Let's go catch us some crawdads, Billy," Everett said, throwing a worried look at Jimmy.

With any luck, Billy wouldn't tell Mama. There would be hell to pay.

Jimmy woke up in a sweat. *Shit!* he thought as he felt his chest constricted in a tight knot. He lay there listening to the night sounds in the barracks knowing it would be another long night. *Goddamn them assholes.* Now he was dreaming about Everett again.

***

It was just past noon when Jimmy, watching from a mess hall window, saw Sergeant Weaver leave his office. *You're right on schedule, Sergeant Weasel. Now look at you. Deserting your post*, he thought with a wry grin. Walking purposefully, he crossed over to the administration building and let himself into the outer office. With a glance at the sergeant's abandoned desk, he burst right through the inner door without pausing to knock. The captain wasn't in. *Well, damn, Captain Eagleshit, SIR. I'll just wait for you.*

Scanning the room, he eyed the plush leather chair then flopped into it, testing how it swiveled and rolled and leaned back at a comfortable angle. *Yes, SIR, this here's one goddamn sweet place to set your ass while you order innocent young men to their death.* Turning his attention to the desk, he discovered a round container that held a selection of cigars. He rifled through the humidor grandly sniffing the pleasant aromas before choosing two cigars and placing them prominently in the pocket of his work shirt. Crossing his arms, he leaned back to anticipate the Captain's return. *No way you're gonna make me sign up, asshole,* he reassured himself while his stomach clenched. As the time stretched out, he distracted himself noticing the beautiful grain of the walnut desk, the soft finish emphasizing the richness of the wood. Leaning further back, he propped his feet on the desktop, his boots leaving gratifying black scuffs on the pristine surface.

The sergeant returned first. Jimmy, waiting quietly, listened to the orderly at work in the outer office. Shortly thereafter Captain Eagleton let himself into his office by the back entrance.

"What the hell!"

"Hey, Captain," Jimmy said, ginning up his courage as his heart raced. "I been waitin for you. Just want to know when I'm gettin out of here."

"Get your ass out of my chair," he bellowed, his face contorted in rage, his sharp brown eyes bulging.

"Sure, sure," Jimmy blustered, settling back with a slow wave of dismissal. "Soon as you tell me when I'm gettin my ticket home."

"You're playing with fire, son," Captain Eagleton sputtered. "Your ticket's going to be for a trip to Leavenworth. Sergeant!"

With lightning speed Jimmy jolted to his feet, braced his hands on the desk and leaned into the face of the startled officer. "You asshole! You've got hundreds of suckers here buyin your snake oil. You been pumping them up with this 'bravery' and 'duty' bullshit so you can send them to die in some godforsaken Korea. What the hell for? My brother didn't deserve to die there. You're not sendin me."

"Sir?" The flustered orderly stood in the doorway.

"Get him out of here, sergeant," the captain said, his voice faltering as he sank into his leather chair.

"Yes, Sir!" the sergeant said, reaching out to grab Jimmy's arm but missing as Jimmy slipped out the door flinging away the pilfered cigars.

"Evans!" he called, scuttling after Jimmy. "You're damn lucky he didn't have you thrown in the brig."

"Listen, Sergeant Weasel, I'm a civilian and I'm never gonna to be under his control or yours neither."

"You're drafted, boy. Make it easy on yourself. No use pissing everyone off. Sign up. Take it like a man."

"Never."

Despite his bravado, Jimmy worried he'd be hauled off any minute to the brig on some kind of charges. He had surely succeeded in getting under the captain's skin, the old hypocrite. He himself was so stirred up that he paced for hours, unable to sit down much less sleep.

As days passed, Jimmy fell into a routine. Mostly, he stayed to himself in the barracks while the steady stream of recruits horsed around, played cards and got acquainted before they rotated out for basic training. About once a week, he got fed up and pulled another ambush on the captain. The required stealth offered an enticing challenge and the officer's outrage was his payoff. His pain-in-the-ass approach was his only strategy. While the days dragged on, the nights were brutal as Jimmy's dreams became relentless. At times he couldn't tell for sure if he lay awake all night remembering or if he was, in fact, dreaming. The tight lid he had kept on his memories had ruptured letting the old memories of his big brother resurface.

***

"Stay behind me," Everett warned.

"There's four of them," Jimmy said as the cocky leader halted his gang a few feet away. Since they had moved to Michigan, they'd had to fight every day after school.

"That's okay. I'm tired a them messin with us. I'm gonna clean that guy's clock," Everett muttered.

At nine, Everett was a big-framed, sturdy kid who was used to hard work and the rough and tumble of fisticuffs. While he had become the protector of his younger brothers, the three had also mixed it up pretty good among themselves. In bearing responsibility for them, he was also the one who meted out punishments, cuffing them into compliance when his brothers got too far out of line.

"Hey, Okie trash," taunted Cliff, a snarling sixth grade bully.
"Leave us alone," Everett growled through clenched teeth.
"You hicks can't even talk right. We're going to send you stupid Okies back to where you came from," Cliff goaded. "Let's get em boys."

Everett was tall for his age and strong, while seven-year-old Jimmy was puny but lithe and feisty. Back-to-back they fought together, giving as good as they got for a while. Everett made sure to nail Cliff, who got a lot madder once his nose was bleeding. The brothers held out as long as they could, but finally made a run for it.

"You dumb ass," Cliff yelled, not opting to take up the chase. "We'll get you and your idiot brother tomorrow."
"How come they're pickin on us?" Jimmy asked. Fleet of foot, he had gotten ahead of his brother.
"Wait up," Everett panted. "Them guys are jerks just pickin on us cause we're new."
"Well I aint goin back to school," Jimmy said, kicking a rock.
"I'm tired of bein beat up, too. But I got a idea," Everett said, ever optimistic, resourceful and fearless.
Jimmy knew he could count on his big brother as they hatched their plan.
"Do you see them coming?" Everett whispered in their hiding spot the next day after school.
"Yeah. They're runnin all around lookin for us."
"Good. Don't let them see you. Tell me when they get just past us."
"Now!" Jimmy hissed, clutching his first chunk of brick.
Together they rose from behind the brick pile with a war whoop, each nailing

one of the bullies right between their shoulder blades. They fired volley after volley, connecting each time as the would-be assailants scattered, howling in pain.

"Don't you never bother us again, you hear!" Everett yelled at Cliff who was in full retreat even as Everett bombarded him with one last missile.

That had been the end of the after-school beatings. The fact that Mama would never know about their little problem went unspoken. Jimmy could trust Everett. He would never tell. Nor would he let on or tease about Jimmy's shameful secret, his failure to learn to read.

Jimmy startled awake in a cold sweat, the tight vice in his chest making his breathing ragged as he lay in the dark on the raw cusp of a dream-memory. His face contorted in a grimace. Everett had been so strong and smart, the one sure thing in his life. *No, not Everett!* He grieved. *He didn't deserve bein killed. He died before he could even live. Damn them all to hell. They filled his head with lies. Suckered him in, 'serve your country, get a education.' Bullshit! And Mama! She signed on for him to enlist. Threw him away.*

***

Everything had changed for the Evans children in 1941 when their mother, Hazel, had taken her six kids and run off with Dan, a soldier twenty years her junior. She had met Dan working as a cook at the military base near their family farm. The three grouped brothers: Everett, Jimmy and Billy had been eight, six and four.

In their new itinerant journey, following Dan to each of his new assignments, the Evans boys had at the very least learned to be resourceful. When they found themselves in Michigan that winter of 1942, the three young brothers had already lived through a tough period, especially Everett and Jimmy. They had lived and worked all their young lives alongside their parents, older brother and older sister on various farms in Arizona, Oklahoma and Texas. They did indeed have a southern drawl.

Jimmy's father, as he remembered him, was a hard man. He could recall times when the farmer and sometime preacher had beaten the children. He also recalled a unforgettable time when his father had threatened to hang himself in the barn. The family story had it that Jimmy, seeing his father make the threat with a knotted rope in hand, advised him, "But that aint how you tie a hangman's noose." As the family endured hardships later, Jimmy was left with a bitter resentment toward his absent father, blaming him for the split in his family.

While Dan had proved to be a kindly soul, the boys had been cut off from their father, their large extended family and the life they knew. In the past they had often been poor while living on the different farms, but they had become truly impoverished as the family followed Dan to successive military training bases in Texas, Louisiana, and Michigan. During all those moves, Dan had been unable to arrange military pay allotments for his new family. There were times in that period when they had lived in the car surviving on bread and peanut butter. While their mother had found work as a cook with each move, the kids had hustled for odd jobs just to eat and help keep a roof over their heads.

During the months in Louisiana, nine-year-old Everett had found work in a nursery shoveling manure and tending plants while Jimmy, at six, had walked a mile every morning to the army base to sell newspapers to the soldiers. In the evening the brothers, toting their kits, had stood outside the local bar earning nickels for shining shoes. Jimmy had vivid memories of walking home in the dark along a deserted railroad spur, shoulder-to-shoulder with Everett, the sharp whining howl of coyotes prickling their nerves while neither owned up to being scared as they hurried along.

Once Dan had finished training as a tank driver, he had shipped out to the front lines to fight the Germans while he was still trying to get his pay allotments arranged. His new family, kids from the South, who wore ill-fitting second-hand shoes, didn't own socks or underwear, was left to face winter in the alien land of Michigan depending on their mother's meager income.

Jimmy had troubles of his own. His first year of school had been interrupted over and over again. Now, he was way behind the other second graders. Mortified when his teachers realized over the months that he couldn't read, he became resentful and disruptive. His shame was so painful that he quit trying to learn. The kid who could hustle newspapers and make correct change at six was moved to the retarded class where he learned basket weaving at seven. Jimmy told himself that he had won, outsmarted his teachers, and quite enjoyed basket weaving. But the hurt and humiliating failure festered even as he became adept at hiding his handicap.

***

"Hey you, Evans! I hear you're too chickenshit to sign up," a new recruit challenged from the next bunk, drawing the attention of all the guys nearby.

"Want to make something of it, Bonehead?" Jimmy asked, leaping to his feet to face the compact-built agitator.

"Well, you'd think a guy would be willing to serve his country," he retorted in a less aggressive tone once he'd seen Jimmy's lean and mean fighting stance.

"Listen asshole, you go right ahead and sign up for a bullet in the head. I'm not that stupid. Get the hell off my ass before you prove just how damn dumb you are," Jimmy warned, his body poised to strike.

"Well, I'm doing the right thing," the gung-ho soldier mumbled as he turned away.

Jimmy let him walk away, but after weeks of biding his time, his nerves were raw and his spirit flagging. He had continued to provoke the captain on a weekly basis without bringing the issue to a head.

After the barracks confrontation, the other guys eyed him suspiciously. He figured that the captain might be counting on that kind of pressure.

Lying on his bunk that afternoon, Jimmy simmered as he watched Bonehead iron his uniforms, creasing the trousers just so and folding his shirts to perfection before packing them with meticulous care in his duffel bag. When the dinner call emptied the barracks, Jimmy lingered just long enough to plug in Bonehead's iron and shove it deep inside the grip. Off by himself in the mess hall, shaking in his boots, he warily picked at his meal until the fire alarms started clanging. Then he went outside to watch as smoke billowed out of the barracks.

"Evans, what do you know about that fire this afternoon?" Captain Eagleton demanded.

"What do you mean?" Jimmy, who had been summoned to his office, bluffed. Shrugging as he stood in the captain's doorway, he crossed his arms to keep his shaking from giving him away.

"I mean you're damn lucky the whole goddamn barracks didn't burn down," the captain said, his voice unaccountably softened.

Unblinking, Jimmy silently met the officer's eye. This was not going as he'd planned. Where was Captain Eagleshit's outrage?

"Just get out," the captain muttered, gesturing toward the door.

Baffled, Jimmy returned to the barracks, which beside the smell of smoke and some water damage was pretty much intact. Bonehead's precious uniforms were, of course, history. The other guys kept their distance, but he'd long since reached the point where he didn't care. At least he'd gotten the ball rolling and he reckoned he'd brought the matter of his fate to a head.

"Evans!" Sergeant Weaver barked.

"Yeah," Jimmy answered, tensing as he shoved away his lunch tray. *Here it comes.*

"Report to Doc Forrest at 1330."

Jimmy had an hour to wonder. *Go see Doc? What've they got up their sleeve?*

"Okay, son. Take off your shirt. I need to have another listen," the old doctor said.

"Why?" Jimmy asked. Riddled with suspicion, he quickly stripped off his shirt.

"It's okay. I'm just checking," Doc said, placing his stethoscope against Jimmy's chest. "Well, son," he said, nodding. "You've got a heart murmur there. I'll have to classify you as 4-F."

"I'm 4-F, Doc? I am?" *Holy shit!* For a moment he couldn't absorb the reality. As relief flooded over him, he grabbed his shirt and buttoned it with trembling hands.

"Hold on," Doc said, peering over his reading glasses as Jimmy held his breath.

"Here," he said handing over a thick envelope. "Your papers are signed. Go home and live your life, son,"

For a moment Jimmy stared into the old man's crinkled eyes. "Okay," he mumbled, grabbing the papers and flying out the door.

2

BACK TO FAIRBANKS

Once he'd boarded the Fairbanks-bound train the next morning, Jimmy never looked back, never pondered his narrow escape. He simply reclaimed his life. During the twelve-hour trip he could hardly contain his zeal, bounding from his seat to explore the train and watch the spectacular views. He reveled in his freedom.

The train had been underway barely half an hour when Mt. McKinley came into view on that bright, clear day. As the train skirted the foot of the mountain, Jimmy was awestruck by its majesty, the stark beauty that dominated the entire landscape for hours as they traveled. Eventually his enthusiasm won over a taciturn conductor who became a reluctant tour guide. As they crossed the nine hundred-foot span on the Hurricane Gulch Trestle, Jimmy glanced down to see the roaring creek a breathtaking three hundred feet below. He was sharply reminded of his own daring adventures in crossing railroad trestles with his brothers, one episode having come close to disaster.

"Damn!" Jimmy exclaimed as he heard the engine begin to strain, chugging on the uphill pull. "Me and my brothers, we used to cross a long trestle over the San Joaquin."

"That so?" the conductor replied in a monotone.

"Yeah. Had to outrun a goddamn freight train one time. That damn trestle seemed real long at the time, but this one's got it beat all to hell."

"Yup" the conductor mumbled, "we're slowing down. Climbing some now. It's quite a pull on up to Broad Pass."

"No shit. I can hear the engine workin. This here's the first time I been a paying passenger. Me and my brothers used to hitch a ride on the Southern Pacific going up to the swimmin hole on the San Joaquin. Them trains would hafta slow down right near our house, way before the bridge. We'd hop on and ride near a mile then jump off just before the bridge."

"Yup. Hopped a few trains myself in my day," the wiry, old conductor said.

"Catchin a ride was harder coming back. Them trains was goin downhill pickin up speed. Trick was jumpin off before the damn thing got to goin too fast."

The conductor just grunted and shook his head in response.

Jimmy knew, could almost taste it, when they drew close to Fairbanks. He watched eagerly as the long single-span Tanana River Bridge came into view. After being away for a month, he felt exhilarated at the familiar sight.

Jimmy turned up the collar of his sturdy wool jacket against the frigid night air as he made his way from the train station to his boardinghouse. It was shortly after nine on that April evening and the sun had just set. As he let himself into the main entrance, he saw that the lights were still on in the Turners' apartment, and he tapped lightly on their door.

"Well, I'll be!" exclaimed his landlady, Mrs. Turner, a tiny bird-like woman. "I thought you was gone for sure."

"Nah! They didn't want me, after all. I'm too damn mean."

"Well, you've still got your bunk and your locker. I figured you'd be back sooner or later. I've been keeping your rent paid up from out of your bank account. Your friend Steve's been around asking about you."

"Yeah. I'll be seein him at work in the morning. What're the chances of getting my laundry done?" he asked, holding up his duffel bag.

"Leave it. I'll have your clothes ready for you after work tomorrow. Two bucks will take care of it. Do you need any cash for now?"

"Yeah. How about a five? I'm going downtown for something to eat after I clean up."

Despite her generally crusty manner, Jimmy knew Mrs. Turner had a soft spot for him. She and her husband were a middle-aged couple who operated the downtown boarding house where a burgeoning population of itinerant workmen found some meals, shelter, and a place to bathe. Jimmy had stayed there off and on for over a year. In that time, Mrs. Turner had become his banker, depositing his paychecks and making withdrawals of cash for him at the local bank. He wasn't sure whether she realized that he couldn't read or write, but with his landlady's help he had figured out a way to manage his money. He kept the passbook and could sign his own name if he decided to make his own withdrawal. But he had not attempted that maneuver as it left him open to possible embarrassment. The last time he had checked the passbook, he had some six thousand dollars in his account.

The next morning at seven sharp Jimmy pushed through the weather-beaten doors of the Electrical Workers Union Hall. Though it was an hour before work call, dozens of men were milling about in the old split-log meeting lodge. Workers sat around the wood stove in straight-back wooden chairs, leaning into their conversations, coffee mugs in hand, the air already thick with cigarette smoke.

"Hey, kid! Where the hell you been?" one of the linemen called out to him.

Jimmy shrugged and waved as he made his way to the office enclosure at the back of the room. Stopping at the railing, he waited to get a clerk's attention while he painstakingly signed his name on the work roster.

"Hey! You got a check for Evans?" he asked when the clerk looked up.

"Yeah. It's been here awhile. Let me take a look."

"How about cashin it for me?" he asked when the guy finally dug out the check from a desk drawer.

"You know we don't usually cash checks here."

"Yeah, but I've been out of town. I need some cash, and I'm trying to get out on a job this morning. It's just a hundred bucks."

"Well, I guess," he agreed reluctantly.

Jimmy waited, watching as the clerk walked to an ancient safe that sat against the back wall of the office enclosure. Standing four feet tall, the double-door black safe had decorative brass handles and etchings in intricate gold patterns that pegged it as a throwback to the Gold Rush days. One door was standing slightly ajar. Jimmy knew that the union always kept plenty of cash. The officials called it their "war chest". He had also seen that the union wielded real power. Without the union there was no way he'd be earning anywhere near two fifty an hour.

Jimmy felt a hearty clap on the shoulder as he tucked his cash in his jeans. "My God! You're back."

"Yeah!" he laughed, turning to look into the impish face of his friend, Steve Turner. "I flunked out of the army."

"You disappeared. Your landlady told me that the army hauled you off. I thought you were gone for sure.

"Naw. Flat feet. Got me a 4-F," Jimmy fabricated, keeping his story simple.

"Our crew's been out at Big Delta stringing new lines into the military base there.

"Shit, that's gotta be a hundred miles out."

"Yeah. We've been staying out there on the base. The food's not fit for dogs. We got in Friday night for the weekend. First time in two weeks. The damn linemen went crazy. They tried to ring me in on their horseshit like always. You know how they are. We were supposed to head back today, but they're all drunk off their asses. Only Fred showed up and he's not looking too damn good. Glen Cochran's the general foreman on the job and he's royally pissed."

"Yeah I bet. That asshole don't treat his men right."

 "Well, he's out there now trying to hunt them down. He'll find them and ream their asses, but they won't be worth a damn until tomorrow. The guys will want you back on the crew for sure."

"Hey Evans! You son of a bitch. I heard the US Army had your ass."

Jimmy wheeled to see Fred Matthews fast approaching. A bull of a man, he was a Texas bullshitter with a heart of gold who couldn't pass up a bet, lived for his next wager. Like the other linemen, he was a rugged wild man who lived on the edge: A daring, hard drinking aficionado of the wager.

"They had me, for damn sure. Didn't like my flat feet, though."

"Yall are goddamn better off, kid. Damn straight. Them military sonsabitches don't know jack shit. Screw them. Yall are one hell of a goddamn good worker. Glad to see you back. My crew's headin out yonder to hell and gone again tomorrow. Could use another grunt. I'll put in a good word for your ass."

"Looks like you're on," Steve Chuckled as they watched Fred dart back toward the office. For a big man he moved through the crowd like a lithe quarterback.

"Damn, Fred moves pretty good for a guy's been on a bender all weekend."

"Yeah, he shows up even when he's half dead. He's always talking about sending money to his girls back in Texas but seems like he's out raising hell with the rest of the linemen most of the time. I've never seen him when he wasn't betting on some damn thing."

"That's for goddamn sure. You goin out on a job today?" Jimmy asked.

"Yeah, I'm just filling in for the day. You know, I've got to work all I can. I'll need the money for school come fall."

"No shit, you miser. You must a learned that penny-pinchin in New York."

"You bet. I saved up big time while you were gone. Didn't get suckered once into blowing my paycheck."

"Christ Almighty! You must a been bored to death."

"That's for damn sure," Steve laughed.

Jimmy left the union hall as soon as he saw that he wouldn't be sent out on a job that day. Walking at his usual brisk pace, he headed out along Third Avenue avoiding dirty patches of snow that still resisted the weak sunlight. As he breathed in the fresh cold air and felt the sun on his back, his spirits soared. He felt young and free, in charge of his own life once more. Turning toward the river on Cushman Street, he caught sight of his destination, the Pastime Cafe.

Red spotted him before he claimed one of the chrome stools at the counter. "Hi, Slim," she said, flashing her radiant smile. "About time you came back."

"Hey, Red. How's it going?"

"Good. Real good. I just got a letter from my husband. I don't know how close he is to the front lines, but he's okay."

"Great," Jimmy encouraged, smiling at the likable waitress. She was funny, and pretty with her fiery red hair, smattering of freckles and dancing brown eyes. He guessed she was in her early twenties.

"You want coffee?"

"Yeah. What kind of pie you got?"

"Blueberry, your favorite. Want ice cream?"

"Sure. Let's go whole hog."

"Where you been, anyway, Slim? I figured you must of run off with some girl. Who could resist those great dimples and those baby blues?"

"Right," Jimmy laughed. "You seen any nice girls around here?"

"No. Those are in short supply now that you mention it. This is a man's town for sure."

Red, who knew most of her customers by name, got back to work in the busy restaurant letting Jimmy slide without giving any explanation for his long absence.

Later as he strolled down Second Avenue, Jimmy skirted clusters of GI's who were in various stages of drunkenness at mid-morning. He hardly noticed the loud arguments and scattered fistfights outside the multiple bars along the street. The daytime action was tame compared with most nights, especially on weekends, when fights raged for blocks.

"Well, I'll be! I been wonderin what become a you," Harvey Edwards grinned, flashing an impressive display of gold capped teeth as he reached out to shake hands.

"I've been away screwin with the military," Jimmy said as he took a chair in Harvey's shoeshine stand.

"Mm, Mm, Mm. I was afeared of that," Harvey said, shaking his head. "How'n hell you loose yerself from them feds?"

"I was too damn mean for them."

Harvey exploded in infectious laughter, his black face crinkling with glee. "Nooo, you be jivin me. Aint no way. Back'n Chicago in Prohibition times dey was plenty a bad peoples, bootleggin, lots a killin in dem gang wars, but thays none meaner'n dem feds."

"You old fox, you was a bootlegger in your time, wasn't you?" Jimmy asked, baiting the old man into a story.

"Sho nuf. But nuthin big time. Bout the onliest way of makin a livin. Most times I was bein muscle, haulin an a totin. Shoulda seed me den. I was strong and smooth. All them ladies had a eye fer me. Yeah, them was da days."

"How long you been up here, Harvey?"

"Be some forty year," Harvey said, frowning as he scratched his head. "Seen lota changin since dem Goal Rush days. Dem prospectors crazier en hell back den. Dem ol grubstakers comin ta town a fightin, an drinkin, an raisin hell alla times. Done shoot one nother dead sometime. Thinkin I's back in Chicago. Now the place runnin over wit dem damn GI' s. Theys mean as snakes. Disrespecful."

"Did you swear off gamblin yet?"

"Not zactly. Ya know. When I gets a hot streak aint nothin stoppin me. Gotta ride it. I been on a roll till las week."

"I hope to God you swore off your damn card tricks," Jimmy said quietly, leaning closer so his voice wouldn't carry.

Harvey gave him a sly smile in answer.

"Christ Almighty, you're gonna get yourself killed one of these days."

"I knows better, but I surely loves ta gamble," he sighed, shaking his head. "It jus that sometime I gets ta owin da wrong peoples."

***

Jimmy was waiting when Steve hopped out of the City Electric crew-truck just before five.

"Hey! Ya ready for a round at the shootin gallery?"

"Yeah, but I'm not betting."

"Sure you are. It's time you broke loose with a couple a bucks."

"No, no, no," Steve protested, breaking into a smile even as he shook his head.

"Come on. Can't be chickenshit all your life."

"Okay. Let's go," Steve agreed with feigned reluctance. "Damn it, Jimmy. You always sucker me," Steve complained good humoredly as they walked away from the gallery a couple hours later.

"You was winning for a while," Jimmy smirked, patting a roll of dollar bills in his shirt pocket.

"Yeah, and then you started that double-up bullshit. I should know better."

"Hey! See that looker comin our way!" Jimmy asked.

"No shit. Where'd she come from?"

"Don't drool all over yourself. She's gotta be a homesteader or farmer coming to town buying supplies. You know, a husband and kids at home."

"Well, I'm not passing this one up," Steve said with a mischievous grin. "Just watch an expert."

Taking three fast strides, arms pumping, Steve launched himself into the air completing a graceful somersault before landing on his feet directly in front of the pretty brunette.

"Good evening miss," he said with a gentlemanly bow. The startled young woman stood wide-eyed for a moment then clamped a hand over her mouth to contain her laughter. Shaking her head, she detoured around Steve and continued on her way. Although she'd undoubtedly encountered many rowdy men in the wild Alaskan Territory, it was unlikely she had ever experienced Steve's novel approach.

"Christ Almighty, how'd you do that?" Jimmy asked, bursting into laughter.

"Well, it didn't get me the girl. It usually works better than that," Steve quipped. "Looks like I'll have to settle for a beer."

"Yeah. Let's go see if Helga's dancin."

"Oh God! I haven't been there in a while," Steve groaned.

Olson's Tavern was already at full throttle when they edged into seats at the bar and ordered beers. It wasn't long before Helga appeared decked out in her elaborate blue and yellow Swedish costume. The full- sized accordion strapped to her chest seemed dwarfed by the girth of the woman who began playing and singing "The Beer Barrel Polka." With each new polka tune, Helga's ample cheeks grew redder and her audience began to stomp and clap to the catchy rhythm. Soon she began to dance, her blond braids flying and her huge body unbelievably graceful in motion.

"Damn!" Jimmy shouted, his second beer already kicking in so that his feet were unconsciously tapping to the beat. "It's a goddamn wonder when she gets all that fat to bouncing."

"Yeah. I think I'll get up and dance with Helga," Steve said with a sly smile.

"You do and I'll have to kick your ass! No, go ahead and then I can tell the crew tomorrow, 'Steve didn't get laid this weekend, but he danced with Helga.'"

They sat back for a while and polished off their beers.

"Christ, I'm hungry," Jimmy said.

"Yeah, let's go. My ears are busted."

"Hey, I'll treat you to a steak at Grifter's," Jimmy offered as they walked along in the frosty twilight.

"Good idea, since you're so flush after beating me out of my money."

"Man, I don't know about you, but I could eat the south end out of a northbound jackass. I haven't had a good meal in a long time."

The waitress at Grifter's set heaping plates in front of Jimmy and Steve. Each had a thick steak that took up most of the platter, leaving little room for a mountain of French fries and some canned green beans.

Jimmy dug in, brandishing his fork and steak knife with eager anticipation. In mere seconds he was savoring the meaty pleasure of a juicy piece of seared steak, chewing with gusto.

Looking across the table he noticed Steve pounding away at a stubborn bottle of steak sauce.

"What the hell are you doing?" he asked, through his mouthful of food.

"Trying to get some damn steak sauce."

"You're going to ruin it with that shit. Oh well, too late," Jimmy said, watching a big gusher of brown sauce slide out of the bottle.

"Goddamn, this steak hits the spot," Jimmy said. "What the hell are you doing now?" he asked, realizing that Steve was having a problem. As he watched, Steve hacked away at his steak without noticeable effect, stopped to examine his steak knife and then determinedly tried again.

"My damn steak is strait off an old bull. The goddamn knife won't even make a dent in it."

"Well, mine's real good," Jimmy taunted.

"Yeah?" Steve said, with a mischievous glint in his eye.

Seizing the steak in both hands, he let out a roar like an attacking grizzly and dropped to the floor biting down and shaking the meat, growling as if to tear it apart. The restaurant became suddenly silent.

An alarmed waitress, who looked worn and harried, approached warily. "Is there a problem?"

"Not if I was a goddamned hyena," Steve said pleasantly, steak sauce running down his chin and on to his shirt. "How about getting me a steak I can eat?"

"Right away, sir," she replied, making an obvious effort to control the smile that pulled at the corners of her mouth.

"Shit, Steve. I think that waitress really likes your style. You could hit on her for a date when she comes back with your tender steak."

"Shut up Evans," he laughed and headed for the bathroom to wash up.

3

BIG DELTA

Jimmy threw his duffel bag into the back of the man-haul and climbed into the rear seat with Steve, the usual place delegated to grunts. Although the sun was just rising, he'd been up for hours, a huge breakfast and several cups of coffee already under his belt. A ragged looking group of five linemen were assembled on the sidewalk where Fred was assigning them to their vehicles and, from the sound of his booming voice, giving them a good reaming.

"Fred looks pissed," Steve said.

"Look at them assholes, they're hung over and all beat to hell," Jimmy said.

"Yeah, the usual," Steve said, laughing.

"If you ask me, Fred don't look so goddamn good either."

Driving the man-haul with Jimmy and Steve in the back, Fred led the four vehicle caravan that set out on the jarring hundred mile trek to Big Delta. The rest of the crew followed in the pole truck loaded with some twenty telephone poles, the lowboy hauling the Caterpillar tractor and boom, and the flatbed truck with supplies of wire, cross arms, hardware and other equipment. Periodically over the three hour drive, the caravan would make a pit stop at one of the rare settlements, mostly isolated roadhouses, along the rough highway. During the long ride, the grunts eventually needled good-natured Fred into a better mood.

The Big Delta job site was in the middle of a wilderness, five miles short of the US Army base at Fort Greely. Once they turned onto the deeply rutted gravel road that ran alongside the City Electric right-of-way, they were forced to slow their speed for those last few miles. Even so, the grab-your-ass-and-hang-on linemen drove true to form, pushing the limits of their vehicles and jarring the hell out of the crew. No one complained.

Proceeding along a parade of upright electrical poles that were in various stages of completion, the caravan finally pulled up at the end of the line. Once they'd arrived at the site, the guys piled out of the trucks, relieved themselves among the scrub spruce that bordered the cleared right-of way, and then got to work.

Although they were still hung over, the strong, tough men threw themselves into the physical activity. Among linemen there was no tolerance for a slacker or a whiner. There was work to be done, new power poles to set and multiple lines to string. With the ongoing Korean War, additional power was needed for the burgeoning army garrison at Fort Greely and for the new secret radar sites being installed in the area.

The men knew their jobs and quickly formed a smooth working team. Dwight, a feisty little bantam lineman, snagged the two grunts to help unload the Cat from the lowboy and attach the auger. Jimmy and Steve knew the drill. Grabbing shovels, they began to clear away the mountain of dirt that welled up as the auger bit into the spongy ground drilling the hole for the first new pole of the day.

"Mosquitoes thick as molasses in this damn muskeg country," Steve yelled over the roar of the Cat.

"Yeah. Taking a crap in the woods is goddamn risky. Bout drilled my ass off," Jimmy hollered.

The Cat bellowed louder as the cavity approached the required six-foot depth. While Steve followed Dwight to the next excavation, Jimmy cleaned out the loose dirt from the bottom of the hole, grappling with the awkward "spoon", a long-handled crook- neck shovel.

As site foreman, it was up to Fred to orchestrate the day's work and make assignments, but the linemen were mainly self-directed. They set to work attaching angle brackets to the crossarms, scaling the already standing poles to secure the assembled crossarms, and installing insulators. Once Dwight had drilled several holes, he exchanged the auger for a boom and started using the Cat to raise new poles. The grunts did the running. Alert and energetic, Jimmy and Steve were adept at anticipating what was needed.

"Hey, Jimmy," Fred called from atop a pole. "Get me some goddamn hardware up here."

Jimmy hustled to the flatbed truck, grabbed his canvas bucket and loaded in nuts and bolts used for securing the crossarms. He quickly sent the bucket up the pole, hand over hand, using a rope attached to a block and tackle.

"Keep an eye out now," Fred hollered down. "Have that damn hardware ready on the next one. I've got a goddamn bet a goin with Dwight. That there shithead's thinkin he kin set another pole afore I get the next goddamn crossarms attached up."

"Yeah. He's yellin for me now. I gotta help Steve fill in and tamp down around that last pole," Jimmy yelled.

"Don't be lettin that asshole get ahead," Fred called.

"Shit!" Jimmy said, as he hustled over to shovel dirt with Steve. "Them damn guys have got a bet on. They're gonna run our asses off."

"What else's new?" Steve laughed.

"Pick it up you guys," Dwight yelled over the roar of the Cat.

"Looks like Fred's getting ahead. He's already climbin the next pole," Jimmy said, as he helped tamp down the dirt around the base of Dwight's newly placed pole.

"Let's go, let's go," Dwight urged.

"Dwight's getting pissed," Steve grinned.

"Yeah. Can't get the next pole set while he's still holdin this one straight with the boom. It's burning his ass."

With the distraction of hard work, the rest of the day passed quickly especially with the added intrigue of competition. The linemen placed their wagers among themselves and no one complained, win or lose when Fred prevailed. However, their enthusiasm waned with the arrival of the noon meal delivered from the army base. The food received harshly profane judgment from one and all of the hungry workers. By quitting time, the men were worn out as they loaded into the crew truck and drove the five miles to Fort Greely.

Passing through the guard station, Jimmy wasn't at all pleased to be back on a military base so soon after his trying encounter. His unease was nothing he would examine or relate even to his friend. Setting his duffel bag on a bunk, he grabbed a quick shower in the barracks before heading to the mess hall with the other guys.

"I'm getting the hell out of here," Mac grumbled as they walked out of the mess hall. "They'll have some real food down at the Buffalo Lodge."

"Hell yes," Fred said. "Ah don't know how them assholes kin eat that shit."

All the crew crowded into the man-haul and headed five miles farther down the road to the old log roadhouse. Jimmy suspected that it had been the plan all along, and he was relieved. He could hardly picture the rough and ready linemen hanging around the barracks all evening, and it sure wasn't any place he wanted to be.

At the Buffalo Lodge the jukebox was blaring out "Mocking' Bird Hill" and a few GI officers were hanging around the rough-hewn wood bar that had been worn smooth with age. The men spread out at a long table and ordered up beer and steaks. It wasn't long before the betting began. First it was over the pinball machine, and then over a series of pool games. The linemen could think of hundreds of ways to wager. Not just who would win, but how many balls a guy could sink in a row, and infinite variations.

Over the next few days, the meager fare served in the mess hall laid the groundwork for a rebellion that wasn't long in coming. When Glen Cochran, the general foreman, arrived at the worksite to bring supplies from Fairbanks and to check on their progress, Fred tackled him.

"Christ Almighty, Glen!" he began, "Eatin that goddamn shit they're servin on base is bullshit. My men'll put up with sleepin in that drafty damn barracks, but they gotta have real fuckin food in their bellies."

All sounds of drilling, shoveling and swearing at the site had gone silent while the whole crew listened. They could clearly hear Fred's booming voice.

"Listen, Fred. You know we have to stay on budget," Glen said, his voice calm while his posture turned rigid.

"Don't gimmy that crap, Glen. You assholes're makin plenty. Best not screw with my crew. My men are gonna be eatin at the goddamn Buffalo Lodge startin today."

"I'll have to get back to you on that," Glen said, with a curt nod.

"Christ Almighty, asshole. I'm not askin. Cut out the bullshit. Just gimmy the goddamn go ahead," Fred shouted, shaking his finger in his boss' face.

"Cool down Fred."

"Quit givin me a ration a shit. You know goddamn well my men are needin real grub. We're the best damn crew ya got and we sure as hell don't got to put up with none of this here bullshit."

"Yeah, yeah. Okay, but your ass in on the line if you fall behind schedule." Glen conceded as he backed up a step.

"The hell you say! My guys're crackin their asses. You damn well know it," Fred hollered, shaking his finger in Glen's face once more.

From that day on, the men ate all their evening meals at the Buffalo Inn putting their drinks on the tab as well. Still, few of them drank too much during the workweek. The hard work and early rising prompted them to roll into the military barracks in time for a good night's sleep. Fred didn't give them a chance to overdo, either, as he herded them into the man-haul before anyone got too involved with wagering, drinking, or baiting the GI's.

Jimmy was in his element. He liked the rough tough linemen, their humor and daring, the camaraderie, the hard-physical labor, the respect from the men and his friendship with Steve. He fell into his bunk at night and slept hard. He didn't dream.

The first Saturday turned into another workday since the guys had messed up by extending their previous weekend in Fairbanks. They would be staying at the jobsite for at least another week or two. Most of the linemen were adventurers at heart who had come to Alaska in search of high paying jobs and who needed their paychecks to support often far-distant families.

By Saturday night the men were ready to let off steam at the Buffalo Lodge, the only local choice for entertainment. They enjoyed some high stakes pool games and pinball competitions that often pitted City Electric workers against soldiers and army officers from the base, putting more on the line than just the wagers. As the night wore on tempers flared, and challenges were laid down with men on both sides spoiling for a fight. In that isolated masculine world, a good brawl was considered just another form of entertainment. No perceived provocation could be ignored after the beer and whiskey had been flowing for some hours.

"Those assholes are going to get a fight started, yet," Steve remarked, setting his empty beer bottle down on the table.

"Oh shit," Jimmy said. "Those damn wild men. We're gonna end up getting our asses kicked. This damn place is overflowin with GI's. Goddamn it, Alex's squarin off with that jackass sergeant."

"When it comes to a fight, you can sure as hell hold your own," Steve said.

"Yeah, but I'm not lookin for a fight. Got my fill a that the first year

I was up here. Them GIs are always itchin to punish somebody. Christ, I been fightin all my life. I'd sooner have a good time. Haven't had enough to drink for a big brawl, anyway."

"I've seen you surprise the hell out of some mean assholes with that long reach of yours. Wham, you smack them, and they can't lay a hand on you," Steve said, true admiration in his voice.

"Yeah, unless some mussel-bound prick gets ahold of me. But there's no pleasure in punching a guy senseless. I only get mad if some dumbshit won't quit ridin my ass. Then I don't care how big he is."

"Looks like the sergeant backed off," Steve observed. "I think he saw the bartender reaching under the bar for his club."

"Yeah, damn good thing. Alex sure as hell wasn't going to back down. That guy's got no reverse."

"Christ, the place is packed with GIs. We'd be way outnumbered," Steve said.

"Talk about no reverse. I once knew a kid in Fresno when I was near about twelve," Jimmy said. "Tough little Mexican shit named Alberto. That kid never backed down. One day I was at the swimmin hole with my little brother and a couple of other kids from my neighborhood. Here comes Alberto with a bunch of Mexican kids. Before I know what the hell's happenin he reaches in his pocket, pulls out a switch-blade and tells us to get our asses out of there."

"Damn, what did you do?"

"Got out. Hell, I was only wearin my bathing suit and that knife looked damn intimidatin. But that wasn't the end of it. The next time I went down there, Alberto and his friends were in there swimmin. I sneaked down and searched through all a their clothes until I found his knife, then threw it as far as I could into a wheat field. Then I stood up an called him. 'Hey Alberto,' I said. 'I just threw your knife away. Come on out you little shitass an fight me like a man.'"

"You should of seen that little hotblooded Mexican come at me like a chargin bull. He was real strong, but not much over half my height even though he was my age. With my long reach he never laid a hand on me. But he kept comin. I'd knock him down an he'd get back up an charge me. Over and over and over. I was ashamed to hit him again, but he wouldn't stop. I kept thinkin, 'just stay down, just stay down.' But he'd drag hisself back up every time."

"Finally, I figured out the only way to make him stop, short of killin him. I put my hands up like I was givin up. 'No mas! No mas! You win,' I told him. Then he smiled and said, 'Si! I win.' After that we was good friends."

"Did you tell him where his knife was?"

"Hell no, but I never seen it again."

As the hour grew late most of the guys gradually migrated back to the table, ordered another beer or a whiskey, and joined in the nightly poker game. Seven-card stud had become their staple entertainment. Whoever was ready to play would retrieve the cards and a box of wooden matches from the man-haul.

While Jimmy seldom joined the wild-ass linemen in their drinking and carousing exploits back in Fairbanks, he did enjoy playing poker with them. He proved to be a worthy adversary surprising the more experienced men. He was a gutsy and aggressive player, constantly raising the bet and often bluffing. But the guys couldn't ever be sure, because he was so damn lucky.

Steve usually folded after a few hands. He couldn't afford to bet the earnings he would need for his college tuition in the fall and couldn't win on scared money. Once he'd lost a few bucks, he sat back to watch the action.

"I'll see Mack's five an raise ya five," Jimmy said.

"You're not bettin that measly pair a duces, are you Jimmy?" Dwight mumbled, scraping his hole cards thoughtfully against the dark stubble of his beard.

"Are you in or out?" Jimmy shot back.

"Well, hell. I'll see you and raise you another five," Dwight blustered.

"It's fifteen to you, Alex," Jimmy prompted.

"What the hell are you betting on kid? Bullshit, that's too rich for my blood," Alex said, throwing in his hand.

"I'm bettin my kings," Fred said. "Yall aint got jack shit. I'll see your fifteen and I'm bumpin it five."

"Damn. I'm out," Mack said, slamming down his cards.

"I'm in," Jimmy said quietly, tossing his matches into the pot.

"Let's see that last shittin hole card," Dwight said, paying up.

"Here they come, down and dirty," Mack said, dealing a final card to each of the three remaining players.

"It's on you, Jimmy," Dwight said expectantly. "Would you quit worryin them goddamn cards and make your bet."

"Okay. I'm bettin ten, sight unseen," Jimmy said as he continued to shuffle his three hole- cards without looking at them.

"Goddamn it. Aren't you gonna to look at them?" Dwight bristled.

"Nope. I made my bet. You gonna to see it?" Jimmy challenged.

"Shit yes," Dwight said, dropping in his matches.

"Well, I'll see ya and it'll cost ya another ten ta take a gander at this here hand," Fred gloated.

"I'm in," Jimmy said.

Tight-lipped, Dwight dropped his matches into the pot.

"Read em and weep," Fred said. "Right here's a full house, kings over fives.

Jimmy dropped his hole cards on the table one by one --- a two, an eight, then another two. "Looks like I got four duces."

"Bullshit! You're one goddamn lucky asshole," Fred said as Dwight quietly folded his hand.

"Yeah, I guess so," Jimmy said, shrugging as he raked in the bulging pot of matchsticks. As far as the other men could tell, Jimmy had never seen that final card before he threw it face-up on the table. At seventeen he was the consummate poker player, daring and closed mouth. His opponents could only wonder how many duces he'd held before that last round.

"I've had enough goddamn cards for the night. How about you buyin us another round, Jimmy?" Fred said.

"Comin up," Jimmy said.

"Where you hale from, kid?" Fred asked, belting down his shot of whiskey.

"Oh shit, all over. Oklahoma, Louisiana, Arizona, Michigan, California," Jimmy answered.

"I, gotta say yall are a hell of a worker. Where bouts yall from, Steve?"

"Hey, I'm a New Yorker," Steve answered with his usual quirky smile.

"Well goddamn, I thought you was talkin strange. What're yall doin way the hell up here?"

"Going to college."

"No shit, we got a college boy here a runnin and a totin for us, guys," Fred remarked to the other linemen who were sitting around the table in various states of inebriation.

"Yeah, well I'm a Texan an damn prouda it," Fred said, his words slurred. "Didn't get me no further than high school. Got a sweet lil wife down ta Amarillo and two lil girls. Had to come up here ta make a decent livin for ma family. Miss em terrible alla time. I'm already thirty-two but fit as a fiddle. I can kick ass good as always. You should a seen me when I was quarterbackin in high school. I was a runnin fool," Fred said and his voice trailed off, his expression becoming vacant.

"Hey Jimmy, yall're a tall drink a water. Ever do any runnin?" Fred asked abruptly.

"Oh yeah, I was damn good at foot racin when I was a kid."

"Think you could beat me?"

"Hell yes."

"Well, you're on. Where ya wanna race to?

"I don't care. You choose."

"Ya think yall can run all the way back ta the army base?"

"Five miles? Easy!" Jimmy answered, confidently.

There was a sudden alertness among the drunken linemen strewn around the table, almost as if they could sense a current of energy connected to an imminent wager. Like hounds getting wind of the scent, they were immediately eager to chase a sporting bet.

"Hey, yall best put ya money where ya mouth be, young buck," Fred slurred.

"Damn right. What're ya bettin?"

"Ah say we make it worth ma while. I can beat your ass real good fer five hundred bucks."

"Christ Almighty, Fred. Your shitfaced. I don't want to take your money."

"What's a matter kid, you got no balls all of a sudden?"

"Hey. I'll put fifty on Fred," Alex blurted.

"I got fifty says Fred'll win," Dwight said, fumbling for his wallet.

"Les go!" Fred said, leaning heavily on the table as he pushed himself upright.

"Hold on, Fred. I'll beat you. Let's do it when you don't have a snout full a whiskey," Jimmy warned.

"Put up or shut up kid. Aint nobody can best me. I cain hold my liquor. Ya gonna run or not?"

"Okay, but it's your funeral," Jimmy shrugged.

It was nearly two in the morning when the City Electric crew poured out of the Buffalo Lodge. Spirits were high as Steve collected money and wrote down the bets. By the light of the moon Fred and Jimmy took their positions at-the-ready on the newly paved road leading back to the army base.

This'll be a cinch, Jimmy thought. *Fred shouldn't of pushed me. I tried to let him off easy. Steve knows to take all bets against me. That miser better damn well do it.*

Jimmy's adrenaline was flowing as he stood on the road and watched Fred prepare for the foot race. The big lineman seemed to deliberate before taking off his flannel work shirt and dropping it in the man-haul.

"Are you ready?" Alex prompted.

"Yeah, let's go," Jimmy answered, shifting restlessly from foot to foot.

"Okay," Fred said. "Bring that damn man-haul round behind us so we got more light."

"Let's get goin. The damn mosquitoes are about to bleed us dry," Dwight shouted as he stopped the vehicle just behind the racers. "On your mark," he called.

"Wait!" Fred yelled. "Gotta get rid a these here heavy boots."

Christ Almighty, now you're messin up big time, Jimmy thought. *This new blacktop's sharp as glass. It's gonna cut your feet to shreds.*

Finally, the race was on. While Fred took off like a rabbit, Jimmy deliberately paced himself. Keeping his heavy work shirt and his boots on, he ran his own race. Behind him the guys were following in the man-haul, cheering and goading and doubling up on bets favoring Fred who was rapidly pulling ahead until he almost disappeared out of sight in the dim moonlight.

It was around the two-mile mark when Jimmy, closing in on a limping Fred, saw him turn around and start back.

He's finished, Jimmy thought.

"My goddamn feet," Fred panted as he went by.

Jimmy heard excited voices from the crew truck and Fred's shout, "I need my goddamn boots."

As the lights of the vehicle fell back behind him, Jimmy ran in a glorious state of pleasure, his body swift and flowing, his confidence soaring. Then the truck was behind him again and the men were cheering him on. As it pulled up to keep pace, a vanquished Fred sat slumped in the passenger seat.

When the lighted gates at Fort Greely came into view, Jimmy was just hitting his stride with plenty of reserve left.

On Monday morning Fred could hardly manage to get his boots on. While he relegated the driving of the man-haul to Alex, he made no complaint as he hobbled around and scaled power poles on his damaged feet. The story was written in the painful grimace that replaced his usually cheerful expression. His glum manner and his silence said it all. His body healed as the days passed, but his mood worsened.

Jimmy suspected the cause. While he had enjoyed the victory, he was feeling bad about Fred and suspecting that the loss of face wasn't bothering the lineman nearly as much as losing the huge five-hundred-dollar bet. He liked Fred, his usual good humor, his bullshit and his infectious enthusiasm.

It was late on the following Thursday night when Jimmy sat down next to Fred who was sitting alone chugging another beer at the bar in the Buffalo Lodge. He knew the foreman had been drinking heavily all week.

"Hey, Fred," Jimmy said, ordering a beer.

"Hey kid," he answered staring down at his empty mug.

"Guess we'll be back in Fairbanks this time tomorrow."

"Yeah."

"I'm gonna see if I can buy me a car when we get back to town," Jimmy said, trying to humor the miserable lineman.

"Look, kid. I caint pay you all what I owe you out a this here paycheck. Can ya wait fer some of it?"

"It's okay. I don't care about the bet."

"Ah gotta send somethin to my family," he said, his voice strained. "I caint leave them broke over ma foolishness. Them kids has got a asshole for a daddy."

"Just forget it, Fred. I made a good lick off the other guys bettin against me."

"The hell I will. A bet's a bet and I'm a man a my word."

"I'm not takin your money, Fred. Send it to your kids. You don't owe me nothin."

"That aint right and ya know it," Fred protested, his face drawn in grim lines.

"It's forgot as of now," Jimmy said, sliding off his seat and walking away without a backward glance.

***

The City Electric convoy headed for Fairbanks right after work on Friday, but since the linemen were hell-bent on stopping at every watering hole along the way, they didn't make it back until the midday on Saturday. When they finally roared into town most of them were well and truly smashed. Once they'd dropped off the company trucks and picked up their paychecks at the union hall, the carousing began in earnest. Some of the men remembered to stop at the Western Union office to send money home before blowing the rest of their wages.

After he'd showered and cashed his check, Jimmy met up with Steve at the Pastime Cafe where Red was busy hassling a Saturday lunch crowd.

"Hey, guys. Guess what! My honey's coming home on leave soon," she beamed, on the run.

"That's great, Red," Jimmy said. "Did you save us any pie?"

"Always got homemade pie for you guys."

"Damn, all the nice girls are taken," Steve lamented quietly, digging into his apple pie a la mode.

"That's for damn sure. She might have five years on me, but I'd like to take her out. Have a few laughs," Jimmy said.

"Maybe more than laughs," Steve said with a grin.

"Yeah. I'd be up for some of that action. But you can see she's stuck on her guy."

"Yup. No nice girls available."

"Hey, I seen a little jeep for sale," Jimmy said. "Let's go see if I can make a deal on it."

"You're on."

At a little past nine that evening with the sun slipping below the horizon, the two friends found themselves cruising around Fairbanks in an old army jeep. The fold-down front windshield, fastened in the "up" position, was their only protection against the freezing night air.

"I can't believe you paid three hundred bucks for this rust bucket," Steve said from the depths of his hooded parka.

"Hey! This little beauty's haulin your ass aint it? And it didn't cost you nothin," Jimmy countered.

"Yeah sure. An ass buster, that's what it is," Steve laughed.

"I'll kick it up. That'll smooth out the ride." Jimmy grinned, jamming down the accelerator as he headed out of town along Farmer's Loop.

"Goddamn," Steve shouted, hunkering down and grabbing hold of the thinly padded metal seat to brace himself.

"You gotta admit this sonofabitch can eat up the road," Jimmy said. He felt exhilarated as he crouched lower over the steering wheel and pushed the old military vehicle up to forty.

"Yeah, I sure as hell like seeing the road fly by right through the floorboard."

"Guess I'll head back toward town. Won't be able to spot any damn moose wanderin onto the road with just one headlight. Let's go pay a little visit to the shootin gallery."

"I'm not betting," Steve groaned.

***

Jimmy was up early on Sunday morning, eager to take advantage of his new freedom to roam. Letting himself in at Steve's boardinghouse, he found nearly everyone passed out in their bunks.

"Roll out. Daylight's burnin. Get your lazy ass dressed," Jimmy said none too quietly as he shook Steve awake.

"Damn," Steve groaned. "You got a wild hair up your ass?"

"Come on. We got some explorin to do."

"Yeah, okay. I'll meet you at The Pastime."

"Taxi leaves in an hour."

"Yeah, yeah," Steve said, staggering to his feet and grabbing a towel from the foot of his bed as he headed for the shower.

Steve made it in half an hour flat, ordering breakfast while Jimmy finished his own and nursed his coffee.

"Hey, let's check out the gun shop," Jimmy said as he parked on a side street. He knew better than to try driving down Second Avenue where a sea of staggering, cursing, fighting GIs and workmen were milling about.

"What the hell did you want that for?" Steve asked as they left the shop with Jimmy's new purchase.

"Aint it a beauty! What's the matter, you choking on the two hundred bucks? Let's go try her out," Jimmy said, stowing his elaborately decorated .44 Smith & Wesson pistol with its leather holster and a supply of ammunition under the back-seat bench in the jeep. Once he'd seen that gun with its carved ivory handles each sporting the image of a Texas Longhorn with ruby red eyes, Jimmy was sold on possessing such a treasure, the very symbol of the free life that the Wild West engendered.

Driving west on Second Avenue the road became even more rough and rutted as they followed the Chena River out of town. After a while Jimmy found a spot where he could drive right down onto the riverbank beside the surging, murky ice-melt water. After getting the feel of the huge pistol by first siting on small spruce trees, they wandered further downstream and found a rusted fifty-gallon oil drum that someone had already dragged there for target practice.

Standing some fifty feet back, Jimmy took aim. "Watch this," he bragged, struggling to keep the gun steady as he extended his arms. "This bastard's heavy," he laughed, rearranging his grip and finally squeezing off a round. Although he was expecting it, the kickback was mulish and the report deafening.

"Missed," Steve said.

"Son of a bitch," Jimmy groaned after he'd emptied the revolver in the direction of the oil drum. "I didn't hit the damn thing once."

"Let me show you how," Steve grinned. Extending the hefty firearm, he sighted down the eight-inch barrel. "Shit, this thing's heavy for damn sure," he said. Shifting more of the weight to his left hand, he still could hardly keep the barrel level. Finally, he squeezed the trigger.

"Great shooting, dead eye," Jimmy said. "Ya missed by a mile."

Undaunted, the friends spent the afternoon perfecting their shooting proficiency. By the time they ran low on ammunition, their arm and shoulder muscles were heavy with fatigue, but neither of them had scored a single hit on the oil drum.

Donning their parkas for the chilly ride, they headed back to town as the temperature dipped toward freezing, the weak evening sunshine having little warming effect.

"What the hell are you doing?" Steve asked as he watched Jimmy tuck the hefty forty-four into his waistband when he got out of the jeep.

"Takin my gun. I'm sure as hell not leaving it here."

"But it's loaded, isn't it?"

"Yeah. Only a dumb sonofabitch would carry a unloaded pistol."

"Well, it doesn't seem like a good idea to take it into The Grifter."

"It'll be fine right here," he said patting the bulky gun butt that protruded over his waistband. "My flannel shirt'll cover it."

On Sunday night The Grifter was packed and noisy. Many a man slumped over the bar prolonging his weekend binge, lamenting his excesses, or drowning his sorrows. At the pool tables and around the poker games the conversations grew rowdy and contentious as the hours passed.

"Goddamn, I'd bet money you never set eyes on a firearm before," Jimmy said as he polished off a second beer and bit into a greasy hamburger.

"My grandpa had a hunting rifle, but my dad wouldn't let me touch it," Steve said. "No one I knew had any kind of handgun in Middletown, New York that's for damn sure. The one time Grandpa took me out target shooting, my father nearly disowned the both of us. When you crossed him there was hell to pay. It was smarter not to get on his bad side."

"Yeah?" Jimmy said, ordering another round as he waited for his friend to continue the story. But the ensuing silence told him that Steve was done. While Jimmy was not in the habit of confiding his own thoughts or feelings, his friend, despite his blithe manner, had a genuine aptitude for being closed-mouth about his personal life.

"When I was a littlebitty kid in Oklahoma my old man could kill a rattlesnake faster than it could strike," Jimmy volunteered, setting his beer bottle on the table and rocking back in his chair. "He kept his twenty-two handy. The tough old bastard was a crack shot. He could kill them with his bare hands, too. Sometimes out in the cotton fields he'd get bit, but mostly he'd see um first and grab ahold of their tail real fast. Whap, he'd whip em against the ground and snap their necks. Them damn rattlers would hang around the irrigation ditch when it was real hot, but once in a while they'd be hidin under the cotton plants. Never seen the old man afraid of a snake. When he got bit, he'd kill the snake first then come up to the house and lie down. Next day he'd be back to work."

"Didn't the venom make him sick?"

"Yeah, but I think his body got kinda used to it," Jimmy continued, the beer loosening his reserve. "One time I was up in my favorite climbin tree, a big old oak sittin out in the front yard. Up I went. When I reached up to the top climbin branch, it felt all smooth and kinda cool. Somethin wasn't right, so I pulled myself up real slow until I could see over the top. I'll be damned if I wasn't face-to-face with a big ol diamondback. I had it clamped down against the branch, just behind the head. Couldn't believe my eyes. I let out a big scream and just let go," he said, throwing his hands up in the air in a gesture of surrender. "Went fallin backwards outa the tree maybe ten feet straight down. Busted my ass good on the wood blocks we kids used for playin trucks. The old man grabbed his twenty-two from off the front porch and shot the bastard right through the head. One shot and the old rattler dropped right outa the tree."

"Damn! I can see you'd need a rifle out there."

"Yeah, the old man had a shotgun and a couple pistols, too. Nobody messed with them. Out in the country you get used to having them around."

"Did he keep them locked up?"

"No. He just put the fear a God into us. We didn't mess around with them, but we got all the shootin practice we wanted with our BB guns. Me and my brothers shot the hell out of each other. It's a damn wonder we didn't shoot each other's eyes out. One time I popped Everett right in the mouth when he was peekin around a corner. He sputtered and coughed and finally spit it out. We laughed our asses off."

"No shit! You'd shoot each other on purpose?"

"Hell yes. It was a hell of a lot more fun than target shootin. We had war games and Cowboys and Indians. There's nothin like sneekin up on a guy and nailin him good while he's lyin in wait to ambush you. Sometimes you'd have to pick BBs out a your hide."

"You kids were tough."

"Yeah. It was Billy nearly shot my ass for real down by the railroad tracks. My brothers and me was walkin along the main line that runs through the San Joaquin Valley on our way to the swimmin hole. Guess I was about twelve and Billy two years younger. He stops and picks up this rusty gun lying by the tracks. 'Hey, lookit this,' he says. 'Somebody dropped a cap pistol.' Then he takes a bead on me, only a couple feet from my face, and starts to pull the trigger. What I see is the cylinder startin to turn and I think 'holy shit' and duck my head real quick thinkin I was about to die. Boom! The thing explodes and my face gets peppered with rusty metal. Billy dropped that pistol like a hot potato and his face turned all white. It scared the crap out a him too."

"What did you do with the gun?"

"We turned it in to the police in Fresno. Turns out it was used in a store robbery where somebody got killed some twenty years before. The robbers had got rid of it along the tracks. It had been lyin there in plain sight all that time and ... "

A sharp blow to the side of his head rudely interrupted Jimmy's story. "What the hell?" he bellowed as he leaped out of his chair. The offender was squaring off to punch him again as the barroom exploded into a melee. Men were shouting, cursing and thumping each other as a mad chaotic wave spread through the entire tavern.

Jimmy, angered by the sucker punch and fired up with beer, moved in on his attacker, stunning him with a quick right cross. The stocky construction worker shook his head as if astonished that the tall, lanky guy had delivered that clean punch while staying clear out of reach. With a roar, he came back at Jimmy swinging. *Okay shithead*, Jimmy thought, landing another right. *Now I'm pissed. Good thing you're drunk off your ass, as big as you are.* The guy kept coming and managed to move in close enough to land a few blows while the fighting raged all around.

Out of the comer of his eye Jimmy saw that Steve was exchanging shots with some uniformed goon and holding his own. *That does it asshole*, Jimmy thought when the construction bozo persisted. Grabbing the guy by the collar, he shoved him back over the bar and nailed him with a hard right and left combination. Cocking his arm back for one more punch, Jimmy felt himself suddenly lifted and slung around. He realized midair that the .44 had dislodged from his waistband. He caught one glance of the pistol hitting the floor and sliding under a barstool before he became fully engaged in another altercation.

Oh shit, I've got to get that damn gun before anyone notices, he thought, the urgency making it hard to concentrate on defending himself in the midst of the brawl. "Goddamn fighting assholes," he mumbled, as he tried to work his way toward the pistol. He caught Steve's eye and saw the wary look. *Yeah, Steve knows the pistol's on the loose.* Inch by inch, blow by blow, he got closer to his goal. Finally, he leaned down and grabbed the hefty .44. Displaying a gun in that tinderbox was risky he knew, but he stuck with his daring plan. His only plan. Quickly he raised the weapon above his head, muzzle to the ceiling and began a slow, deliberate walk to the door. Steve fell in behind him, as a hush spread through the tavern and men stepped out of their way. Their luck held. Pushing through the door, they broke into a dead run.

***

The next morning when Jimmy walked into the union hall the mood of the place was subdued as befitted a blustery Monday. Still suffering the effects of their weekend excesses, the workers were predictably churlish and downcast. Despite being biffed-up a bit, Jimmy was rarin to go. He grabbed a cup of coffee and, toting his duffel bag full of clean work clothes, sat down quietly next to Fred who looked the worse for wear and in no mood for conversation as they waited for the crew to show up.

"Christ," Fred mumbled, "here comes Glen Cochran. Looks like he's got his ass in a knot."

"Where the hell's your crew?" the company foreman demanded.

"Yall spect me ta know? I aint their keeper."

"Well they damn well better show up. We aren't losing another day on the job."

While Glen paced and cursed under his breath, Jimmy spotted Steve ease in the front door and head for the coffeepot.

"Weren't you out tearing up the town with them all weekend?" Glen asked, pointing at Fred accusingly.

"Yeah, most a the time."

"It's getting late. Where did you see them last?" Glen demanded.

"Well," Fred said, hesitating and dropping his eyes, "they was goin over ta Miss Laverne's place."

"Goddamn, those damn assholes. They're not going to be worth a fart in a whirlwind."

"Hold on now. You know goddamn well they're real good workers. They just get ta raisin hell."

"You," Glen said, pointing at Jimmy, "get on over to that whorehouse and drag those screwups out of there. Tell them to be here in an hour or they're fired."

Oh shit! "You mean that cabin down on Fourth?" he asked, stalling while he searched for some way out.

"Yeah. Get a move on. Daylight's burning," Glen ordered.

"Nice shiner ya got there," Jimmy said, pausing as Steve caught up outside the union hall. "You comin?"

"Yeah. From the looks of your jaw, that charging bull nailed you pretty good last night," Steve observed, as he fell in step.

"I didn't see that big bastard comin. He blindsided me. And then he wouldn't take no for an answer."

"Christ Almighty, when you picked up that pistol, I thought you'd gone crazy. I was thinking 'now somebody'll get shot for sure.' No shit, you got some brass balls. I couldn't believe we walked right out of there," Steve said, shaking his head.

"Yeah, it was a real close call. That pistol's never gonna see the inside of a bar again. But one thing for damn sure, I aint lookin to bust into no goddamn whorehouse. Seems like it oughta be your turn."

"Oh no," Steve grinned. "The boss gave you the job."

"I noticed you sure as hell was makin yourself scarce back there at the union hall."

"Hey, I figured no use sticking my nose in when Glen's got a splinter up his ass.

"Yeah, well right here's goddamn Miss Laverne's place."

"Good luck, buddy. I'll wait out here," Steve said, crossing his arms.

With a withering look at his friend, Jimmy approached the sagging one-room log cabin, the warped plywood front door sitting only inches back from the street. Knuckles raised, Jimmy paused for a moment before giving a token knock and pushing into the dark interior.

"Hey honey," a disembodied throaty voice greeted.

He stood still, blinking. As his eyes adjusted to the darkness, the potent smell of unwashed bodies and the pungent odor of sexual encounter assaulted him. He could hear moans and rustlings and as his eyes cleared, could make out someone going at it on the crude dining table.

"Hey! You City Electric Assholes!" he shouted, thankful all at once for the dim lighting.

"That you, Jimmy?" slurred Alex's familiar voice from the area of the dining table where the action seemed to have stopped. "You finally comin down to try this stuff out?"

"Listen here! Glen Cochran sent my ass down here to tell you screw-ups you got one hour to be down to the union hall, or you're all fired," he blurted then headed back out the door.

He beat a hasty retreat as he greedily breathed in fresh air on the brisk walk back to the union hall.

"What's it like in there?" Steve grilled as he kept pace.   .

"You could of seen for yourself if you wasn't so chickenshit."

"Come on, tell me."

"Christ, it's dark and it stinks. I'd have to be drunk out of my goddamn mind to buy what they're sellin."

As they entered the union hall Glen stopped mid-pace and rushed up to them.

"Did you find them?" he demanded.

"Yeah. I told them."

"Well, are they coming?"

"Yeah, I think so."

"Were they all there?"

"Shit, Glen. I didn't take roll. I told Alex and best I can tell the rest of them shoulda heard me."

"Well, those dumbshits have another forty-five minutes. That's it. If they don't show, I'll can them."

"They'll be here," Fred said, stabbing out his cigarette. "Cool off. Ah don't give a good goddamn that yall 're the shittin boss. Yall 're getting on my goddamn nerves now."

Glen stalked away without another word.

"So, did yall get a good look inside Laverne's?" Fred asked, his mouth twitching into a smirk.

Jimmy shrugged and dropped into a chair while he fished in his shirt pocket for a cigarette.

"Aint no different from all them other whorehouses down there on Fourth," the salty lineman said as the two younger men remained silent.

"Sure aint no other willin women around these here parts," Fred continued, his voice becoming soft and reflective. "When guys're gettin the urge, they got no goddamn sense once they're all liquored up. Workin so far from home, theys times when a man's gotta break the dry spell," he finished, trailing off to silence.

Within the hour, the bedraggled crew drifted into the union hall. Glen followed hot on their heels. His clamped jaw worked as he eyed them, sizing them up before he began barking out their driving assignments. The men stared back defiantly. When the caravan was finally on its way to Big Delta, they were running three hours late.

Over the next two weeks the unrepentant crew practiced their new sport of badgering the grunts. On the job and after hours at the Buffalo Lodge they never let up about the whorehouse raid.

"Hey Jimmy," Dwight started in as he dealt another hand of poker. "Miss Laverne says you're real cute. She says you should stay a little longer next time."

"Yeah," Alex chimed in, " Alma Sue says 'yall come any time.'"

"Christ Almighty, was she the one you was humpin on the dinner table?"

"Could be. It's hard to remember," Alex laughed. "But those girls could teach you lots a tricks."

"Goddamn, how'd you get past the stink?" Jimmy retorted.

"What's a little stink when you're after hot pussy? Nothin better. I'd say bein a little drunk helps."

"You mean blind drunk, don't you?" Jimmy asked.

"Hey, we'll take you down there next time we're in town. A good piece of ass'll make a man of the both of ya," Dwight goaded.

"Forget it. You damn hounds are out a your minds paying for rotten pussy. I sure as hell don't want any that I gotta pay for."

"Yeah, paying is bullshit. Besides, those hags are old and ugly as sin," Steve said.

"Yeah. Payin queers the deal for him," Jimmy grinned.

"You gotta be referrin to 'The Crane,'" Mack said. "Her neck's so long she looks damned deformed. But that's not what I'm thinkin about when I'm with her. You got to learn to overlook some things."

"Yeah. She can give you a real good time," Alex prodded.

"Not me. She'd be as likely as not to give you the clap," Steve said.

"What'd you know about the clap?" Dwight asked.

"Nothin. And that's how its gonna stay," Steve said.

"You're missin out. Them girls'll break you young bucks in right," Mack said.

"I'm broke in just fine. When it comes to pussy, I'm damn picky." Jimmy retorted. "But I can understand why it was so damn dark in that stinkin cabin."

"Sure, sure. You're sounding mighty like a virgin."

"Think what you like. You won't be gettin me down there to Miss Laverne's and that's the end of it," Jimmy said with finality.

But there was no end to the ribbing the linemen inflicted on the grunts. While the crew worked hard on building the power lines by day and played hard at the Buffalo Lodge by night, the whorehouse subject simmered, flared, and persisted for two solid weeks, but it never died. When the crew packed up for their return to Fairbanks, they already knew their rotation was at an end. After the weekend, a fresh crew would take over the Big Delta project.

4

THE CABIN

In Fairbanks the month of May finally brought some welcome warmth along with the expanding hours of daylight. The sun rode higher in the sky and a breath of spring pulsed in the air.

Keeping his name on the work roster at the Electrical Workers Union Hall, Jimmy was assigned to local jobs working nearly every day. While he and Steve often found themselves picked for different crews, they usually hung around together after work and on weekends.

On the job with the temperatures approached sixty degrees by midday, Jimmy could often shed his flannel work-shirt and settle for working in his tee shirt and Levi's. His winter gear, the heavy parka, insulated boots, woolen long-johns and socks, were already stowed in his locker at the boarding house where he kept the pistol and all his other belongings under lock and key. Even with his recent extravagant purchases he continued to give Mrs. Turner some of his paychecks to deposit in his savings account.

For Jimmy, roaming around in his jeep became a favorite pastime. He loved to explore and now he had transportation. Driving in that open vehicle still called for a warm jacket especially in the chill evening air. He found that the swarms of mosquitoes were kept at bay as long as he was in motion.

One Saturday afternoon he was kicking around by himself out along Steele Creek Road when he came upon an old pickup off in the ditch.

Spotting a woman and a teenage girl hiking further up the road, he pulled alongside and stopped short to avoid immersing them in a swirl of dust.

"Hey, you need some help?" he called.

"Oh yes," the dark-haired woman answered as relief softened her pretty face. "I had a blowout and the darn truck slid right off into the ditch before I could stop. Could you tow us out? There's a spare in the back of the truck."

"Sure. Where do you live?" he asked, enjoying the view of the attractive woman in some kind of uniform and the sweet-faced teenage girl dressed in a flannel shirt, jeans and work boots, her dishwater blond hair pulled back in a thick ponytail.

"We live just up the road a couple of miles. I've got to get the supplies home and the animals need to be fed. I'm running late."

"Jump in. We'll grab your stuff and I'll run you home."

"Thanks. It's so kind of you. I'm Margaret Watkins and this is my daughter, Lilly," she said, extending her hand.

"Nice to meet you Mrs. Watkins. Hi Lilly. I'm Jimmy Evans," he said, flashing his dimpled smile.

"Hi," Lilly answered shyly, dropping her gaze.

"That's our place on the right. Thanks for the ride. My husband can go after the truck later."

"I don't mind, Mrs. Watkins" Jimmy volunteered as he delivered them to their isolated cabin. "I just need to run into town for my tow chain. I'll be right back."

Steve, my hard workin friend, you are damn well missin out, he thought as he hightailed it back to town and pulled in at the Big Tire Store.

"Hey Dan," Jimmy said, catching the attention of a gray-haired tire salesman who looked to be fifty but who he knew for a fact was barely thirty. Dan was, after all, his stepfather.

"Jimmy! Well I'll be goddamned. Where the hell you been?" Dan asked, pumping his hand.

"Oh, just around."

"What the hell do you mean 'around'? We haven't laid eyes on you for a year. You're mama's been all worked up worrying about you."

"Yeah, yeah. I've been busy."

"Well, are you working?"

"Did you ever see me when I wasn't workin?"

"No," Dan laughed, shaking his head. "You're a goddamn hard worker Jimmy."

"A while back I got on at City Electric. Been up to Big Delta. The job pays good," Jimmy said. "Hey, I'm in kind of a hurry. I need a tow chain, a carjack, and a nut wrench."

"Come on. I'll fix you up," Dan said, gathering the items and ringing up the purchase himself.

"Thanks," Jimmy said, turning quickly toward the door.

"Son! Go see your mama. Don't be a stranger," Dan called after him.

It didn't take Jimmy very long to yank the old Chevy pickup out of the ditch and change the tire. And he quite enjoyed the welcome the Watkins family gave him as pulled into their rutted dirt driveway.

At the sound of his engine, Mrs. Watkins, three kids and two mongrel dogs poured out of the gold-rush-era log cabin to greet him.

"You're truck's out of the ditch and I got the spare on her. She's off to the side of the road. Hop in and I'll drive you down to get her."

"Wonderful!" Mrs. Watkins exclaimed, clapping her hands and hugging them to her chest in a gesture of delight as they made the short trip to retrieve her truck. "Now I can get to my job on Monday. With my husband out of town working construction, I wasn't sure how I'd get that old wreck of a truck back home."

"Here, here, come on in," Mrs. Watkins insisted when Jimmy pulled back into the driveway in her wake.

He stepped onto a low add-on front porch while the kids stared curiously and the dogs sniffed him, wagging their tails once they'd judged him safe. As he followed the family into the tidy one room cabin, a younger girl, who was the brown-eyed, blond picture of her older sister, shut the heavy, sturdily reinforced front door behind them.

"Have to keep those pesky mosquitoes out," she said at a barely discernible whisper. "I don't like them."

"Me either," Jimmy laughed. "They're real mean at this time of year."

"Jimmy, this is Molly. She's nine. And Charles here is eleven. You've already met Lilly," Mrs. Watkins said.

The kids nodded as their names were mentioned, then remained silent as they looked at Jimmy expectantly. Jimmy shook hands with each of them bringing smiles of surprise at being treated in such an adult manner.

"We are expecting you to stay for dinner," Mrs. Watkins said.

"No need for that, but I won't turn you down. What smells so good, anyway?" he asked, glancing at the bubbling pot on the wood stove. The rising steam wafted a delectably meaty fragrance.

"We're having stew. Dinner will be ready in half an hour. Kids, it's time to get your chores done," she said.

"Hey, I'm good at chores," Jimmy said. "I'll help you guys."

Jimmy was in his element as he carried several armloads of firewood to fill the wood-box near the stove. Charles took great joy in loading him up to his chin, standing on tiptoe to reach. He helped the young boy pump water from the well and tote in two full pails. Meanwhile the sisters were occupied with watering and spreading feed for the chickens in a tightly constructed pen and coop.

"Hey Jimmy," Lilly called, her brown eyes dancing mischievously. Aren't you going to help us too?"

"Sure," he answered, sliding through the gate into the wire mesh pen taking care to block the eager dogs from entering.

"Here's the basket. Why don't you check the nests in the coop and see if they laid any more eggs this afternoon?"

"What if those old hens want to peck me?" he asked innocently.

"Oh, they can be real mean," she warned with mock sincerity.

"Yeah," Molly piped in. "I'll do it," she said heroically, holding out her hand for the basket.

Pulling the basket back, Jimmy shot them a worried look and darted into the coop in two long strides. "Ouch, ouch, give me that darn egg you miserable chicken," he hollered in a falsetto. Hearing the girls' giggles, he kept up the charade until there were gales of laughter.

"I only got two eggs," he said in a sad voice as he emerged. "And I think I'm bleeding."

"Where?" Lilly asked, hands on hips.

"You are not," Molly laughed, taking the basket from him as she examined his hands.

"Dinner's ready," Mrs. Watkins called from the porch. "What's all the commotion?"

"Jimmy's being a knothead," Charles said. "He's afraid of the chickens."

"No, he's not," the girls said in unison.

"Be sure to wash up before dinner," a smiling Mrs. Watkins said, indicating the wash basin, water pitcher, and soap sitting on the front porch railing above which a towel hung from a nail.

"I haven't milked Heidi yet, Mom," Lilly said.

"That's okay. The goat will have to wait until after dinner. Charles, you run on down to the root cellar and bring back the chilled milk from this morning. Remember to shut the doors tight."

Head bowed, Jimmy silently endured the blessing that included each person giving fervent prayers for Stuart and William, and, it seemed everyone else of their acquaintance. His mouth watered at the tantalizing fragrances wafting through the small cabin. He couldn't remember the last time he'd had a home-cooked dinner. The stew proved delicious beyond his expectations, rich, full of meat and vegetables and the yeast rolls tasted heavenly, light and buttery.

"That's the best stew I ever tasted, Mrs. Watkins."

"Thank you. I used the last of the moose that William shot in the fall. With the permafrost the meat stays good in the root cellar. When he gets home, I expect he'll hunt another moose and likely make sausage of it to keep it good over the summer."

"Would you like some more?" she asked reaching for his plate.

"Oh, no thanks. I already had seconds and lots of those great rolls," he said, patting his stomach. "I don't know where I'd put another bite," he groaned.

"Jimmy, you remind me so much of Stuart, our oldest son," she said, smiling wistfully. "He's full of mischief, tall and lanky and strong, just like you. We all say he must have a hollow leg the way he eats."

"Yeah. I heard about my hollow leg before," Jimmy said, feeling comfortable and welcome. Is Stuart working on the construction job with your husband?"

"No," Lilly answered, sadness resonating in her voice. "He's off in Korea. We miss him."

"We're waiting to hear from him. It's been over a month," Mrs. Watkins said.

"Oh. He got drafted?" Jimmy asked.

"No. He enlisted last fall when he turned eighteen," Mrs. Watkins explained. "We believe in serving our country. He'll come home safe and sound. Our whole church is praying for him," she said, her tense expression belying her confident words.

Oh shit. We won't be seein eye to eye on that. You got me all wrong. I'm nothin like your Stuart, he thought. In the silence that followed Jimmy swallowed hard, choking back his own convictions and painful grief.

"Lilly, it's time to milk Heidi. You kids are on kitchen cleanup," she said, putting an end to the subject.

"I'm comin with you Lilly, milkin beats kitchen duty hands down," Jimmy said.

"Aw, that's not fair," Charles complained.

"So how old are you anyway?" Lilly asked, grabbing the milk bucked off the porch on the way to the goat shed.

"I'm - uh- eighteen. I had a birthday a few weeks back and clean forgot about it till just now. How old are you?"

"Almost sixteen, in a few months. You seem like you're a lot older," she said, watching him intently.

"Well, I been on my own takin care of myself for a long time now. Already been lots of places and done lots of things."

"That so? Ever milked a goat?" she challenged, her eyes dancing with mischief.

"Well, no, but I milked a cow. Can't be that different."

"Here we are," she said, opening the gate to a high-fenced enclosure and handing him the milk bucket.

A scrappy goat standing about three feet high was in the far corner of the paddock. It seemed to Jimmy that Heidi had fixed him with a baleful stare the moment he'd stepped inside.

"Why don't I just watch you awhile?"

"You don't know how," she laughed. "Okay, grab a handful of that bailed grass from inside the shed. That'll keep her busy while I milk her."

"Heiiiidi!" was all Jimmy heard between the time he turned his back and the moment his rump was impacted and lifted clear off the ground.

"Oh! I'm so sorry, I'm so sorry" Lilly said, her voice crackling with suppressed laughter as she dragged the errant goat back by her collar and chained her to a stake. "Are you okay?"

"Yeah, I'm fine," Jimmy said already on his feet and brushing himself off. "Guess I shouldn't of turned my back, huh?" he asked. *The joke's on me,* he thought. *Feisty girl. Pretty. Did she set me up? We'll see.*

"She hasn't pulled that trick for a long time," she said, breaking into outright laughter as she pulled up a stool and put the bucket in place. "Settle down, girl," she said dropping her voice into a quiet caressing tone as she began massaging the teats.

Jimmy watched in silence while Lilly milked. She expressed the warm liquid with skilled hands while she murmured calming phrases, her voice weaving a rhythmic melody in counterpoint to the hissing cadence produced as each pulse of milk hit the side of the pail. Jimmy was mesmerized.

"Want a turn?" she challenged, breaking the spell.

Jimmy, at a total loss for words, just shook his head. His sudden arousal had taken him by surprise. *Christ! What the hell am I thinkin? God no! She's a nice girl. I'm sure as hell not lookin for that kind of trouble*, Jimmy thought fighting back his lustful impulse. He was confident in his ability to control his own bodily urges. Unlike his liaisons with the older, experienced girls who had taught him the ropes in the fields of Fresno, he knew that messing with this girl could mean a kind of involvement he wasn't ready to handle.

"All done," she announced, moving the bucket clear of the goat before releasing it from the tether.

"What's the matter?" she asked noticing his wary look. "Oh! She won't butt you again."

"Not while I'm watchin," he said, laughing as he sidestepped toward the gate.

"Mom," Lilly called out when she got near the house. "Heidi popped Jimmy."

Jimmy saw that the family had gathered at the front door awaiting their return. At the news, Molly broke into a big smile that she covered quickly with her hand. Charles, however, guffawed and demanded a play-by-play.

"Oh no. I thought she was over that," Mrs. Watkins said. "I'm so sorry. Here Charles, take the fresh milk out to the root cellar, please."

"That littlebitty goat couldn't hurt a guy much, but she sure took me by surprise," Jimmy said waving a hand dismissively.

"Come on in," Mrs. Watkins said, making an obvious effort not to laugh. "Lilly's made a blueberry pie. I'll bet you'd like a piece."

"It's my favorite," Jimmy said. "I'll manage to stuff it down."

"Can you play some rummy with us after I take the milk out?"

Charles asked.

"Sure. I'm kinda rusty, but I bet you can straighten me out on the rules."

The evening passed quickly as they got better acquainted over the card game. Seated at the rough wooden table, they absorbed the warmth radiating from the nearby wood stove, a kerosene lantern illuminating the players as the cabin darkened.

"Where are you from, Jimmy?" Mrs. Watkins asked between hands.

"I'm from all over, but I moved here from California last year. Have you guys been here long?"

"Yeah," Charles answered, "seems like we've been here all my life."

"We've been in Alaska for five years now," Mrs. Watkins explained. "We came up from Montana so my husband could find work."

"Lots of the guys I'm workin with come up here from all over looking for jobs."

"Do your folks live here?"

"Yeah. I helped move them up last year. They got a homestead about five miles further out on Steele."

"So, you live with them?"

"Oh no. I live in town. I'm workin for City Electric."

"I know where that is. I work mornings just over on Third Street at the Miner's Cafe. Thanks to you I can get to work on Monday. You know it's hard to keep these homesteads afloat. We have ninety acres but it's not good for growing much of anything."

"Mom, deal," Molly said impatiently.

"Okay," she said, shuffling the deck. "Stuart tried to get a summer job at City Electric last year. But they wouldn't take him on since he was only seventeen. Have you worked there long?"

"Just this year. Last year I worked for F&J Mining," Jimmy said, aware of Lilly watching him as she had all afternoon.

"Did you work down in a mine?" Charles asked, perking up.

"No. I worked on a gold dredge."

"What's that?" Charles asked, the card game forgotten.

"Were you digging up gold?" Molly asked.

"Well, the dredge was. A gold dredge's a big barge, like a boat. When they know there's gold under the ground, they dig a big hole and pump it full of water. Then they drag the barge in, so it floats."

"But how do they get the gold?" Molly asked.

"Well, there's an arm at the front that has buckets with sharp claws. Them buckets scoop up chunks of dirt right down to the bedrock where the gold is and dump it into the hopper."

"What's a hopper?" Charles asked.

"It's an open place in the deck where the dirt drops down into a barrel that's full of holes. While the barrel keeps turnin, powerful sprayers inside go to washin the gold free from the rocks and mud. The heavy gold drops down into the sluice boxes and all the rest a the stuff, the slag, dumps out the back of the dredge."

"So what makes it run?" Molly asked.

"Huge, steam engines. It kinda moves forward like a monster eating up everything in its path."

"What was your job?" Lilly asked.

"Oh, I was a roustabout, helped out with all kinds of things."

"Like what?" she persisted.

"Well, I helped out the mechanics and electricians with their equipment. They was always havin to fix stuff. I was haulin the welder around most of the time. The operation there went on twenty- four hours a day and everything had to be workin. The whole crew was workin twelve-on and twelve-off for ten days straight. Since the mine was near thirty miles north of here, they had a big lodge for us to stay in. It was swell. We had all the food we could eat. That hard work made you real hungry."

"Did you get to see the gold?" Charles asked impatiently.

"Man alive, that was the best part of the job. When they shut her down after ten days, they'd do repairs like weld new teeth on the buckets and grease everything up. But the main thing was gettin the gold out of the sluice boxes. We'd go down inside the dredge and shovel the gold into these long, skinny canvas sacks. There was still a lot of black sand mixed in. Once they was filled up, them sacks was heavier than hell." *Damn it!* Jimmy thought, realizing he'd let slip a curse after carefully controlling his rough language all evening.

"Anyway," he continued after an awkward silence, "it was all a guy could do to throw just one of them bags over your shoulder and tote it up out of there. We'd pile them in the back of a pickup and they'd drive it off to the smelter."

"You tell good stories just like Stuart," Molly said adoringly.

"Didn't you like that job?" Lilly asked.

"Yeah. I loved it."

"Then why did you quit?"

"When the ground froze up last winter, they had to close it down."

That night Jimmy drove back to town by the light of his one headlight, his stomach still filled near to bursting with blueberry pie and his heart singing with a rare contentment.

***

"Hey Steve, see that old geezer playin cards over yonder?" Jimmy said, setting his beer bottle down on the bar.

"You mean that little wizened up guy with the stringy beard?"

"Yeah. Old Pete there's a legend. He prospected for years, then sometime back he struck it rich, found a huge vein of gold."

"Well, he looks like he's down and out."

"Yeah. He is. Lost every penny includin the deed to his mine on a single hand of poker," Jimmy said, delivering the dramatic punch line that was sure to goad his miserly friend.

"No shit!" Steve said in disbelief.

"Yup," Jimmy said, grinning. "He laid it all on the line and lost. Said he had no regrets and went back to prospectin."

"Where'd you hear that?" Steve asked, looking askance as if the story, inconceivable to him, might be a whopper.

"Old Harvey Edwards pointed him out one day."

"You mean the old shoeshine guy down on second?"

"Yeah, he's a old-timer. Knows everybody. He can tell you lots of stories."

"Do you think it's true?"

"Yeah. Them big time gamblers are crazy as hell."

"I guess so," Steve said, taking a pull on his beer as he watched the old prospector playing cards. "You still working local jobs?"

"Yeah. We've been puttin in a new line off Farmer's Loop," Jimmy said. "The work's good. I like kickin around after work with the days gettin long."

"Yeah. Matter of fact it's getting late. I'd better turn in. I'm signed up for another stint at Big Delta tomorrow. I'd rather be working with the old wild-man crew out there. I kinda miss their bullshit, but the money's good. Why don't you sign up again? We're a good team."

"Naw. I'm takin a break from being stuck day and night with a crew. All they want to do is get drunk, fight and blow their wages on makin stupid bets. Hey, tomorrow's Monday morning. Maybe Glen'll have to send you down to Miss Laverne's to haul the crew out of there."

"God, I hope not," Steve grimaced.

***

With time on his hands, long days and plenty of youthful energy even after a hard day's work, Jimmy began to explore the area around Fairbanks in earnest. His trusty jeep negotiated the rutted back roads, at times mired in mud with the spring rains. The ride was rough but satisfying as he wandered through the swampy muskeg along the Tanana River. He drove through stands of birch trees and scrappy spruce that had topped out at twenty feet as they stubbornly withstood the yearly onslaught of brutal winters.

Jimmy had taken to carrying a Winchester thirty-aught-six rifle as his wilderness companion. So it was that he undertook the moose hunt, or moose chase as it turned out. One day as he meandered near a small creek on a particularly primitive road, a bull moose came charging out of the brush, crossed in front of the jeep and took off toward the river. Startled, Jimmy grabbed his rifle and got off one quick shot. Jumping from his jeep, he chased after the beast, which he thought he might have hit in the rump, at best. Still, he couldn't leave it wounded or so he told himself.

Charged for action, he plunged through the head-high brush in hot pursuit. Stopping to listen, he heard crashing and snorting sounds ahead to the right. He stepped up his pace, attempting to follow the path the moose had plowed through the scrappy, brittle undergrowth, sometimes running alongside or crossing the tumbling stream. Each time he paused he could hear the behemoth charging ahead. He had kept up the chase for what seemed like hours, hearing but never catching sight of his target, when it dawned on him that he was hopelessly lost.

Wondering how long and how far he had ranged; Jimmy gave up on his quarry as he tried to get his bearings. The high brush seemed a solid barrier blocking his view in every direction. Going on gut instinct, he bulldozed his way across the creek and headed due east according to his reckoning. As his stamina began to flag, his earlier enthusiasm for the hot pursuit of wild game was transformed into a fervent desire to discover any sign of civilization.

His rifle was becoming heavier by the mile when he finally stumbled across an overgrown dirt lane. Spurred on by a jolt of relief, he eventually intersected a more traveled road, the very road beside which he would find his jeep some eight miles further down. Tired, but confident that he was on the right track, he slowed momentarily to check out a deserted miner's cabin. The isolated dwelling caught his interest, but his focus remained riveted on finding his vehicle. After he'd slogged another five miles down the road, he rounded a bend to see his waiting jeep, a welcome sight as semi-darkness closed in.

***

"Where yall been, sonny?" Harvey Edwards asked when he saw Jimmy slide into one of his shoeshine chairs.

"Yesterday I was wanderin around in the goddamn wilderness."

"Why you was ya doin dat?"

"I took a notion to hunt a damn moose and got myself lost."

"Uh, uh, uh," Harvey said, shaking his head.

"It was a dumbass trick," Jimmy admitted.

"Sho nuf. Hey, yall see dat ol lady?" he said, pointing to an ancient woman determinedly making her way down Second Avenue, leaning heavily on her carved wooden cane. "Dat be ol Miz Ford. She be one ol- time madam herebouts."

"No shit," Jimmy said, eyeing the hunched, frail woman shabbily dressed all in black, except for the dirty red stocking cap on her head. "She looks like she's fell on hard times."

"Ha! She be one feisty ol woman. Make a fortune wit her whorehouse back in Goal Rush days. She end up ownin bout half a dis here town."

"Yeah? She must a been one damn smart whore."

"Mmm hmm. Dem layars ala time now tryn ta say she crazy, taken her ta court."

"Is she crazy?"

"Sho nuf, she be some daft. But them layars jus schemin on her moneys. Miz Ford, she gots a heart a gold for chillins. All the time findin some family down on dare luck an lettin um stay in one a her ol cabins. She like ta hide a bag full a moneys inside for them ta find. Den she sayin not her moneys so they cain be keepin it."

"Where does she live?"

"Right in dat buildin, she ownin dat whole damn thing."

"She looks like she's broke."

"Naw. She jus old."

"Hey, Harvey. I was down to Laverne's a couple weeks ago."

"Naw, ya wasn't."

"Sure as hell was."

"Youse best be watchin yo ass round dem whores, sonny. They be up ta teachin dem tricks what aint no good for younins. They be rollin ya in da bargain."

"Yeah, I figured," Jimmy laughed. "My boss sent me down there to roust out some of the linemen a couple weeks back. None of them guys had a dime left in their pockets. Just between us, them girls damn well scare the hell outa me."

"Den ya aint so dumb afer all. Dem whores be eatin ya alive," Harvey said, breaking into deep rumble of laughter as he flashed his gold-capped smile.

"You been winnin any card games lately Harvey?"

"Mmm hmm. Been wild-ass lucky."

"Soon you'll be rich as Mrs. Ford. Be able to sell out your shoeshine stand here and live like a king."

"Naw," he said, shaking his head. "I be workin this stan til da day I dies."

***

It wasn't long before wanderlust and curiosity brought Jimmy back to the deserted cabin. Taking a better look at the place, he saw a sturdy log hut with an intact sod roof. The door, a reinforced sheet of plywood with a simple metal handle, had no lock. With hinges squealing as he opened the door, he peered into the dark windowless interior. Propping it open so that he could see, Jimmy sized up the accouterments which consisted of a wood stove, a raised sleeping platform, some crude shelving on one wall. A myriad of cobwebs swayed gently as fresh air flowed into the little cabin. It seemed that nobody had lived there for years. Even so, he found little sign of any leaks and the chinking between the logs seemed intact. As he scouted the surrounding thick woods of stunted spruce and the clear gurgling creek some hundred feet away, he found something about the remote location that called to his need for independence and stimulated a primitive urge bonding him to the place.

The next day he moved in. Having withdrawn two hundred dollars from Jimmy's bank account for him, Mrs. Turner agreed to sell him a used mattress and a couple of chrome kitchen chairs. As always, he would continue to be a steady boarder, paying his monthly rent, coming and going as he pleased. His bed in the dorm and his locker would be reserved for him.

At Roy's Mercantile, Jimmy stocked up on everything he could think of to set up housekeeping: a double-bit ax, a kerosene lantern, a full can of kerosene, wooden matches, pans and cooking utensils, a can opener, canned food, eggs and bacon, a flashlight, a sleeping bag and pillow, and a bucket to carry water. Loading his jeep with supplies, he set out on his foray into the wilderness.

By the time the late setting sun slid toward the horizon, he had collected, chopped and stacked a pile of firewood next to the front door. With a sense of sweet satisfaction, he wiped away the sweat that was coursing down his face in rivulets after his hours of exertion. Now the mosquitoes were swarming, and an immense hunger was driving him. By the light of his lantern he started a fire in the old wood stove, tending it carefully as the tinder caught, then stoking it as the flames licked higher. Searching through the jumble of purchases scattered on the floor, he found a pan, a can of beans and the can opener before he realized that the cabin was filling with smoke. He hurriedly adjusted the damper to no avail before throwing the cabin door wide open. On closer inspection with the aid of his lantern, Jimmy discovered that the tin stovepipe was rusted through. Once he'd doused the fire, he used a shirt to fan out the smoke. Then the mosquitoes had to be eliminated with the rest of the energy he could muster. That night he settled on cold beans for dinner and curled up in his sleeping bag. Exhausted and elated he fell into a sound sleep.

Jimmy's trusty internal clock got him up in time for the twelve-mile drive back to the boardinghouse for a shower and breakfast before he reported for work at the union hall. That afternoon he was back at the mercantile buying a new stovepipe and tools. While he was there, he picked up a loaf of bread, toilet paper, soap and a wash basin, necessities he'd forgotten the day before.

As he fixed up the cabin, Jimmy began to think of the place as his private hideaway. Chopping wood, hauling water, bathing in the ice-cold creek, relieving himself while doing battle with the voracious mosquitoes were all part of the experience. He had, after all, lived in situations just as primitive. He enjoyed the challenge, the self-sufficiency, and the solitude.

***

"What's new, Red?" Jimmy asked, as his favorite waitress hustled to serve a Saturday lunch crowd at The Pastime Cafe.

"Hi Slim. I'm real good," Red answered, flashing her pretty smile. "My husband finally got leave. Two weeks. I was real thankful to see him safe and sound. He's shipping out again tomorrow, but I couldn't get any more time off."

"It's swell that he could come home."

"Wish he could stay. It's been rough on him."

"Yeah."

"Where have you been, Slim?"

"Been workin at City Electric. Found a little cabin in the woods out past Steele Creek. I cleaned it up real good. Been stayin out there part time."

"Yeah? Who does it belong to?"

"I don't know. Seems deserted. It's nice and quiet out there."

"Yeah. It's pretty wild here in town day and night," she said, looking down to total a bill on her order pad. "Oh, damnit!" she mumbled as her pencil lead broke. "Have you got a little penknife in your pocket?" she asked.

Patting down his pockets Jimmy finally came up with a long switchblade he sometimes carried in his jacket. Never without some kind of knife in his pocket, he thought of it as an essential tool.

"Here," he said, releasing the blade. "It's a little big for the job, but it'll sharpen your pencil."

"I guess so," she laughed.

"I'll do it," he said, making a pile of shavings as the shaped the pencil to a sharp point.

Laying the knife on the counter, he sipped his coffee while Red caught up on her duties.

"Thanks," Red said, leaning on the counter across from him. "Sharpest pencil I've had in some time. Do you always carry that thing?"

"Hell no. I forgot it was in my coat pocket. But I always carry a pocketknife. Have since I was a littlebitty kid. My old man gave all us boys one. Carried it all the time."

"What's a little kid do with a knife?"

"Whittle if nothin else. But around the farm seems like there's always somethin you need to cut. It come in handy. In fact, I ended up usin it my first year of school."

"At school?" she asked looking doubtful.

"Oh yeah," he said with a smirk. "There was this big kid named Manuel. He decided one day he wanted to sit on me. Every damn recess he'd catch me and sit. I was kinda puny. For weeks it was always the same. He didn't get tired of it and I couldn't get away from him. One day when I was trying to throw him off, I felt that knife in my pocket. Somehow I managed to get it open and I stabbed him in the ass."

"You didn't!"

"Oh yeah! He jumped up and went to hollerin. The teacher was madder than a wet hen. She took the knife and come to my house that night. Shit, I was afraid to go home. When she come in, she handed the knife to my old man and spouted off about the terrible thing I done. He listened for a while, then asked me what happened. All I could say was that I was tired of Manuel sittin on me every recess. The old man looked at me real mean, then handed over the knife. Told me to do the same thing if it was to ever happen again."

Red was laughing. "Oh boy!"

"The teacher was real pissed. She slammed the door when she left. But the old man just laughed."

"Hey you! I been waitin for service over here," a uniformed Air Force sergeant sitting a few seats down slurred in a belligerent tone.

"Be right there," Red said, waving pleasantly.

"What the hell you got there on the bar, buddy, a goddamn switchblade?"

"Yeah. What's it to you?" Jimmy challenged, sizing up the plastered sergeant who looked muscular and mean.

"Only a punk would carry a lowdown weapon like that," he persisted.

"Yeah, Yeah." *Christ Almighty! This dumbass aint gonna let it go. Looks like a mean sonofabitch, used to knockin heads.*

"What did you want to order, sir?" Red asked.

"I wanna know what that scum's doin in here with that chickenshit weapon."

Jimmy jumped to his feet leaving the switchblade on the counter. "Okay, asshole. Let's take it outside," he said, making a beeline for the door before the guy jumped him and they wreaked havoc in the restaurant.

As soon as the hostile sergeant staggered out onto Cushman Street, Jimmy settled the matter rapidly. Staying out of the hulking soldier's reach, he nailed him with a couple of well-placed punches and the agitator went down like a rock. *Damn good thing he's drunk off his ass, Jimmy thought. This guy could beat the livin shit outa me. The poor assholes under his command are gonna pay tomorrow.*

***

Driving out to the cabin after stocking up on supplies, Jimmy passed the Watkins' place and was tempted to stop. He liked the family and was drawn to the lively Lilly, but he thought better of it and drove on. He had things to do at the cabin, he told himself. As he loaded his arms with groceries, he noticed that the cabin door stood wide open. Puzzled, he stepped into the dimly lit room and was taken aback by the scene. The place had been ransacked. *Goddamn! What the hell's been goin on here?* he thought, glancing around hastily. It didn't take him long to deduce the identity of his intruder. Every can had been knocked off the makeshift shelves and strewn about the cabin. And each had distinctive puncture holes through which most of the gravy had been drained from the canned stew and the juice from the canned peaches. *Oh shit. Some goddamn bear 's come callin,* Jimmy thought as he surveyed the damage. While the kerosene lantern lay on its side and his sleeping bag and clothes had all been thrown around, nothing was broken. He would have to replace his stock of canned goods.

The satisfying "thunk" reverberating with each swing of his ax improved Jimmy's mood as a respectable pile of firewood gathered at his feet. He'd finished cleaning up the cabin, all the while brooding over the intruder.

No damn bear was going to drive him out of that place. But with any luck the marauder was just passing through. Now that he had made the cabin livable, he'd become downright territorial. Had he thought of it, he'd have circled the place pissing on trees to leave his mark. The cabin was his, unless of course the real owner showed up. That night Jimmy slept as soundly as ever in the welcome quiet of the wilderness, but from that time on he always kept the Winchester handy beside his bunk.

***

On a Saturday afternoon early in June, Jimmy, freshly showered, shaved and slathered up with Mennen Skin Bracer, stopped to pick up a dozen doughnuts at Spudnut's. As he climbed back into his jeep, he felt a little sheepish when he spotted the Big Tire Store just across the street. *Goddamnit!* he thought averting his gaze. He would have liked seeing Dan, but he knew his kindhearted stepfather would jump on him about coming to see Mama. And he wasn't ready.

As he covered the five miles to the Watkins' place, he was tantalized by the yeasty smell of fresh doughnuts wafting from the box on the passenger seat. Although he was a hearty eater, he seldom acknowledged his own hunger. Somehow his control over his physical needs and his stamina were a matter of pride. He could go for days without sleep, work all day without eating and resolutely curb his sexual urges. He valued his independence and guarded it with an iron will.

As Jimmy drove along, Dan's kindly face came to mind. He remembered him as a sharp young soldier, just nineteen and Mama's new husband when they followed him to Texas for basic training.

Jimmy nodded at a memory as it played through his mind. It was early one morning when Dan and Mama went off to shop at the base commissary leaving a sleeping thirteen year old Iris in charge of the three younger brothers. The boys put their plan into action as soon as the car was out of sight.

Now Jimmy laughed out loud at the daring and stealth. How he and Billy struggled to stay quiet while eight year old Everett slipped into Iris's bedroom and carefully pulled the window shade down so she wouldn't be awakened by the rising sun. Already the day was turning Texas hot. Gleefully they raced down to the river tasting the sweet flavor of the forbidden. As they frolicked in the swift flowing water, time got away. The next thing they knew, Mama was standing on the riverbank and they froze in their tracks knowing there would be hell to pay.

Dumb kids, Jimmy thought shaking his head. *We had to go swimmin where the riverbank was thick with little willows. Just right for a mean switch. She whipped our bare asses good. Put a hustle on us runnin back to the house.*

But six year old Jimmy hadn't run, and he hadn't hollered like his brothers. No, he'd set his own pace as he marched deliberately before the lash, his jaw set in a stubborn mask of defiance, his hands fisted at his sides as he repeated his mantra, "that don't hurt, that don't hurt, that don't hurt." He had thereby gotten the worst of the punishment. Having to glean his own switch from the riverbank had seemed the greatest indignity. In his mind he could still see Dan sitting on the porch steps, shaking his head. "I know they deserve it. I know you gotta do it," he kept saying. With his back, and buttocks, and legs on fire, Jimmy looked at his stepfather and was amazed to see that tears were streaming down his face.

Jimmy remembered how changed, how silent Dan had been when he came home for good at the end of World War II. He had served six years fighting in Germany and then in the Pacific. Had two tanks shot out from under him. That was all Jimmy knew about his stepfather's war experience. For a while Dan had done strange things like dragging Mama into a ditch when a low flying plane flew over them. When his stepfather came home, Jimmy was nearly twelve. After that Dan had worked hard to provide for his family, for a houseful of kids only one of which was his own.

Yeah, Dan's a good man, Jimmy thought. *He always done his best. Christ! Us kids waitin in the car watchin Mama going into the motel room with that slimy preacher. Damn it, why couldn't Mama do right by Dan?*

***

The Watkins' dogs greeted Jimmy enthusiastically before any of the family could gather at the front door. The kids welcomed him as they vied to see the package he was retrieving from the jeep.

"Hey, who wants something sweet?" he asked proffering the fragrant box of doughnuts as he stepped onto the front porch.

"Jimmy! How nice to see you. Come and meet my husband, William," Mrs. Watkins said, introducing the two.

"Nice to make your acquaintance. I've heard a lot about you. It seems you rescued my family while I was gone," William Watkins said, giving him a firm handshake, his expression serious.

"It wasn't nothin. I got the best of the deal. Mrs. Watkins' home cookin hit the spot," Jimmy said, sizing up the tall, powerfully built man.

"We've been getting the garden ready for planting. Want to help?" Lilly challenged with the same mischievous sparkle in her eyes that intrigued him.

"Sure. I'll pitch in," Jimmy agreed as he held out his offering.

"First we'll enjoy Jimmy's doughnuts," Mrs. Watkins said. "Molly, take the box and set it up on the porch rail. We'll sit out here in the warm sunshine and have out treat."

"We'll have a picnic," Molly said, her expression adoring as she took the box from him.

"Charles, you can bring up some milk from the root cellar while I go put on a pot of coffee. Everyone wash up please," Mrs. Watkins directed.

"Grab a chair," Mr. Watkins said settling into an ancient rocker on the front porch. "I hear you're working for City Electric."

"Yeah. I like the job," Jimmy answered, sitting on a hard wooden chair, and noting to his amusement that the sisters had quietly competed for the seat next to him, Lilly winning out.

"Did you finish school, son?" Mr. Watkins asked, getting down to business.

"No. I quit and went to work." *Oh shit. It's gonna be the third degree. He wants to know who the hell I am.*

"We got a letter from Stuart last week, Jimmy," Mrs. Watkins interrupted as she pushed through the front screen door holding two steaming mugs of coffee. "He didn't tell us anything about what's happening there, but at least we know he's okay,"

"That's good to hear, Mrs. Watkins."

"The garden still needs lots of work," Charles said. "Pretty soon we can put in the potatoes and carrots and peas."

"Do you know how to hoe?" Molly asked earnestly.

"Oh yeah. I'm a expert. I believe I had a hoe in my hand before I could even walk."

"Well," Lilly said, "we need an expert to help us. This year we want our best garden yet. But someone's got to shovel the chicken manure, too."

"You lived on a farm?" Mr. Watkins asked in his solemn voice.

"All my life," Jimmy answered, prickling under the close scrutiny. The man had a poker face, unreadable. It was hard to tell if disapproval lurked behind the mask.

Over the long afternoon Jimmy worked up a sweat while proving his mastery over the hoe and the shovel. He worked with the family in their modest garden plot, breaking up the winter packed soil, mixing in sand gleaned from the river and home-grown chicken poop, hoeing, raking, and finally forming raised beds. The kids threw themselves into the work, sharing spirited banter and friendly teasing as they put out their best effort with an eye to drawing Jimmy's approval. Jimmy had the time of his life.

When Mrs. Watkins urged him to stay for dinner, he turned her down having had quite enough of Mr. Watkins scrutiny.

***

"I'm so hungry I could eat a horse," Jimmy said, dropping into a booth at The Grifter that night. Reenergized after his shower at the boardinghouse, he was ready for a little hell raising.

"Let's see, it's probably on the menu," Steve laughed. "What kind of trouble have you been up to since I've been out of town?"

"You been missin out, partner," he said.

"Yeah. Like what?"

"Well, I got a girlfriend," Jimmy said, waving at the waitress to bring them each a beer.

"Where the hell did you find a girl?" Steve asked skeptically.

"Right here in town. And she's filthy rich."

"Bullshit. You're pulling my leg."

"No. Last week I had a beer with her at the Klondike Hotel. Turns out she owns the place," Jimmy said, taking a big bite out of his hamburger.

"How the hell old is this phantom woman?"

"Oh, round about ninety I'd guess," Jimmy said, mumbling through his food.

"Ninety? Goddamnit, Jimmy. You nearly had me."

"Yeah," Jimmy said, laughing until he nearly choked. "You ever seen old Mrs. Ford?"

"No. Who the hell is she?"

"She's the ol bent-over lady wanderin around most of the time down on Second, always wearin a long black coat, black boots, and a red stocking cap. Uses that big carved cane."

"Yeah, I guess I've seen her. How the hell did you get to know her?"

"Just started talkin to her one day," Jimmy said, signaling for another round. "Way back in the gold rush days she was a prostitute, but a smart one. She moved up and become a powerful madam, all the time buyin up property. She owns damn near half a this town."

"You think it's true?" Steve asked, taking of long pull on his beer.

"Yeah. Old Harvey says it is. He says she's always helpin people down on their luck, especially the ones with kids."

"God, is she that ancient lady who looks like a derelict?"

"She's the one. I don't think she cares much about her looks anymore," Jimmy said, laughing. "She smells kinda ripe and her teeth are all black and broken. But she can tell a hell of a story. How she got to be powerful in this town when there was even less women and all the guys wantin to marry her. She even had some English Duke that wanted to take care of her. Figured most of them wanted to take care of her money. Never married any of them. She had guts, for damn sure."

"So, did she buy you a beer?"

"Hell no. She made me pay."

By the time they got to the shooting gallery, Jimmy had done his best to ply his friend with enough beer to loosen him up. He himself was feeling no pain as bets were laid down and he extracted some of Steve's hard-earned money. Much later they drifted into Helga's, chugging more beer and tapping their feet to the pounding rhythm in the smoky, clamorous tavern. Whether either of them actually got up and danced with Helga became the subject of a running debate later when they tried to recall the events of the evening.

***

Jimmy came wide awake. *What the hell's that noise?* It seemed like he'd been hearing it for some time. He opened his eyes then slammed them shut against the pain. *God, my head's about to explode. I'm at the cabin, but how the hell did I get here? Christ! What is that goddamn noise?* Opening his eyes, he raised his head slowly and found the source of the disturbance. *What the hell!* He couldn't believe his eyes, didn't want to. There beside him in the bed was an old toothless Eskimo woman sound asleep. His mind was paralyzed by the implications. Jimmy could only stare in horrified fascination as he watched her slack lips vibrate noisily with each exhaled breath.

After a moment he discovered Steve sleeping soundly on the opposite side of their new bedmate. With great care lest he disturb their guest, he reached across and gave Steve a sharp tap on the shoulder. He watched as his friend's eyes popped open and then saw the growing revulsion on Steve's face as he came to full awareness. As if by mutual plan they crept out of bed, gathered their clothes and slid out the door soundlessly.

The only plan of action that came to Jimmy's muddled mind was to run away and leave the nightmare behind. They walked several miles before either spoke.

"What the hell happened?" Steve demanded.

"God. I don't know."

"Was that your cabin?"

"Yeah. It's the one I been fixin up."

"How the hell did we get out here?"

"I don't know, but my jeep wasn't there so we must of took a cab. We got about twelve miles walkin back to town."

"Who was that?"

"Never seen her before. You must a picked her up."

"Goddamnit, Jimmy! You don't think we-uh?"

"I hope to hell not," Jimmy said, shaking his head. "But that aint the question."

"What do you mean?"

"I'll tell ya the goddamn question. Who the hell do ya think saw us with her?"

***

Early Monday morning with Steve trailing behind, Jimmy entered the union hall ready to take his medicine. While he dreaded the taunts that he felt doomed to endure from the ribald linemen, he held his head high. *God, they're gonna be brutal*, he thought, squaring his shoulders as he sauntered over to the coffeepot. He glanced warily at each familiar face expecting the drubbing to begin at any moment. Yet nobody said a thing. Here and there he heard a cheerful greeting as they crossed the room and eased into chairs. A small seed of hope began to grow in the depths of Jimmy's pride. Was it possible that by some miracle none of the linemen had seen the two of them cavorting around town on Saturday night, drunk off their asses and in the company of a toothless Eskimo woman?

"Damn," he mumbled to Steve as his optimism grew, "I think we're in the clear."

"God, I hope so," Steve said, breathing a sigh of relief.

***

Red didn't look at all good when Jimmy dropped into The Pastime Cafe on a Friday evening for dinner. He noticed right away that the pretty redhead seemed even more pale than usual.

"How's it goin, Red?" he asked, seeing her slow down and seem to rest against the counter.

"It's goin good, Slim," she said, giving him a wan smile.

"I'm up for blueberry pie. Ya got some?"

"Sure. In a minute," she said breaking off abruptly to make a run for the bathroom.

"You sick?" he asked when she came back looking ghostly white.

"No," she said quietly with a soft laugh. "I'm pregnant. But I'm not telling anyone. I need to keep my job. We weren't planning on a baby so soon, what with Chris off fighting on the front lines."

"Christ Almighty, now you're gonna have a hard row to hoe. When's your husband supposed to come home?"

"He's still got more than a year to serve. I'll be okay once I get to feeling better," she said forcing a smile. "Just don't tell anyone. So, you ready for pie?"

"You up to it?"

"Oh yeah," she said swallowing hard.

"You know anything about old Harvey Edwards?" he asked as she set his dessert in front of him and reached for the coffeepot. "I was down by his shoeshine stand a little while ago and he wasn't there. I never seen a time when he wasn't around," he continued, stopping when he saw the thunderstruck look on her face.

"What?"

"He got shot," she said in a horse whisper.

"Shot? Where is he?"

"He's dead. Somebody blew his head off in his own house."

"Oh shit! That goddamn card game. Jesus Christ! I tried to tell the old man," he blurted, stopping as his throat constricted.

"He was a friend to everybody. I don't know why anyone would kill him," Red murmured.

"Yeah," Jimmy whispered, pushing his pie away. *Goddamnit old man, you really fucked up.*

***

When Jimmy pulled up at the cabin and saw the door standing wide open, he knew the marauding bear had made another visit. It had left its mark once again, tearing the hell out of the place. All the evidence was there. The canned food all ruined, the empty bacon package torn to shreds and the broken eggs splattered over the rough-hewn floorboards.

It was the last straw for Jimmy. He declared war. As he cleaned up the place, he made his plan. By Saturday night he had the cabin restocked and his roost set up for his stakeout in a nearby tree. Although he would have no cover of darkness at that time of year, around two in the morning he crawled into his hiding place and, cradling his trusty Winchester, kept himself awake and ready for the ambush. He was stiff, tired and frustrated, his need for vengeance unsatisfied when he retreated from the tree and crawled into his bunk as full daylight returned. But he wasn't done with the bear and, as it turned out, the bear wasn't done with him. It seemed to him that his nemesis knew when he was gone, but he vowed to find a way to outsmart the wily troublemaker.

The next week, Jimmy got sent out on a local job with Steve and the affable lineman, Fred. Working with them seemed almost like old times at Big Delta. August days had turned hot, nearly eighty degrees. As they worked steadily, Fred was his usual bullshitting self, joking around, bragging, and drumming up endless wagers.

"I got a goddamn bear tearin up my cabin every time I stock the place up," Jimmy said as the crew strung lines into a new area off Farmer's Loop.

"Hey, hoist up them insulators," Fred called down, knowing Jimmy would have them ready. "Do ya lock er up when ya leave?"

"Naw. Door don't lock. The other night I sat up waitin for the damn thing to show. Had my thirty-aught-six ready to shoot the bastard."

"Ma money's on that there bear," Fred said, laughing.

"I'd a damn well shot em if I'd a seen him."

"Shit, Jimmy. You want to hope you never see that bear," Steve said.

"I swear that goddamn bear watches and waits for me to leave."

"He likely does. Ya suppose he shits in the woods?" Fred prodded.

"Wouldn't surprise me if he shit in my cabin," Jimmy said, cheering up.

***

On a warm afternoon in early fall Jimmy dropped in at the Watkins' homestead.

"Hey, had to see how the garden's goin," he said by way of greeting as the kids and dogs enthusiastically surrounded him.

"Where've you been?" Charles asked. "We thought you'd come back and try our carrots. They grew okay, but they were kinda bitter."

"Then I hope you didn't save any for me," Jimmy laughed. "I been busy workin hard," he added, catching Lilly's eye and giving her a wink. He could hardly look away from the sweet sight of her standing there barefoot in a cotton shirt and shorts.

"The garden's really come along better this year, thanks to your help," Mrs. Watkins said. "The soil is still poor, but we got a good crop of peas and the potatoes look pretty good."

"Yeah, but we were looking for you when all the weeds came up," Molly added.

"Come on in and visit with us, Jimmy," Mrs. Watkins urged. "You'll stay for dinner. We're not taking 'no' for an answer."

"Yeah. I'll need some help milking Heidi," Lilly teased.

"Oh, no," Jimmy protested. "She's tougher than me."

"Lilly! You know she's dried up," Molly said, drawing a laugh from everyone.

For several hours Jimmy played cards with the kids on the front porch while Molly flirted outrageously and Charles tried to entice him into telling a story.

"Come on Jimmy," Lilly said, grabbing a pail as she slipped her shoes on. "Let's go pick some blueberries and I'll make you a pie for dessert."

"My favorite. Let's go," he said, jumping up.

"Wait for me," Molly and Charles said at almost the same time.

"Oh no. You two are doing chores and helping with dinner," Mrs. Watkins said with finality, to a chorus of protests.

"I know a blueberry patch just waiting to be picked," Lilly said with a saucy grin as they hiked along the brushy terrain.

"That right?"

"Yes. I been saving it in case you came," she said, meeting his gaze with her soft brown eyes.

"Oh. Well, I've been working," he stalled.

"Can you keep on working outside all winter?"

"I think City Electric keeps the crews going until it gets twenty below or so. Seems like somebody's gotta fix the lines even when everything's all iced up."

"Stuart's a hard worker. Maybe he can get a job there when he comes home," she said earnestly. "I know he'd like you."

"You think so? I guess you like me, too."

"Oh yes," she said, stopping midstride.

Before he realized what was happening, she had planted a quick kiss on his lips and taken off like a gazelle, her long shapely legs and firm buttocks a devastating sight as she ran ahead.

"Hey, wait a minute," he called after her, sprinting to catch up as he reigned in a surge of desire.

"Here we are," she said indicating a bountiful patch of blueberry bushes. She rushed forward to grab a handful of ripe berries and presented them to him. "Here, taste these. Open your mouth."

The tangy sweetness hit Jimmy's tongue in a burst of flavor. "Mmm. Best thing I tasted since eatin watermelon hearts right out of the farmer's field," he said watching Lilly empty a handful of berries into her mouth.

"Did the farmer know?" she asked, munching.

"He must of found out. Us kids didn't stick around."

"You were a bad boy, purple lips," she teased.

"Let's see your lips," he said, pulling her close and giving her a soft, tender kiss. "You taste good," he said, flashing his dimpled grin. Too good, he thought and let go of her. "Let's pick those berries."

"I'm starting back to school on Monday," Lilly said softly as she dropped a handful of blueberries into the bucket.

"Do you like school?"

"Yeah. I've been studying really hard so I can go to college."

"College? What do you want to do?" he asked as they gleaned side-by-side. He liked her easy familiarity, the sound of her animated voice and her spirited attitude.

"I love animals. I think I'd like to be a veterinarian. When we still lived in Montana, I had my own horse and I took good care of her, even when she had her foal."

"You got big plans for a little girl," he said, brushing away a stray lock of hair that had escaped her ponytail. *Back off! You got no business with her. Don 't be a asshole,* he warned himself.

"My dad says it's a waste for a girl to get a college education. But Mom thinks I should be able to take care of myself."

"She's right."

"I think so. But in church they're always acting like the only thing a girl's supposed to do is get married and stay at home with kids. My mom has to clean rooms at the hotel, so we have enough money. Dad doesn't like it."

"There's nothin wrong with decidin what's best for your own life. It takes some guts."

"That's what I want, to be independent," she said, her whole body animated with resolve. "I can't talk to Dad about it much. He's crabby most of the time. We're all worried about Stuart. But it seems like Dad has it on his mind that Stuart won't come back. Two of his friends have already been killed."

"What are you studying in school?" he asked, abruptly changing the painful subject.

"I've been taking all the science classes I can, but I also like writing. I keep a diary and I write in it every day. Sometimes I write poems," she said with a mysterious smile; "Here," she said, fishing a folded paper from her pocket.

"What's this?"

"It's for you. Read it."

"You wrote me a poem?" he asked, stalling. *Oh shit. How can I get out of this?*

"Yes. Read it."

"Read it to me," he said, starting to panic as he held the paper out to her.

"No. Don't embarrass me. You have to read it yourself," she insisted, ducking her head as a rosy blush crept across her cheeks.

"I never had a pretty girl write me a poem before. I'm gonna save it," he said, sliding the paper into his shirt pocket.

Setting the brimming pail on the ground, he wrapped his long arms around her waist, drawing her against him. "You're some special girl, Lilly," he said, looking down into her trusting face. He kissed her then with a sweet sincerity that escalated into blind lust when she returned his kiss with startling passion.

"Whoa, little girl. You're some kisser," he said, releasing her from the embrace. Keeping his voice steady, he turned abruptly and picked up the pail to hide the embarrassing evidence of his arousal. *And I'm workin hard on bein a asshole. Aint right to take advantage. I can't make no promises.* "Are you makin me a blueberry pie or what?"

"Yes," she said, taking his hand. "Let's start back before those pesky kids come after us."

***

Leaving the Watkins' place shortly after dinner, Jimmy willed himself to turn toward his folks' homestead rather than head to the cabin. Driving along, he patted the paper in his shirt pocket and wondered if he'd ever know what Lilly had written. As he pulled up at his parents' cabin, he could see that they had made little progress toward proving-it-up. The cabin was now a crude plywood shack with a tin roof and a door, but still looked unfinished. Even the outhouse looked off kilter and hastily thrown together. He could see that the surrounding acreage had been partially cleared of brush and scrappy spruce trees, the piles of debris waiting to be burned. It seemed to him that his folks had only one year left to make the required improvements for gaining title and he could see there was lots yet to be done.

"Hey, good to see you Jimmy," Dan called from the front doorway.

"Yeah. Had to come out and see what you done to the place."

"Well, it's comin along slow. Come on in and say howdy to your mama."

"Well I'll be. It's a stranger come a callin. Though ya was getting too good for the likes a us. You livin in the same town an all. And caint come an see your ol Mama."

"Yeah, Mama. I been workin. What's Billy up to these days?" he asked. Unable to bring himself to look her in the eye, he glanced around noticing the skeletal interior with its exposed studs and open rafters.

"Oh, he's off an workin up ta Stevens Crick fer some minin company. Up an quit school. He got the idea his shit don't stink neither. Don't come round ta see his mama. After all I done fer you kids. Totin your lil asses round on a cotton sack tryin ta feed yall."

"Yeah, you told me Mama. Startin before I was five years old, I remember workin my ass off to help out, too."

"Come on and sit," Dan said, shuffling a pile of dishes crusted with dried food to the far end of the makeshift plywood table.

"No, I'm okay," he said leaning against the doorjamb. "When ya gonna finish the inside here? It's cold as hell even with the wood stove goin. I thought you was gonna build yourself a cistern to cut back on the water you hafta haul," he said, directing the conversation to Dan.

"I'm not planning to do any more on the place this year. Soon we'll be moving back to town for the winter. This here's not much of a place. Can't grow a damn thing. And it's too far out for me to get to work on bad roads."

"Yeah. I can see that."

"What's your hurry? Don't be huggin that there door. Set down a dangnab minute. Caint ya spare your mama a few minutes? Been keepin sumpin fer ya."

"What, Mama?" Jimmy said, pulling a straight-backed wooden chair from under the table and planting himself.

"Dan, fetch me that brown box over yonder," she ordered, pointing toward a pile of stuff in a corner of the cluttered cabin. "See, now aint these purdy?" she said, producing a pair of custom doeskin boots from the box. "Lookit here. I bet ya never seed the likes a these handmade boots. Real soft, fur linin an all. These here are fer you."

"I don't want em, Mama," he said, bristling. "Why'd you go and spend all that money? Take em back. I'll buy my own goddamn boots. Dan's workin hard. Don't just blow his money on shit like this," he said, bolting to his feet.

"No. These here come from my money. It done come from the

goverment settlement. Everett's life insurance. I bought them boots so's you'd be getting sumpin from him."

"Everett's money?" he growled, rage blooming. "Goddamn blood money? I sure as hell don't want those fucking boots," he yelled, glaring into her brilliant blue eyes, the mirror of his own.

"Why you bein so mean?" Mama said, tears trickling down her once-pretty face. "I'm hurtin terrible what with ma boy bein kilt. Why you wanna put more hurtin on me?"

"It aint right, Mama. Everett's goddamn dead. And you just goin right ahead and blowin his goddamn insurance money. Why can't you ever do right, Mama?" he exploded.

"I just got to thinkin you ought ta have sumpin a his," she said, shaking her head.

"Your mama meant to do good for you, son," Dan said.

"You sent him off to slaughter, Mama," Jimmy blurted, shaking as the full power of his grief and rage gripped him. "You encouraged him to sign up when you knew better. Let him swallow all that bullshit about duty and servin his country. He wanted to live, Mama. You let him get took advantage of. He was the best one, Mama. The best one in this whole goddamn family and he had to go get his fucking brains blown out."

"Aint my fault. He wanted to sign up," she sobbed.

"You shoulda stopped him. He was so damn smart. Had a girl he wanted to marry. He woulda had a good life. Dan, you coulda stopped him. Look what the war done to you."

"I had no say in the matter, son," Dan said, quietly.

"I was only thinkin a you," Mama wailed, holding out the boots.

"Goddamnit! You didn't do right by him, Mama," he said in a hoarse whisper, choking on his anger as he snatched the boots from her hands and stalked out the door.

Slinging the reviled boots under the back seat, he jumped in the jeep and roared away. The weight on his chest was so heavy he could barely breathe.

Back at the cabin he dragged the despised boots inside, flung them into a corner and started to frantically pace as his whole body screamed with rage. The pair of exquisite custom boots tore open his grief, exposing his raw convictions: Everett's death had been a senseless waste; his brother's life had been far more precious than his own; and the boots were an extravagant symbol of Mama's neglect and careless whims. Those stupid boots were a maddening reminder of what losing Everett had meant to him.

Stirring himself from his frenzy of agony, Jimmy rushed to the wood stove and started a fire. He threw in chunks of firewood, stoking the fire until the stove glowed cherry red. Then he pulled on the boots. Sitting down on the cabin floor, he propped his booted feet against the inferno, denying the pain as long as he could. It hurt. It hurt like hell he realized as unacknowledged tears coursed down his cheeks .

He would repeat the exorcism from time to time until the damn boots were destroyed.

***

Jimmy tapped on the hotel counter startling Steve who was so entrenched in his textbook that he had failed to hear his friend come into the lobby.

"What the hell! You scared the shit out of me," Steve said in a subdued voice.

"Yeah. Your nose was buried in that book. How's the job?"

"Hell, it's a gravy job. Night clerking doesn't take much beside keeping an eye on the door."

"Yeah. You was doin a good job of that."

"Usually there's nobody coming in late or even calling the desk. So I can sit here and study. My room's free, too. Problem is staying awake."

"Looks like you got homework," Jimmy said, keeping his voice low to match Steve's tone.

"God yes. This accounting assignment's got me shaking my head. But I'll figure it out."

"I don't know why you want to crap up your mind with all that horseshit."

"Hey, I'll get my business degree. Then my whole damn family will respect me."

"You gonna go back to New York an turn into a tight-ass businessman?"

"I don't know. Alaska's an interesting place and the people are a lot different from anybody I ever met at home. I always wanted to come here just for the hell of it. How did the job go at Big Delta?" Steve asked.

"We got it wound up in two weeks. Put the whole damn line in for another radar site. Was working with old Fred and Dwight and Alex, too. Them guys're still up to the same bullshit, but it was so damn cold we was freezing our asses off most of the time."

"Did Fred bulldog Glen into letting you stay at Buffalo Lodge?"

"Oh yeah. They had it out right there in the union hall before we ever left."

"Well, being in school's not so bad. Those linemen can damn well wear you out after a while with all their horseshit."

"Yeah, but they do keep it interestin. Hey, you won't believe somethin we saw out there last week. It was early one mornin. The sun was just risin and it was colder than a witch's tit when we started workin. All at once somethin comes crashin outa the trees and chargin into the right of way. It's bellowin. Christ! Nearly crapped my pants. This thing stands maybe fifty feet away snortin and stompin and pawin the ground. You can't see what the hell it is on account of all the steam rollin outa its nostrils, but its head is huge, and it's got shaggy fur all crusted in ice. The only thing I could see real clear was this big bloodshot eyeball just a rollin. The damn thing stood there bellowin like a banshee. It didn't take any of us on the ground long to get into the man-haul. The linemen on the poles was hanging on for dear life wishin for a rifle," Jimmy said, laughing and pausing for dramatic effect.

"So, what was it?" Steve asked, taking the bait.

"It was a goddamn bull buffalo. The damn thing stood there intimidatin the crap outa us, then turned around and disappeared into the brush.

"A buffalo?"

"Yeah. I never heard a no damn buffalo in Alaska before. But come to find out, a whole herd had been brung in and turned loose sometime in the thirties."

"Come to think of it, I guess that's how the Buffalo Lodge got its name. Did you make a killing at poker this time?" Steve asked.

"I done okay. The guys were drinkin too damn heavy out there. With days so short, they'd get started early."

"Yeah. The time gets long when you're with a bunch of drunken assholes. Who was the other grunt?"

"That stupid ass Tommy. He don't work worth a damn."

"Yeah. I know. He was out there the last time I went. He's a worse drunk than the linemen."

"You aint heard the worst of it. When we was comin back yesterday, Fred was drivin the pole truck and a couple of us was ridin in the back. It was damn cold back there. Well, every time we come to a roadhouse the guys're all yellin to stop and then you can't get them out of there till they drunk the damn place dry. So Fred gets tired of it and says no more stops. Pretty soon Dwight goes to hollerin he's gotta take a piss. Fred aint stoppin and Dwight's drunk off his ass. Dwight finally takes matters into his own hands. He crawls out onto the truck bed, works his way to the tail end and pisses over the back while the truck's runnin full out. I'm thinkin he's gonna make it and that's when we hit the frost boil. Damn truck hits that bump and tosses that asshole clear into the air."

"Was he okay?"

"Yeah. We all thought it might of killed him when he went flying and landed about twenty feet off the road. Snow must a softened the blow. He jumped right up. We had to yell like hell to get Fred ta stop. He was madder than a wet hen."

"I bet. A job from hell. Glad I missed it. Are you still staying out at that cabin?"

"Naw, it's got too cold. When do you get a night off?"

"I can't get off unless I find a replacement."

"Guess that puts a monkey-wrench in your gettin out an raisin hell."

"That and having to study. But you know where I am. You can always come and keep me awake."

***

On a frigid Monday morning near the end of December Jimmy was sitting in the union hall with some of the lineman as he waited for his job assignment. With temperatures dipping well below zero, City Electric was only running a couple of crews solely for repairs and maintenance.

"Oh shit, looks like Glen Cochran's got a splinter up his ass," Dwight mumbled as the foreman stalked toward them."

"He's loaded for bear," Fred said with a chuckle.

"Evans!" Glen said, stopping abruptly in front of Jimmy. "How many times do you goddamn grunts have to be told to take care of the equipment?"

Jimmy clenched his jaw as he silently came to his feet, facing his boss eyeball to eyeball as the room fell silent.

"You left the valves open on the goddamn cutting tanks in manhaul number three. Damn things froze and exploded all to hell. What do we pay you idiots for if you can't do the goddamn job!" he exploded, then turned on his heel.

When Jimmy kicked him in the ass it was pure reflex. No warning, just the thud of impact and the unceremonious sight of Glen lifting off the ground. Even the tough linemen couldn't believe their eyes.

When Glen whirled around, Jimmy's face was inches away from his.

"Listen you dumbshit," he said, jabbing his finger in the foreman's face. "You'd best get your story straight before you ream some guy a new asshole. Screw you. I aint leanin over. Have my paycheck ready. I'll pick it up at City Electric in a hour," he said, walking around the wide-eyed foreman and picking his parka off the rack as he headed out into the dark morning.

5

CALIFORNIA BREAK

Jimmy was ready for a change of scene. The memories of warm days in the sunshine and the loose, fun-loving girls of his Fresno, California roots beckoned loud and clear. While it was easy for him to make a decision to break out of the confining climate and the stagnant social morass he'd fallen into, leaving Alaska in the dead of winter proved no small fete.

The very day he explosively quit his job, Jimmy took an old travel trunk containing his winter gear, his gaudy .44 Smith & Wesson pistol, his Remington rifle, and a few personal papers including Lilly's unread poem, over to his parents' rented place in town. Saying his brief goodbyes, he gave them a thousand dollars of his savings. He didn't bother to retrieve the contents of his appropriated cabin retreat.

That afternoon Steve, Red and Mrs. Turner each wished him well as he made his rounds, reassuring them that he expected to come back in the spring. Steve would have the use of his jeep until his return. Hard as he tried, though, he couldn't rid himself of a gnawing unease about Red. Her pregnancy was showing, and he feared that the damn war would rob her of her husband, and she would be left alone.

Jimmy caught a cab that evening to the little Fairbanks Airport. Wearing his heavy wool jacket, carrying just over five thousand dollars in his pocket, and toting his duffel bag filled with summer clothing, he was chilled to the bone by the time he arrived at the airport on that clear, frigid Monday just before Christmas in 1953. Jimmy's new adventure had only begun.

Hopping on the plane, a two-engine taildragger, Jimmy planted himself by the window just behind the wing and savored thoughts of warm sunshine and footloose fun. He had worked hard, and he damn well deserved a real vacation.

The plane was packed, nearly filled with some thirty holiday travelers when they roared into the sky. Jimmy watched as the cherry-red flame of exhaust shot from the engine, the glow illuminating the wing against the cold black sky. As the plane rapidly gained altitude, he could hear the engines straining. Knowing they would be climbing over the Alaska Range to reach Anchorage, he settled back to enjoy the flight. Before long the plane seemed to buck and tilt, and he noticed that the colorful light display he had been observing had changed from a flame to a barely discernible glow. As the plane tilted, then corrected, then tilted again, he could hear the screaming rev of the opposite engine. Jimmy remained cool as he concluded they were flying on the power of the opposite engine. He could only wonder what that meant, but he fervently hoped that the sucker was up to the job.

The flight turned back as the stewardess explained that the one remaining engine wasn't powerful enough to take them over the mountains. They were on their way back to Fairbanks. Jimmy watched as the familiar Fairbanks runway lights came into view. And the plane continued right on past.

What the hell? Jimmy wondered, finally feeling the crumbling of his bravado. *We missed the goddamn airport.* When the aircraft started into a sudden steep dive, his heart began to race. *Christ, I've bought the goddamn farm*, he thought.

All he could see through the velvet darkness was some backlit treetops coming at them fast. Too fast. With a death grip on the armrests and a clenched jaw, he listened to the frightful sounds of general panic all around him.

Then he felt the wheels hit the pavement on what turned out to be a small landing strip just a mile from the main airport. The plane taxied to a gradual stop. For a sterling moment the entire plane was deadly silent except for the rough thrum of the one idling engine.

"Keep your seats, please," a stewardess announced in a shaky voice. "They'll be sending out a bus to take you to a hotel. The mechanics are going to work on the engine, and they say we should be able to take off again by midnight."

While Jimmy ate his dinner in the hotel restaurant, he avoided thinking about his narrow escape. It had all worked out. He was damn well going to have his vacation and thaw out for a while.

At midnight he was again on the airplane headed for Anchorage. He noticed that there were a few more vacant seats this time, but he couldn't let those chickenshit quitters discourage him. This time the plane got only as far as the runway. They sat perched at the head of the runway with the pilot revving the engines for a long while. Jimmy was pretty sure the engine on his side was still dead as a doornail. It would clatter and backfire when they poured the coal to it, but it showed no sign of actually running. He watched it like a hawk, fully prepared to wise them up if the crew decided the flight was a go.

Back at the hotel once again, exhausted, Jimmy grabbed a few hours of sleep before returning for an eight o'clock takeoff time. As he buckled himself into the now familiar airplane, he noticed that fully half of the seats were vacant. Embracing a Buck Rogers sense of adventure, he jauntily sat back and waited for takeoff. Not to say that he didn't keep a sharp eye on the rogue engine. On that clear, crisp morning the plane lifted into the sky swift as a bird. Reassured by the comforting cherry red flame of the engine's exhaust, he began to watch the frozen wonderland as it passed below.

They were halfway to Anchorage when the heat went out. It didn't take long to notice. All at once, Jimmy felt chilled to the bone as passengers began jumping up and digging their jackets out of the overhead compartments. The blankets went fast, the coffee ran out and everyone had to make do. The rest of the flight was a matter of staving off hypothermia and everyone was damn glad when they finally landed in Anchorage.

For Jimmy there was another night in a hotel, once again waiting for his plane to be repaired. He was onboard yet again at noon the next day. With the heating system fixed and both engines in working order, the much-delayed flight continued on to Seattle with stops in Juneau and Ketchikan. As the troublesome airplane made the approach to the Seattle Airport, Jimmy was sick of delays and quite ready to switch to more reliable ground transportation. By that time he was pretty well convinced that air travel in 1953 was not all that it was cracked up to be. Still, it was the only viable way to travel from the Alaska Territory to the lower forty-eight states in the dead of winter. If you lived through it.

Little did he suspect there would be one more turn of events. It seemed that Seattle was socked in with fog and a tricky instrument landing would be on the agenda. There was no gentle landing in store for the survivors of the odyssey. Making a steep dive, the pilot brought her down for an abrupt landing without the benefit of changing pressurization in the cabin. On the quick trip down, Jimmy along with all the rest of the passengers gripped his ears in agony. He was weary to the bone when he finally got on the Greyhound Bus headed for Sacramento. It would be a long trip, but he could sleep and when he awoke, he'd be in sunny, warm California.

Having left behind the Alaskan frontier wrapped in its brittle Arctic chill, Jimmy could never have imagined the specter of his long journey back.

***

Some twenty hours later, stiff and groggy, Jimmy hopped off the bus in Sacramento. He was truly road-weary, but even in his muddled state, he felt lifted by the luxurious warmth of a sunny afternoon with the temperature hovering close to sixty degrees. Toting his duffel bag, he walked nearly a mile inhaling the balmy air before he spotted a motel where he decided to crash for the night.

The shower felt good. He stood in the pounding spray until the water turned cold. Finally dressed and refreshed, he found a little diner where he ate his meal before returning to the motel and falling into a deep sleep.

The next morning, Jimmy bought a car. Strolling around town after breakfast, he happened on a sales lot where he took a shine to a little beige '41 Chevy business coup. A run-down battery made starting her up something of a challenge, but Jimmy wasn't put off by that minor problem. He and the salesman push-started the compact car and after a trip around the block he judged it to be a little under-powered but road worthy. The car was his for two hundred bucks.

Once he had wheels, Jimmy started to give some thought to where he was heading. Taking care to keep the engine running until the battery had charged up, he turned south on Highway 99 in the direction of his old stomping grounds.

Four hours later he crossed the San Joaquin River craning his neck to glimpse the swimming hole, an old gravel pit beside the river, where he and his brothers had come to cool off on hot summer days. Seeing the interlaced steel girders of the railroad bridge, he thought of how they had gotten down to the river many times by hitching a ride on a Southern Pacific freight. Another mile down the road he turned off on Main Street and cruised into Herndon, a little community just north of Fresno where he had grown up once his Mama and Dan had settled after the war.

The neighborhood hardly seemed changed in the two years since his folks had sold the house located at the far end of Main. Cruising by Schmidt's Grocery, he pulled over and parked, deciding on a whim to drop in. The neat two-story white clapboard structure, with the general store occupying the first floor and living quarters upstairs, had served as the local meeting place. Jimmy remembered how involved, the proprietors, Mr. and Mrs. Schmidt, had been in sponsoring the local adult softball league. It seemed to him that each summer the whole town had turned out on weekends for softball games down at the grade school ballfield. The Schmidts also owned the huge white water tower looming behind the building, which supplied the water system for the area. It suddenly dawned on Jimmy that the enterprising couple had been the backbone of the community.

Passing the fading potted petunias and geraniums that still lingered atop the front railings of the store, he stepped up on the covered porch enjoying the familiar sight of assorted benches and wooden chairs, standing ashtrays and scattered newspapers. He nodded to a few kibitzing old geezers whom he recognized and opened the wooden screen door, hearing the tinkle of a bell announcing his presence. The proprietor, a tall athletic man in his late forties, glanced up from behind the counter.

"Hey, Mr. Schmidt," Jimmy greeted.

"Long time no see, son."

"Do you remember me?"

"Sure. You're one of the Evans boys."

"Yeah. I'm Jimmy."

"Oh yes. The pitcher," he said, his face lighting up with recognition.

"That's right," Jimmy said, surprised and pleased at the mention of his pitching prowess.

"You've turned into a tall drink of water. You down visiting for Christmas?"

"Yeah," he said, although the holiday hadn't even crossed his mind. "Thought I'd look up some of the neighborhood hoodlums. Albert and Hazel and Wesley still around?"

"Oh sure. Where have you been?"

"Up in Alaska. Thought I'd take a break from the cold for a little. You still got your dog pickin up the mail?" Jimmy asked, remembering how the clever shopkeeper, who also ran the local post office from his store, had trained his dog to retrieve the mail sack.

"Sure do. Gretchen's getting old but she still loves to go after the mail sack."

With a big double-scoop ice cream cone in hand, Jimmy settled into an old rocker on the front porch. Watching Mr. Schmidt build the cone had taken him back to times when he'd been eleven or twelve and walked over to the little store to spend his precious hard-earned nickel on a treat.

As he looked across Main Street, he saw the big empty field where huge revival tents had sprouted periodically as well as traveling carnivals, which seemed about the same deal to him. He remembered how they had brought the buzz of excitement to town especially on the hot humid late days of summer. Beyond the field lay the Southern Pacific Railroad tracks running parallel with Main. He could see the post that sported a hooked arm where Mr. Schmidt hung the out-going mailbag to be snatched by a passing train from which the in-coming mail was also tossed onto the landing. Jimmy shook his head admiring the efficiency and quirkiness of the shopkeeper sending his dog after the mail pouch.

Behind the wheel once again, Jimmy drove a few blocks down Main to take a look at his old house, which sat near the front of a deep, narrow lot that stretched some two-hundred feet back to the railroad tracks. The place still looked pretty good, the rough-cut siding was freshly painted white and the green shutters, scroll-cut with Christmas tree shapes, were still in place. The new owners had let Mama's yard go to hell, though. She had been so proud of her yard, the only house on the block with a manicured front lawn and beds of fragrant roses. He remembered her being out there watering every morning before dawn.

Looking beyond the house, Jimmy could see that the old makeshift bunkhouse, where he and his brothers had slept, had been torn down. Having moved out on his own at fourteen, it had been nearly four years since he'd actually lived there.

His mind reeled back to the time when his family had moved to California. As soon as Dan had mustered out of the army late in the spring of 1945, they had left the hostile confines of Michigan and migrated to the Fresno area. Jimmy had just turned eleven. With barely enough money to buy the lot in Herndon, his parents had set up housekeeping in a tent purchased from the army surplus store.

With Dan getting hired on at the Highway 99 Truck Stop and Mama working the swing shift as a cook at the adjoining cafe, the family got established. The three young brothers hustled up jobs to help out. Everett, already a six-footer at thirteen, got a job washing dishes in a local restaurant. Jimmy, dragging Billy along, went to work in the huge fig orchards that occupied the acreage across the street and all the land to the south where Main Street dead ended. He liked growing things, liked learning about pollinating the trees and pruning and harvesting. With his eager energy, Jimmy would end up getting seasonal work in the fig orchards, in vineyards, and wheat fields over the next few years. He remembered being a favorite employee of one grower who would come to pick him up, put him in charge of a crew of grown men, and feed him with his own family.

***

That summer of 1945 had been a busy time. Under Mama's direction, they had harnessed their energy and resources to build an unconventional house starting from scratch. Much of the wood came from huge army surplus packing crates, which they tore down salvaging the one-by-six boards, the plywood lids and bottoms, and most of the nails, which had to be pounded straight. The first construction project was the outhouse, which proved a learning experience but turned out reasonably sturdy. The makeshift home with its wood stove, electricity, running water, linoleum floors, rolled tarpaper roof and composition siding of fake brick was finished before winter. It seemed more comfortable and livable in comparison to the tent. The family was used to roughing it. Jimmy was proud of the accomplishment. He'd worked enthusiastically, eager to learn, full of can-do. In those times and in that neighborhood, building your own home wasn't uncommon. Most of the neighbors were also barely getting by.

The next summer the family would build the present house with a real bathroom. With his newly acquired construction skills, Jimmy had thrown himself into helping build the new house while he also worked in the fig orchards. He thought the sculpted shutters were fine finishing touches. It made the place home. The new house provided room for his parents and two younger sisters while the three young brothers were assigned to the original hodgepodge structure as their sleeping quarters. The boys liked having their own territory with Everett riding herd. Both of their older siblings had already taken off on their own.

Well the goddamn place belongs to somebody else now, Jimmy thought. They was doin good here. Owned the place. I don't know why in hell Mama and Dan give it up, got talked out of it by her goddamn sneaky brother. Look at them now. Trying to make a go of it on some piece a crap land and a lousy cabin won't keep them warm in winter. Got no goddamn sense. They aint never gonna learn.

***

"My God, Jimmy! Ya stayed away long enough," Albert said, as he opened his kitchen door in response to Jimmy's tapping knock.

"Guess you still recognize me," he said, shaking his old friend's extended hand.

"Had to be you. Who the hell else ever pecked on my back door like that? Christ! Ya got even taller," Albert said with his easy smile.

"Well you're short and stubby as ever," Jimmy said clapping him on the back. "What the hell you doin these days?"

"I been working down at the truck stop since I graduated last summer. How's Alaska treatin ya?"

"It's a goddamn wild kind of place. It's great. Thought I'd come down an soak up some sun for a while. Wesley an Hazel still around?"

"Yeah. Let's go round em up."

By afternoon, the four old friends were hanging around in Albert's kitchen drinking beer, smoking, and catching up while Mrs. Herman put a ham in the oven for Christmas Eve dinner. She smiled at them indulgently and put out a can of salted peanuts before leaving them to visit.

"Albert said you was workin up to Shasta Winery," Jimmy said to Hazel who, he noticed, was finally a little smaller than him.

"Yeah. I'm headin up the work crews out in the vineyards," she said, her thin face drawn into her usual serious frown.

"Well, I'm bettin you keep them guys towin the mark," Jimmy teased.

"What do ya mean?" she asked, with the hair-trigger look that all the neighborhood boys had learned to dread.

"I mean, how many of their asses did you have to kick before they figured out you was the boss?"

"Oh, only a few," Hazel said, breaking into surprisingly hearty laughter that made her face light up.

"Well, I remember many a time when ol Albert here had to sneak in the back door cause you was mad and gonna beat the shit outa him," Jimmy prodded at his own peril.

"You damn boys was only getting what ya was askin for," she said, crossing her well-muscled arms.

"We didn't make the mistake a pissin ya off too often," Albert said, laughing.

"Ya never did catch me," Wesley said. "I seen ya beat up Albert. I'm not sure how the hell he found the guts ta show his face again, but I knew to get the hell out a your way."

"Yeah, ya weasel, always jumpin on that damn bike."

"I'll tell ya, Hazel. You got my undyin admiration the day you beat up Raymond," Jimmy chortled. "I couldn't believe it. He was mean as shit and three times my size. Always pickin on me. Then one day he must of said somethin to piss you off. I saw you light into him and you sure as hell put him on the run. Best day of my life. Laughed my ass off."

"Surprised the hell outa him, didn't I?" she laughed. "So, how's Alaska been treatin ya Jimmy?"

"It's a real wilderness. I found me a cabin to stay in for a while and there was this damn bear kept on raidin the place. I was layin in wait trying to shoot him, but the bastard never come near until I left for town."

"Sounds wild for damn sure. What kinda work did you find up there?" Wesley asked.

As the afternoon wore on, Jimmy told his friends about his adventures on the gold dredge and the line crew, giving them a lively account of some of his wilderness experiences.

"Hey, I hear you're goin to college, Wesley," Jimmy said.

"Yeah. I'm takin classes out at Fresno State. My dad wanted me to go, but I'm not sure what I'll end up studying yet. I'll be workin this summer to save up for next year."

"You been playin any softball since ya left here?" Albert asked

"No. Never picked up a bat."

"Well, that's a damn shame. With you pitchin, we used to beat the hell out a everybody come up against us. Let's us run down and hit a few."

"You're on," Jimmy said.

For Jimmy, playing work-up softball with his old friends on the school-yard diamond truly felt like a return to the best of his childhood. Pitching wildly at first, he soon had his rhythm back sending zingers across the plate.

"Damn," Albert said after striking out, "now I remember why you was always on our team."

It wasn't long before some neighbors of varying ages joined the work-up game. Those who remembered him were reminded that Jimmy could bat as well as he pitched, and he ran like the wind. As always, he had mercy on the younger kids and fed them easier pitches.

Christmas Eve with Albert's family turned into a reunion with so many friends and family dropping by that the crowd filled the little cottage and spilled out into the rustic back yard. The revelers were full of fun and cheer and strong spirits. The atmosphere of welcome and goodwill momentarily stilled the demands of Jimmy's restless striving.

***

After bunking on Albert's couch for the night, Jimmy set out Christmas morning for Porterville. He wasn't quite sure where Uncle Grady and Aunt Ida lived now, but he would ask around for directions to Jackson Farms Ranch once he got into town.

On the familiar drive along the fertile eastern reaches of the San Joaquin Valley that skirted the base of the chiseled Sierra Nevada Mountains, Jimmy kept company with his memories. School days at Herndon Elementary came back vividly to his mind.

Mr. Dupuis, the poor bastard, Jimmy thought. *I give him fits.* He remembered when he'd showed up at school with his brothers in the fall that first year and they'd put him in Mr. Dupuis' fifth grade class. While Jimmy managed the basic math, the truth of his reading disability rapidly came to light though he did his level best to disguise his problem. Disruption became his ineffective cover.

He and Wesley had been stealthily targeting classmates with rubber-band-propelled paper clips when Mr. Dupuis caught them red-handed. As he recalled, his teacher had reached his limit that afternoon. Old Wesley had caved right away, owning up and taking detention as punishment. But Jimmy had sullenly denied his involvement. When the teacher marched the unrepentant hellion into the library, he'd given him one more chance to confess before bending him over, then breaking two stacked wooden rulers across his butt. Jimmy had taken his punishment in his usual silent, stoic manner. He'd had plenty of experience with Mama's punishments and could call up his "that don't hurt" angry resolve. He couldn't remember quite how the next event happened. Somehow, he had been knocked off his feet.

That's when ol Dupuis made his mistake, Jimmy grinned to himself with a shrug of chagrin as he remembered. *He must of been goin to help me up when he stepped over and straddled me. Wham! I kicked him right in the balls and he went down like a wounded bull. God, I run like hell. Then I was shit outa luck. Scared to go home. Sure I was gonna catch bloody hell from Mama. When I finally come home, everyone was actin normal. Couldn't figure it out.*

After ditching school for a couple more days, Jimmy, dumbfounded, had concluded that Mr. Dupuis actually hadn't told. Mustering his nerve, he'd gone back to class and slipped into his desk. For weeks after that, his teacher had utterly and completely ignored him, a punishment that Jimmy, to his surprise, found worse than any he'd experienced.

Jimmy remembered the relief he'd felt when one day Mr. Dupuis called him aside and explained the project he would head up. He would be in charge of creating a huge map of California on a full sheet of plywood. For the rest of the school year Jimmy directed teams who etched the topography of the state with woodburning tools: the mountains, rivers and lakes; the counties and cities; and the natural resources and products. When the map was coated with several layers of varnish, the finished project was a work of art that was displayed in the school hallway. For Jimmy it was a rare source of pride.

Driving along, he marveled at Mr. Dupuis' tolerance and the kindness he'd shown in allowing the unruly kid to save face and stay in school. In the process Jimmy had been able to learn and to demonstrate his abilities.

Goddamn, he was a hell of a teacher and a real man, Jimmy thought. *He must of really liked us kids. That Wesley was a pain in the ass, too. Never sittin still for a minute. I don't know why in hell he bothered to take us to the track meet.*

With satisfaction he remembered going to the all-city competition that had been held at Fresno High School when he was twelve, how Mr. Dupuis had encouraged Jimmy, Wesley and Hazel to participate and taken them in his car. Representing their small school, they had all made a good showing. Squirrely little Wesley had placed in the hundred-yard dash and lithe, determined Hazel had shined in the girls' long jump, the high jump and the mile race. While he'd participated in the other events, it was in the boys' mile when Jimmy charged into the limelight. Floating through the eight laps on the track, he left the other kids his age in the dust and, pulling away at the end, delighted in the thrill of victory.

Everett, who was in his first year at the high school, had gone along to the meet. For Jimmy it had been especially gratifying to have his steadfast older brother see him breeze to a win. In the last year Everett had become progressively less available as he'd grown more serious about school, juggling homework and his dishwashing job. Jimmy had turned more and more to his buddies for companionship as his big brother developed a love for reading that drove him nuts. No matter how he pestered and prodded, the times when Everett would break away to go swimming or play ball had become fewer as time wore on. And Billy was no use. Jimmy had decided that the kid was a slacker and eventually gave up on dragging him along to work in the fig orchards.

Yeah. Next time I go through Herndon, Jimmy thought as he rolled past vivid green fields of alfalfa, *I'm gonna have to look up Mr. Dupuis. I'd never of stayed in school through the sixth grade except for him. The poor bastard put up with my shit for two whole years.*

While he watched for a place to get directions as he approached the town of Porterville on Christmas Day, Jimmy remembered his final day of school. He'd only lasted a few weeks in Miss Bates seventh grade class. One morning his defiance had pushed her over the edge. When she whipped her hand back to slap his face, he caught it in his grasp before she connected. He left school that day and never went back.

Jimmy stopped to ask some neighborhood kids who were playing basketball in the street for directions to Jackson Farms Ranch. Since street signs were of no use to him, he kept asking as he got closer to the right area. Most local people gave "country" directions, anyway.

"Turn right at the second stop sign, left at the old oak tree, and left again at the big pink house."

When Jimmy pulled up at Uncle Grady and Aunt Ida's house, there was no mistaking he'd found the right location. The place was packed with relatives.

The front door was wide open, and as he walked in a hail of welcomes greeted him.

"Good God! Look what the cat dragged in. "

"How in the hell are ya?"

"Thought ya was up ta Alaska."

He'd forgotten how boisterous the family gatherings could be. As he laughed and shot back similar greetings, most of the conversation was lost in the hubbub. There was food everywhere. He was happy to see that the aunts had topped themselves in a well-established competition to outdo each other for the holiday feast. Grabbing a plate, he circulated through the overwhelming banquet of choices before he worked his way to the back yard in hopes of scrounging up a seat. On the way he noticed his oldest brother, Earl, and many cousins, aunts and uncles, some on his list of favorites and some on his other list. He'd long been aware that not all of his relatives were too fond or approving of him.

Grabbing a spot at a picnic table, Jimmy settled in for a feast. Most of the older men, including Uncle Grady, were sitting nearby visiting while they smoked and drank beer. Troops of younger cousins were horsing around in the sparsely landscaped back yard.

"Hey, Jimmy! How 're the folks doin?" Uncle Grady called over.

"Workin hard, Uncle Grady. They moved into town for the winter. Too damn cold to stay in the cabin now."

"This here country life suits me fine. Don't know what possessed them ta move way on up yonder. Too damn cold fer me. "

"Yeah, it's harsh cold for damn sure."

"Here you are, Jimmy," Aunt Ida said with a smile as she handed him a glass of lemonade.

"That hits the spot, " he said, smiling back at the aunt who had always been kind and welcoming.

"Where's Glenda hidin out?"

"She's been helpin in the kitchen. Must a missed you comin in the door. She'll be glad to see you."

It was only moments before his favorite cousin came charging out the back door and gave him a big hug before sitting down next to him at the picnic table.

"It's good to see you, Jimmy," Glenda said, her smiling face a mask of sincerity, her expressive brown eyes sparkling. "I didn't know you were coming. "

"I didn't either" Jimmy laughed, basking in her gentle favor. "Just decided to come down and get some sun. "

"What's it like in Alaska, Jimmy?"

"It's this great big wilderness, like the old-time wild west. Not too many rules up there. You kinda do what you want. I been workin for the electric company helpin string electric lines way out in the middle of nowhere. Them linemen I been workin with, now there's some tough guys. All of them work real hard and they don't put up with any slackin off "

"I hear it's real cold. " Glenda said.

"Oh yeah. I been out workin in twenty below. Just a while back my crew was workin way out stringin electric lines and all at once we heard all this horrible bellowin an stompin an snortin comin at us. Couldn't see a damn thing. It's twenty below and whatever's comin our way is making so much fog with all that snortin, no one can make out what it is," Jimmy said, noticing that everyone around him had abandoned their conversations and were leaning forward to listen in. "The damn beast just stood there bellowin somethin horrible. Then it turned around and disappeared into the scrub," he said with a mysterious smirk and leaned back in the chair folding his arms as if the story were finished.

"So, what was it?" Glenda asked, taking the bait.

"Guess, " he teased, knowing all along that his kindhearted cousin would be the first to break. *Gullible as always*, he thought. But he loved her for it, that steady earnestness so rare in the family.

"It turned out to be a bull buffalo, " he laughed

"That's bullshit, Jimmy. You're makin that up," his brother Earl interjected. "Everybody knows there aint no buffalo in Alaska. Sounds to me like a big old moose."

"Buffalo in Alaska. It was news to us," Jimmy laughed, ignoring his brother's jibe. "Seems a herd a buffalo was turned loose up there sometime in the thirties. " *Yeah, brother. You're still a asshole.*

"It sounds like the wild west all right," Uncle Clete chimed in.

Jimmy stiffened, quietly refusing to respond to his comment. He had no use for Uncle Clete, the uncle who had persuaded Mama and Dan to sell him their hard-earned Herndon home. It turned his stomach to think of where his folks were now, just scraping by and sliding toward losing their useless homestead claim. It took all his effort to reign in the urge to confront the weasel then and there. Holding back was a rare move for him, but love and respect for Aunt Ida and Uncle Grady gave him pause.

"Come on, Glenda," he said, abruptly rising from his chair. "Let's go see what those other knothead cousins have been up to."

***

By the time the Christmas guests were leaving, Jimmy had made the effort to connect with a number of the relatives. Some of them he hadn't seen in years. In his short interaction with Earl, the oldest brother ten years his senior, he'd gotten plenty of exposure to the sibling he'd seen as a bully. Nothing, he could tell, had really changed about Earl. *Still the blowhard asshole,* he concluded. Later Christmas night Jimmy got a real chance to visit with his favorite relatives, the ones who showed him love and respect. Aunt Ida and Uncle Grady always had made him welcome.

"How do ya keep the equipment runnin in that kinda cold," Uncle Grady asked.

"They was hard startin, but they had em fitted up for the weather, electric heaters and stuff."

"I got enough trouble keeping machines going around here. Sure wouldn't want to fight weather like that."

"You got your eye on a boy around here?" Jimmy asked in a teasing voice turning to Glenda.

"Go on!" she said, elbowing him. "I can't be bothered with the rowdy guys around here. All they're up to is drinking and driving fast. I'm going to graduate high school this year. "

"Already? What ya gonna do then?"

"I'm going to nursing school. I've been saving up and I can work all summer for Dad. "

"That's a good idea. You'll make a good nurse."

"Yeah. It'll take me a year of classes to go for a license as a practical nurse. The hard part will be having to live away from home."

"I know. Mean as your little brothers are, you're still a real homebody."

"You been workin this ranch lots a years now, Uncle Grady," Jimmy said.

"Yeah, I'm in charge a runnin the whole damn machinery barn now. Got a crew and all."

"Now! There's no call for cussin, Grady," Aunt Ida admonished.

"You're a sharp mechanic. They're lucky to have you," Jimmy said to the man who had once struck fear in his heart.

"Well, I aint doin bad for a guy can't read nor write. Got a steady job to support ma family an the company even lets us live in this here house."

"You work awful hard, Daddy," Glenda said.

"Yup. Takes seven days a week durin busy times. A man does what he needs to. Besides, I like mechanic work. I kin keep them trucks an tractors an combines purrin like kittens."

"Seems like you was working like a mule every time I ever seen you. Can't remember you takin a whole day off to sit around to talk before today," Jimmy said, admiration in his expression.

"Well, I saw you was always willin ta work hard, not afraid ta get your hands dirty. Got a stubborn streak in ya too, " Uncle Grady said, nodding at the truth of it.

"How do you figure?"

"Oh, I remember when your folks was in that real bad car wreck down ta Arizona. You was one tough kid. "

"Yeah, I remember. I must of been around five. I remember wakin up right at the edge of a irrigation ditch. God, I was scared."

"It was real bad what with the little neighbor girl bein kilt. Your Mama's arm was all smashed up and both a your Daddy's legs was broke," Uncle Grady said.

"We come from Chandler to get you after they taken everybody to the hospital and you was the only one could go home," Aunt Ida said.

"Yeah. I remember Everett's face bein all raw like it was sandpapered, and Billy had his front teeth knocked clear out," Jimmy added nodding at the picture in his mind.

"Well it was your Daddy done pulled yall out. That Marvin was a tough man draggin his family ta safety on two broke legs," Uncle Grady said.

"Yeah," Jimmy said, sharp sarcasm in his voice. "Seems like he coulda showed some concern when us kids was clear across the country starvin."

"You don't know the whole story, son," his uncle said.

"So far as I can tell a man should see to it his kids get fed," he said, bitterly.

"That night after the wreck, you was real high strung. Started cryin and raisin hell. Nobody could get a wink a sleep, " Uncle Grady continued, ignoring Jimmy's stinging reproach of his father.

"Mind your tongue. He was scared to death of the thunder and lightenin," Aunt Ida said, throwing her husband a piercing look.

"Seems like I told ya ta shut up or I'd put ya outside in the storm. Next day I come ta regret sayin that," his uncle said.

Jimmy nodded silently as he remembered the panic he'd felt that night, the flashing and booming of the storm and the uncertainty of separation from his family after the frightening accident. While his uncle had terrified him, he had also laid bare the deep reserve of resilience in Jimmy's nature. It was only later that Jimmy had come to recognize the kind heart hidden beneath his uncle's rough exterior.

"My heart near ta stopped when we couldn't find you the next mornin," Aunt Ida said with a sigh.

"Yeah. I remember walkin all day. Seems like I was real mad," Jimmy said, smiling.

"You was one stubborn little shit," his uncle said with admiration. "We was looking all over fer ya close ta home when it finally come to us ya must a struck out fer the hospital way off in Mesa, for cryin out loud. It was some seven mile on down. "

"We was heading down to the hospital when the nurse called to say you was there," Aunt Ida said. "Like ta broke my heart thinkin about you out there all by yourself. But you was alright when we took all three of you boys home that night. "

"Yeah," Uncle Grady laughed. "You was plum wore out, slept real sound the next night. "

Later, as Jimmy drifted off to sleep on a pallet in the boys' room, he thought about his aunt and uncle taking in the six Evans kids during the months when both of his parents were recovering in the hospital.

God, that must a been tough, he thought. *Uncle Grady scared the crap outa me, but he always done right by his family. Tough old bastard pulled out his own goddamn teeth with a pair a pliers when they got to hurtin him too bad,* Jimmy thought, smiling as he lay there half asleep. *Now that's what ya call brass balls.*

***

After two phone calls to get directions, Jimmy finally pulled up in front of his sister Iris's place on the outskirts of San Bernardino. Luckily, he'd thought to ask Aunt Ida for his sister's phone number. Navigating the huge Los Angeles metropolitan area was daunting even for a traveler who could actually read the road signs.

Getting out of the car, Jimmy stretched, releasing the tension from his road-weary mind and body. *Goddamn, what a dump*, he thought looking over the rundown rental. The bungalow had a squat profile typical of a slab foundation. He walked past the tired, ungated picket fence and through the parched front yard. The peeling front door stood ajar.

"Hey, Iris," he called, giving a quick knock as he walked in.

"Jimmy! I was so surprised to hear from you. What're you doin down here, anyway?" she called excitedly as she emerged from another room, a toddler hitched on her hip.

"Hi Sis," he said walking into a warm hug and returning it. "Just look at you guys," he said, smiling at his young niece and nephew who had come eagerly to their mother's side.

"You remember Uncle Jimmy," Iris said to the little girl and boy who were both looking dubiously at the tall stranger. "You filled out some," she said, turning back to Jimmy. "Heartbreakin handsome as ever."

"Yeah. Couple a day's at Aunt Ida's can fatten you up," he laughed. "But I stay on the go. Keeps me lean and mean." He'd forgotten how pretty his sister was with her thick dark hair, high widow's peak and clear blue eyes. *God, she looks wore out. I hope this new husband's worth a damn. Not another loser like the last two. Guess she was hell bent get away from home, with her and Mama always buttin heads. Both of them bein so headstrong.*

"Who's this little guy?" he asked, his attention causing the one-year-old to duck his head into his mother.

"He's Charlie," Sissy said, drawing closer. "He's shy."

"Well you aint shy are you Sissy?" Jimmy laughed, as the five-year-old smiled back. "Don't you remember me?"

Sissy gave him a quizzical look, shaking her head.

"Tell me what you've been up to," Iris said as she settled the baby on the floor with a bowl of Cheerios and threw a pot of coffee on the stove to percolate.

"I been workin my ass off for the last couple of years," he said, seating himself at the battered chrome dinette. "Alaska's a ass-kickin place, but not much goin on in the dead of winter. Thought I'd come down and mess around here for a while. Soak up some sun. I never felt cold like they got in Alaska. Think I could bunk on your couch?"

"Sure. How's Mama and Dan doin?" she asked as she cleared the old crusted dishes from the kitchen table, stacking them in the sink.

"Okay, I guess. Can't for the life of me figure why they give up the place in Herndon. It's damn hard gettin by up there. Ground aint worth a damn for growin stuff."

"Well, you remember how they got took by Uncle Clete. Went and traded for his place in Sacramento then had a hell of a time keepin up on the payments." Iris said.

"The Herndon place was paid for. How did that snake talk them into that kind of deal?"

"I don't know," she said, shaking her head. "But with Everett getting killed, Mama just wanted to leave. Gettin free land in Alaska sounded like a new start, I guess."

"Yeah. Well, I guess so," Jimmy said, as he realized that the older kids had taken seats at the table and were big-eyed watching his every move.

"Everett was really gonna make somethin of himself," Iris said, setting a cup of coffee in front of Jimmy. "I loved that boy," she continued in a choked voice. "It just don't seem right that he aint never comin back."

"Don't, goddamnit!" Jimmy erupted, holding up his hand in a desperate effort to make her stop talking as he felt his molten rage rise. Seeing the kids jump and flinch and the crestfallen look on his sister's face, he felt ashamed of his harsh outburst.

"Listen," he said, swallowing hard as he avoided looking at Iris, "I saw a little grocery store down the block. How bout I take these two down for a ice cream?"

"Sure. That'll give me time to clean up," Jane agreed.

Although four-year-old Tim had yet to talk to him, he warmed up a bit at the promise of a treat. While his pretty older sister seemed hungry for attention, the handsome boy with startling blue eyes was not so easily won over. Jimmy enjoyed the warmth of small hands slipping into his own as they walked the few blocks to the store. Sissy chose an Eskimo Pie, while Tim insisted on a Hershey Bar for his treat, and Jimmy decided to buy himself a pack of cigarettes and a gallon of milk for the household.

The first evening at Iris's place turned out to be strained to say the least. Less than an hour after her husband, Alan, came home from his job at George Air Force Base, she left for her evening work as a waitress. Jimmy couldn't get a handle on the problem, but over the hastily consumed dinner there had been a hostile static between the couple. Now he sat at the table smoking while he tried to make conversation with his brother-in-law.

"You been workin at the base for long?" Jimmy asked, watching Alan finger a flight magazine he'd obviously rather be reading.

"Three years, now. It's steady, but bein a supply clerk don't pay worth a shit. Want a beer?" he asked, pulling two bottles from the small refrigerator and opening both at Jimmy's nod.

"Yeah, good jobs're hard to find. There's lots a guys up in Alaska went there for work," he said, settling the baby in his lap after the kid's father had ignored his cries to be picked up. "Can't deny little Charlie here. Looks a hell of a lot like his old man."

"Yeah," he muttered. "Hey! You kids shut up!" he yelled at Sissy and Tim who were squabbling over some crayons and a coloring book. "Christ Almighty, I'm stuck here every night with these damn kids. There's never enough money. Iris is raisin hell cause I want to take some flyin lessons. Wanted to be a pilot all my life. Could be one a them, what ya call em, 'bush pilots' flying in supplies and stuff up there in Alaska. But she thinks I should give it up."

"Hard job, takin care of your family," Jimmy said, taking an intense dislike to the man who had yet to look him directly in the eye. *You prick!* "I'll be payin rent so long as I'm stayin here."

It wasn't long before Jimmy left the house, breathing a sigh of relief. He wouldn't be spending much time there with Alan. Cruising down the road he spotted a bar with lots of cars in the parking lot and decided to stop in. At eight o'clock The Longhorn was jumping, the jukebox cranking and lots of action going on around the pool tables. Jimmy ordered an on-tap mug of beer at the bar and checked the place out.

As he sipped his ice-cold beer, he watched a fat, bald guy hustle some pool players. Jimmy was wise to him right away, watching him throw a couple of games until the bets got high enough. He smiled when the con artist cleared the table while the chumps looked mighty downhearted to be walking away with empty pockets.

Jimmy noticed a big guy come in and sit down at the bar a few seats away and observed how he commanded attention. Looking like a football player, all muscle with a head of curly blond hair and a knowing smile, his cock-sure attitude matched his Hollywood good looks. Jimmy was impressed how the women flocked to the guy, surrounding him within minutes.

"Hey, babe," Jimmy heard the jock say to a petite blond who seemed to be hanging on his every word, "what ya doin later?"

"Well that depends," she teased. "You taking me to the game on Friday?"

"I'd take you in a minute, but nobody can get Rose Bowl tickets. Hey, I'll come over to your place on New Year's and we'll listen to the game on the radio."

"Are you sure you'll be listening the game?" another pretty girl teased suggestively.

"Well, we know USC's going to skin Wisconsin. They don't even have a fighting chance."

"Hey, don't be discountin them Wisconsin boys. My money's on them," Jimmy yelled over the hubbub.

"You betting?"

"Sure. I got ten bucks says Wisconsin runs away with it," Jimmy challenged, drawing a few speculative looks from the women.

"You're on, buddy. Name's Dwayne," he said, extending his hand across his flock of admirers.

"I'm Jimmy," he said, returning the firm handshake.

"You meeting me down here to pay off?" Dwayne asked, giving a pleasant laugh.

"Sure. I'll be here."

"Haven't seen you around before. Where you from?"

"Oh, I'm down from Alaska," he said, noticing a pleasant shift in the women's attention.

For the rest of the evening Jimmy entertained the group with stories about his Alaskan adventures. He found that Dwayne was a local guy who was about the same age. Before he left the bar, they agreed to meet there and firm up their bet the next night. It seemed that they would be able to hear the game on the radio at The Longhorn on New Year's Day.

When Jimmy got back to Iris's place, she was still up waiting for him.

"Where'd you go?" she asked quietly.

"Just out for a while," Jimmy answered.

"Alan didn't piss you off, did he?

"No. I didn't have no trouble with him," he said with a shrug. "I won't cause you no problem. Here's twenty bucks to help out with food."

"Thanks."

"Listen. I'll be keepin my own schedule, so don't be waitin up for me."

"Okay. Your still my little brother, you know. You were such a puny little thing and so stubborn. I looked after you three boys for lots of years. There's a blanket and a pillow on the couch for you."

Jimmy woke to the sound of heavy footsteps and the front door slamming. He bolted upright. Squinting at the brightness of early morning sunlight that beamed in on him through the living room window, he could barely make out the silhouette of his sister sitting hunched at the kitchen table.

"What's a matter, Sis?" he asked.

"That guy's such an asshole," she said, swiping at her eyes with the back of her hand.

"I was gonna try to avoid mentionin that."

"Yeah. You're a real diplomat," she said, giving an ironic laugh. "How long did you plan to last before givin your opinion of that selfish jerk?"

"Well, I aint too good at coverin up my true feelins, but I aint here to bring you no grief. I got savings. I can find a place to stay."

"No. I like having you here. And the kids could use some attention. Listen, I'm goin out to do laundry later. It's my day off. Just leave your dirty clothes and I wash them along with mine."

"No need for that."

"Hey, I washed your dirty drawers many a time."

"I guess so," he laughed.

When he had showered and dressed, Jimmy played with the kids for a little while before setting out to cruise the used car lots. With the prospect of available females and blatant plans for seduction, he decided that his little Chevy two-seater just wasn't going to make the grade. Several hours later, Jimmy rolled off the lot in a spiffy white '47 Chevy convertible. It had set him back another thirteen hundred bucks, but, what the hell, he'd worked hard for it. With the warm sunshine pouring in on him and a balmy breeze ruffling his dark, slicked-back hair, he drove around for hours exploring the mountains northeast of the city. *Goddamn, this is great*, he thought. *Now I'm livin high on the hog.*

Stopping for something to eat in Big Bear, he walked around enjoying the woodsy feel of the place, the welcome familiarity of openness in contrast to the confines of the city. He noticed that the temperature had dropped a bit but refused to acknowledge feeling cold. It was nothing compared to the deep chill he'd left behind in Alaska. *Now if I can only find my way back to Iris's place, I'll be doin real good*, he thought with a whimsical smile. Although he'd found the huge metropolitan area intimidating, he was confident in his ability to navigate. Over the years he'd fine-tuned his memory for landmarks and direction. Once he'd been to a place, he seldom got lost.

Iris and the kids loved his new car. After he'd taken them for a ride, stopping to pick up some groceries, they didn't want to get out. They looked pitifully sad when he pulled up in front of the house. Having cleaned up and left before Alan got home that afternoon, Jimmy took a spin around town for a while and ended up at The Longhorn nursing a beer. When Dwayne sauntered in later, he sat down next to Jimmy and took up the conversation where they'd left off the night before. The guy was full of bull and full of himself, fun and funny, and Jimmy was up for a good time. Once they'd settled on the Rose Bowl bet, which grew to thirty dollars, they agreed to meet the next day, New Year's Day 1953, at the bar and listen to the game.

As the night wore on, Jimmy watched Dwayne in action, the way he energized everyone nearby. He was amazed at the bevy of pretty young women hovering around them, drawn, it seemed, like bees to honey. *Goddamn, that Dwayne's got em droolin. How the hell's he doin it? They're plum throwin theirselves at him*, he thought. Although he noticed that he was getting a fair share of attention himself, he modestly laid it off on his new buddy's charm and his own fat bankroll that he doled out generously.

When Dwayne and three attractive women, who proved to be roommates, piled into his neat little convertible, Jimmy knew he was going to get lucky. Margie, the redhead with big blue eyes and a low-cut blouse that showed off some of her assets, was all over him as he drove to the duplex where the three women lived. He marshaled all his powers of concentration to watch where he was driving, which seemed inordinately far in his current state. *It's been a long dry spell, but I'm finally gonna get some*, he thought. *How the hell far is this place anyway?*

***

"Where've you been? I was worried about you," Iris said as Jimmy let himself into the house around ten the next morning.

"Out bringin in the New Year. I told you not to be waitin up."

"You've been out catting around. Can't fool me."

"You caught me," Jimmy said, grinning at his sister.

"You be careful."

"Always. It's okay, Sis. I'm just havin a little fun. Where's Alan?"

"Down at the damn bar," she said, pushing the kitchen door wide open to keep an eye on her kids playing out back. "We can't keep up with the bills and he thinks nothing of blowing 'his' money on drinking and playing pool. Says it's his holiday and he needs to get away from them noisy kids. I'm sick a livin poor."

"We already done plenty of that," Jimmy agreed.

"Yeah. Thought I'd get away from living dirt poor when I left home. Have to say, Mama was clever at thinkin of ways to make a buck, but she was always pissin it away as fast as it come in."

"Yeah. And we worked our asses off in the fields to help out. You was stuck watching us boys some of the time. But me and Everett turned over all our pay from farming jobs and got a nickel for the movies or to spend at Schmidts. Remember way back when we was first followin Dan down to Texas? Seems like he was doin his basic trainin. I remember Mama sellin stuff on the sly to the soldiers." Jimmy said.

"Oh yeah. I remember. Camp Howze. We was livin in a tiny town just outside of Gainesville. I forget the name of the place. I was thirteen and you must a been round about five or six. Mama had me damn near tied to the stove fryin up chicken. It was hotter then hell."

"Yeah. Them soldiers was out there runnin and sweatin up a storm. Comin right by the house. They was supposed to make do with just a canteen of water and some rations. Their tongues was hanging out by the time they got to our place. The Army even had a MP stationed outside the little grocery store so the men couldn't stop and buy stuff. That's where me and Everett come in. We'd hide by the road and take orders for soda pop and candy bars, then walk out of the store all loaded down right past the MP. We'd have to run like hell to catch up with them soldiers, but it paid good. Them guys was damn happy to get the stuff," Jimmy said, the crafty smirk of a sneaky little boy lighting his face.

"Mama even had us filling canteens when they was going by. Then she got the idea of feeding them. Set up a regular outdoor cafe. Once word got out, them hungry soldiers that was bivouacked on down the road would sneak back after dark for a plate a fried chicken and beans and cornbread. Lots of nights we had the back yard full of GIs sitting on the ground chowing down. Yeah, Mama had lots of schemes for making a buck. Kept us kids workin like fools."

"Yeah. It was never easy on us kids. I know sometimes you got the worst of it, but you done your best for us boys," Jimmy said.

Iris, her looks already fading at twenty-five, stood still nodding.

***

An hour later Jimmy was showered, shaved and on his way down to The Longhorn. Getting some sleep never occurred to him. He was flying high on excitement and anticipation. Having been far too occupied with Margie, he wasn't sure what had become of Dwayne and the two roommates last night. *The game'll be on soon*, he thought. *They should be down at the bar by now. Damn, I hope it don't last too long. I got more on my mind that any damn football game. Best be thinkin a somethin else, pussy hound,* he warned himself with a wolfish grin, *or you'll be embarrassin yourself walkin in there.*

Although the bar was packed, Jimmy managed to work his way onto a stool beside the group from last night who had staked out their own territory. With the New Year's revelers having a rollicking good time, the noise level was incredible. From what he could tell, there was a tight gathering of maybe eight young women, regulars it seemed. Among them sat Dwayne, the cock of the walk. He was laughing and cracking jokes. All eyes were on him and he was playing to each of them. Jimmy spotted Margie in the group, but her attention was focused on Dwayne. As the evening developed, he realized that the women were buying the drinks. *Goddamn, them girls are all over Dwayne. Eager aint the word for it. That guy's a real operator. How the hell many of them do you suppose he's been screwin?"*

It was hard to hear the narration of the Rose Bowl game even with the radio turned up full blast and set out on the bar. The patrons were predictably partial to the Southern California team, cheering wildly with each yardage gain.

"Damn, Dwayne," Jimmy shouted above the uproar, "you put your money on a bunch a fumble-bums."

"What'd ya mean?" Dwayne asked.

"Oh, come on! They're playing way out a their league," Jimmy baited. Though he had no interest in football and knew nothing about the teams, he took the opportunity to stir the pot, which was one of his favorite sports.

"You're gonna get yourself beat up talkin like that in this crowd," Margie said, sidling up next to him.

"It's okay, hon." he said, wrapping an arm around her waist and giving her his dimpled smile. "I'm just pumpin them up a little."

"Save a little of that pumping for me," she said, putting her lips close to his ear.

"You like that do ya?" he asked, looking her in the eye.

"Yes!"

"Touchdown!" Dwayne screamed, as the crowd roared.

Although Jimmy's team never scored, he kept up his derisive banter throughout the game and graciously paid off the bet at the end. That night at Margie's, his payoff was far better.

Over the next few weeks Jimmy spent a lot of time hanging around with Dwayne, going out on the town every night. One thing he discovered early on; the guy never paid his own way. With his looks, charm and enthusiasm for life, he just seemed to be sliding along with no job and no car. Jimmy was wise to the fact that his girl-friendly Chevy convertible and his fat bankroll were basic to the friendship, but he figured, what the hell, he was having fun.

"Hey," Dwayne said, jumping into the passenger seat on a Saturday morning. "Let's swing over by Rosemont."

"Okay, just tell me when to turn. Where're we goin anyway?"

"I'm thinkin about havin some turkey," he said, with a mysterious smirk. "The girls can roast one up real good."

"Yeah. So, where're we goin?"

"Depends on whether you know how to butcher and dress out a turkey," Dwayne said, breaking into his infectious laughter.

"You're full of shit. But it just so happens I butchered chickens lots of times," Jimmy chuckled, having fun with the guessing game.

"Hot damn! I thought so. Well, fill up the tank, we're headin out toward the desert a ways."

"Yeah, yeah. Surprise me," Jimmy said, gunning it until the warm air whipped their hair.

"How long you known them girls," Jimmy shouted over the roar of the wind.

"Damn near a year. They like to take care of me and all of them's a good lay."

"That's gotta make them the most open-minded women I ever seen," Jimmy said, shaking his head in amazement.

"Yeah, well, they kinda compete for my favors. Works out good for me. Don't cost me nothin. The three of em work at a insurance company downtown."

Jimmy digested the idea of the strange relationship silently for a while. As they drove into the desert, the terrain began to look forbidding, with barren rocky outcroppings and clumps of strange looking yucca trees surrounded by patches of tumbleweeds. On the long stretches of straight road there were sudden dips periodically, where it dropped into dry washes and rose back out. An irresistible temptation for Jimmy.

"Hey, you didn't tell me about the road," Jimmy grinned, jamming the accelerator as they approached another series of dips.

If Dwayne answered, Jimmy didn't hear him as they roared into the first dip, feeling the stomach-turning sensation of being suspended, the sudden drop and the force exerted as they ripped up the other side. The roller coaster effect was exhilarating. They burst into laughter just as they entered the next dip.

"Christ Almighty! You drive like a maniac," Dwayne yelled, mid-laugh as he tried to catch his breath when the road finally leveled out.

"Car just eats up the road," Jimmy replied gleefully. "Ya gonna tell me where we're goin?"

"You'll see. Goddamn, ya gonna wreck us," Dwayne hollered as he felt the car accelerate toward the next series of dips.

"Hang on!"

Jimmy was pouring the coal to her as he crested the third dip and shot toward the next. Just as they roared over the brink, he saw the group of range cattle dead ahead in the bottom of the depression.

"Shit!" Dwayne hollered.

Clenching his jaw, Jimmy made an instant inventory of his options.

Hitting a cow at a hundred miles an hour was not one of them. Aiming for a narrow strip of clear pavement on the left side of the road, he held his breath cutting the right wheel as close to the cattle as he could without hitting them while trying at the same time to keep the left wheel from dropping off the edge into the gravel shoulder. *Don't you bastards move*, he thought as time slowed while he held steady and threaded the needle. Next thing he knew, they were past the cattle, but the left wheel was digging into the gravel, pulling them off the road to the left. Knowing he was losing control; he picked a level spot and drove off into the desert.

"Damn! Damn!" Dwayne kept repeating, shaking his head. He looked decidedly pale when Jimmy slowed the car to a stop a few seconds later.

"Hey, no harm done," Jimmy said lightly. "What'd ya do, shit your britches?"

"God, I thought we was dead meat."

"Guess it paid off learnin to drive in them old muddy fig orchards. Kinda sharpens up your reflexes," Jimmy said, gripping the steering wheel to still his trembling hands. "I think the car's okay. Should be able to drive right back on to the road. Think I'll take a piss before we start out."

"Yeah."

Dwayne was uncharacteristically quiet for the next few miles but came to life as they approached an isolated factory, a huge cement building with several belching smokestacks.

"Okay country boy, turn right on the road up there," Dwayne said, his confident smile back.

"We drove all the way out to the middle of the goddamn desert to visit a factory?"

"Yup. We're pickin up my friend Rufus. Works out here all week at the borax plant."

The long drive back to San Bernardino was positively dull in comparison to the excitement they'd already had. Rufus seemed like a fun-loving guy from what Jimmy could hear of the conversation. On the way back, Dwayne gave his friend a blow-by-blow description of their harrowing narrow escape, making it sound more like a lark than a brush with death. His admiration of Jimmy's driving skills rang loud and clear in the telling.

Just before they reached town, Dwayne directed Jimmy to turn onto a little dirt road that wound off to the east. A mile down, they stopped and got out.

"Get ready to catch us some turkeys," Dwayne said.

Jimmy followed his lead, stealthily climbing a brushy hill until they could peer down on an enclosure that contained row upon row of Quonset-hut-like structures surrounded by barbed wire. It seemed that Rufus already knew the drill. From what they could see, the coast was clear with no vehicles parked nearby on a Saturday afternoon. When they slipped quietly down to the fence, Dwayne produced a pair of wire cutters from his pocket and quickly snipped the lowest rows of barbed wire. The door to the nearest hut was unlocked and in minutes they emerged with two squawking turkeys in hand, passing them off as they crawled under the fence. Stifling laughter, the three raced for the car.

"Kinda like shootin fish in a barrel," Dwayne grinned. "Hurry up and open the trunk."

"Squawkin damn birds," Jimmy laughed, as he fumbled with the lock.

Jumping into the car, the guys flew down the road, giddy with exhilaration at their prankish foray. At Dwayne's direction Jimmy pulled into a little wayside area and stopped out of sight from the road.

"Okay, Jimmy. Time to demonstrate your butcherin skills. The girls don't want no noisy birds getting hauled into their place."

Opening the trunk, Dwayne and Rufus scrambled to grab the flapping, squawking turkeys. Jimmy settled for wringing their necks. At first, he had grabbed his trusty pocketknife, but decided against turning the trunk of his car into a bloody mess.

At the women's duplex they smuggled the limp, feathered creatures in through the back door. Jimmy was amazed to see how unconcerned the young working women were especially after their bathtub was filled with blood, guts and feathers. Some hours later the six of them feasted on roast turkey out in the backyard. They all swore it was the best they'd ever tasted, but the case of beer that Jimmy had run out to buy early in the evening may have influenced their judgment.

Jimmy kept so busy running that he avoided most of the conflict at Iris's place. When he dragged himself home and collapsed on the living room couch, he was usually so exhausted he could have slept through an earthquake. He often spent the mornings with his sister once he'd managed three hours sleep more or less, and he enjoyed the kids even when they pestered him awake. Sissy and Tim looked forward to rides in his convertible with the top down, and he was a dependable source of treats at the neighborhood grocery.

Jimmy tried to make sure he was out of the house before Alan got home. The sound of the guy's voice yelling at the kid's or making snide remarks to Iris was enough to spark his anger. *What a selfish prick*, he'd think any number of times as his hands clenched into fists. For Jimmy, who seldom held back his venom, it was a strain to keep his mouth shut. He hesitated to interfere and cause more trouble, besides his sister wasn't likely to listen to his advice. She was as bullheaded as the rest of the clan. He just kept giving her money. It was the best he could do.

Spending time with Dwayne was a blast. The guy was a charming trickster, always happy and up to something. He couldn't get over his astonishment at the way Dwayne could sweet-talk girls right out of their panties wherever they went. The guy was a regular gigolo.

"Hey, see that looker over there waitin for a Greyhound?" Dwayne said one afternoon as they were cruising around downtown San Bernardino.

"Yeah."

"Well, pull over and get out. I need the car. I'm getting some of that."

"Sure," Jimmy said, shaking his head as he pulled to the curb.

"Hey, pick you up in an hour over there at the cafe," Dwayne called, pulling a quick U-turn.

Standing at the curb, Jimmy watched as his friend pulled alongside the well-dressed blond. After a short conversation, she opened the passenger door and got in. *Goddamn amazin*, he thought as he watched them drive away.

"What the hell did you say to her?" Jimmy asked as soon as Dwayne reappeared a couple hours later.

"Hey, I'm just a natural lover," he smirked. "See, she's back to standin out there waitin for her bus. But now she's got a big satisfied smile on her pretty face."

"Damn. Where's she goin, anyway?"

"She's on her way to meet her husband up in San Francisco. He's some kinda serviceman. Man, she was hot to trot. Really liked the roomy back seat in your car. Took me a minute to figure out how to put up the top, but I took her to a real private place anyway."

"Ya coulda left the top up. It's kinda cold today."

"No. We need it down. I got a idea. Come on. Let's go," he said. "Keys are in the car."

"Okay, ya gonna tell me why we're needin all this fresh air?" Jimmy asked as he pulled away from the curb.

"Yeah. Just hang on a minute. Okay now, slow down and ease into that alley. Stop right by that beer truck. Now!"

Dwayne already had his door open before they came to a stop. In one smooth motion his feet hit the alley, he grabbed two cases of beer, one after the other, lowering them swiftly into the open back seat, and slid back into his seat.

"Go," he hissed.

They were out of the alley, and around the corner well before the delivery man could discover his loss.

"Damn. You must of done that before."

"Oh yeah. We'll be havin a real good time with the girls tonight."

They were pretty well smashed by the time they left the duplex in the early morning hours. While Jimmy intended to drop Dwayne off at his house where he lived with his mother, his high-flying friend hadn't had quite enough excitement for the day.

"Listen, I wanna get me a couple of turkeys," Dwayne slurred.

"Yeah, let's go tomorrow," Jimmy said, thinking more about hitting the sack than embarking on a new adventure. His eyes felt heavy.

"No!" Dwayne insisted. "We're gonna get us some lavender turkeys."

Shit, he wants to steal some a Gorgeous George's goddamn purple turkeys. Oh, what the hell. "Okay."

Jimmy had driven by the turkey ranch before. Located some six miles out of town, the spread was well known in the area, mostly because of the flamboyant wrestler's penchant to paint everything on the place a gaudy shade of bright lavender. The ranch-style house, the barn, the tractors, the trucks, and even the rail fencing, all were painted in "orchid," Gorgeous George's signature color. The final touch at the front of the property was the hog-wire cage containing the turkeys, which were also dyed a brilliant purple.

Still feeling no pain, Jimmy and Dwayne made fast work of kidnapping the fowl. With the cage located right at the roadside, it was a simple matter of opening the unlocked cage, grabbing a couple of the gobblers and stuffing them in the trunk. As tired as he was, the caper hardly produced any sense of excitement for Jimmy.

***

"Goddamnit, Jimmy," Iris yelled, shaking his shoulder.

"What!" he said, bolting up, startled at her tone.

"What the hell've you been up to?"

"What'd you mean, Sis? Something wrong?" he said, still groggy even as he heart raced.

"Hey! I borrowed your damn car this morning needing some milk for the kids."

"Did it break down? Tell me what the hell's goin on," he demanded.

"Yeah. Well, when I parked downtown, I started hearing this godawful commotion. Sounded like it was comin from the trunk. Well, I had to look."

"Yeah?"

"You jackass! I opened it up and these damn purple turkeys come busting out at me. Scared the life outa me. Then they're runnin down the street, flappin and squawkin, attractin all kinds of attention and all at once I figure out where they come from. Damn it, Jimmy! What the hell are you doin?"

"You let my turkeys get away?" Jimmy asked, innocently.

"Your turkeys were purple, Uncle Jimmy," Sissy said from the doorway where she and her brother were standing wide-eyed.

"People were looking at me," Iris ranted, switching the baby to her other hip, "and I'm knowin goddamn well where they come from," she said, her lips twitching as she began to lose her mad.

"I guess you ought to stay out of a guy's trunk," he said, busting up. "Your reputation's likely ruined in this town."

"I knew you boys would be the death of me," Iris said, succumbing to hysterical laughter. She laughed until tears rolled down her cheeks.

"You're gettin awful damn fussy about the groceries I'm bringin home," Jimmy commented, setting his sister off again. "You coulda cooked the damn things if you hadn't let them loose."

Jimmy loved his sister. Seeing up close how miserable her life was, how overwhelmed she was with trying to care for her three children and deal with another loser husband wore on him. It was all he could do to resist the urge to bring his own chaos to the situation. He couldn't fix it.

March in Southern California brought sunny warm days with balmy ocean breezes that swept the air, clearing away the stubborn layer of smog. Despite the easy living, Jimmy began to feel his old restlessness once more. While he still had plenty of cash, he hadn't worked or done anything productive in a couple of months. He thought he was having fun as he sported around in his classy car, enjoyed his glib charismatic friend, and indulged in the pleasure of frequent sexual liaisons, but somehow the afterglow had faded, and he was feeling empty and adrift.

6

EXPLORING WITH EDDY

Jimmy hit the road again as casually as he'd blown into town. His decision to abandon the San Bernardino "good life" had been spur of the moment, driven by his growing discontent.

Iris had been sad to see him leave and the kids had been genuinely upset. They were his only regret. He was worried about his older sister, but she would make her own decisions, good or bad, just like she always had. All he could do was give her a couple hundred bucks and wish her well.

Damn glad to be leavin that stinkhole of a city behind, he thought. *Too many damn people packed in. Christ! Iris ought to throw that selfish prick out on his ass. Useless whiner. He's goddamn mean to them little kids. I'd of kicked his worthless ass myself if it a done any good*, he thought, clenching his jaw against the anger threatening to surface. *Damn near did it a couple of times. Yeah, it's past time I was on my way.*

His restless mind calmed as he covered the miles, soothed by the wind in his hair, country music on the radio, and the open road ahead. He loved driving. *Wonder what old Eddy's up to these days*, he thought with a growing sense of anticipation as he headed up Highway 99 toward Fresno. He thought that his old buddy, who he'd run around with after quitting school at twelve, would still be living near Highway City.

As it turned out, Eddy still lived at home. He was out in the driveway working on a motorcycle when Jimmy pulled up in his spiffy convertible.

"Well goddamn, Jimmy. What the hell're ya doin in these parts?" Eddie greeted, wiping his hands on a rag before giving him a greasy handshake.

"Come to check up on you," Jimmy said smiling at his affable friend.

"Shit, I aint seen you in years."

"Looks like you become some kinda motorcycle nut. All of these belong to you?"

"Hell no. I sorta worked my way inta runnin a cycle shop right here outa the garage. Man, look at your wheels. Ya come inta some money or somethin?"

"Sure. Struck it rich in Alaska," Jimmy teased. "Hell no. I just decided to come down an kick around a while. Which one a them bikes is yours?"

"This here Harley 61's mine," he said pointing out a well-maintained canary yellow cycle. "Hey, hang on. I'll take ya for a spin."

Jimmy ducked his face behind Eddy's shoulder, squinting to keep flying debris out of his eyes and nose as they flew along the highway going out toward Kerman. Perched on the leather saddle behind his sturdily built, smaller friend, he had only the tips of his boots braced against the terminus of the running boards for purchase.

"Goddamn, we're about flyin," he yelled gleefully over the deafening roar of the powerful engine.

Eddy slowed, then turned into the gravel parking lot at Harry's Tavern, their old hangout.

"Hey, ya need to get a cycle," Eddy said over a beer.

"Yeah, maybe," Jimmy said, taking a big bite of his burger. "You been practicin your pinball? Bet I can still beat your ass."

"You always could. Man, I remember you pickin me up ta come out here ta play foosball and all them arcade games. Seems like I was only sixteen, so you was what, somethin like fourteen? And you driving your own car," Eddy said as he smiled at the memory, his clear blue eyes earnest and his windblown strawberry-blond hair settled in waves.

"Them was the days. Shit, I was workin up to Manteca, livin in a hotel right there on Main Street, makin it on my own. That night job workin in the Spreckels warehouse was a pushover. No shit, all I had to do was grease the chute with a hunk of bees' wax. Was runnin all day sometimes haulin beans to the cannery, then I'd crawl way up in them rafters and set the alarm to wake me up every two hours. Didn't eat too regular, but I saved enough to buy me that little '41 Ford."

"Yeah. The both a us was full a bullshit them days," Eddie laughed.

"Remember goin to the Dixie Theater? We had our own reserved seats to watch them shoot-em-up cowboy shows. Like we owned the place."

"Yeah, everybody had his spot staked out of a Saturday night," Eddy said.

"But you was the damn joker. Brought your aunt's pet skunk and turned it loose. Everybody broke into a panic. You emptied the place," Jimmy said, laughing.

"Damn. I got in trouble for that. But we had em goin. All them kids was screaming, sure they was gonna get squirted," Eddy said.

"Johnny didn't think it was so damn funny when you put us up to hidin his little toy-size car."

"Oh yeah. Forgot about that," Eddy laughed. "Man, he was pissed. But it was too temptin. Seems like it took four of us to pick it up and move it. And him so careful ta lock it up."

"You was always thinkin up some kind of bullshit. So, where's Johnny these days?" Jimmy asked.

"He got drafted and sent to Korea. Damnit, I heard he was missin in action."

"Goddamn shame," Jimmy said, withdrawing into a solemn silence as the sounds of jukebox music and the cheers of game-players seemed to press in on him all at once.

Over the next few days Jimmy got reacquainted with Eddy, discovering that his friend lived a casual life, free and easy. He lived with his folks, tinkered with motorcycles and worked in the fields to earn a few bucks, but his passion was riding his bike. Full of friendly good humor, he seemed content.

Jimmy rented a cottage in a little motel that was tucked behind a grocery and gas station on Highway 99 on the outskirts of Highway City. When Eddy refused to ride around in Jimmy's car, he parked his classy convertible at the motel and started hitching on the back of Eddy's cycle. It took only a few days before they were at the motorcycle shop in Fresno buying Jimmy his first bike.

The midnight-blue Harley 74 was bigger, heavier, and less

maneuverable than his friend's, but Jimmy liked the powerful feel and the challenge of it. His first hurdle was driving the sucker out of the parking lot. Learning to coordinate the mechanics of engaging the clutch with a foot pedal, shifting gears with a side-mounted stick, and goosing the throttle while actually staying in control was tricky, but he ate up the challenge. Thrilled to it. Took command of it. From that moment forward, he rode the machine full boar every chance he got. The leather jacket, goggles and saddlebags turned out to be wise investments.

Jimmy and Eddy started roaming the countryside, traveling to local scenic destinations on their bikes. Loading up sleeping bags, a few Cokes and Dr. Peppers, a loaf of bread and a package of hot- dogs in their saddlebags, they were set to go. All through the month of March and into April they headed out for days at a time. During that period Jimmy's nineteenth birthday passed without his noticing. On their scenic forays they ventured into the rugged riches of Yosemite National Park hiking the partly ice-clad falls' trails and taking in the spectacular vistas. They rode through Sequoia National Park to view the towering giants and traveled west to Morrow Bay to cruise along the Pacific Ocean. Jockeying the powerful cycles was hard work, and many times, utterly exhausted, they pulled off the road and slept under the trees.

Once they had explored the wide-open reaches of Central California from the Sierra Nevada Mountains to the Pacific Ocean, they started ranging farther afield. Over a hot meal in a little country cafe or sacking out by a campfire, Jimmy spun his stories about his adventures in Alaska. The warm weather and the lengthening days reminded him that soon it would be time to head north to Alaska again for a summer job.

Jimmy continued to spend generously as he paid more than his share of expenses. When he started getting low on funds, he sold his convertible and restored the twelve hundred dollars to his shrinking bankroll. He wasn't attached to the car. What he valued was the life he was living on the road. Exploring the countryside with the wind in his face satisfied his wanderlust, riding the powerful machine as it roared beneath him challenged his strong body while embracing the element of risk, and the companionship of his happy-go-lucky friend brought a rare contentment. He was savoring life again and feeling his freedom.

As time passed, Jimmy and Eddy hit on another plan to extend the adventure. They would tour through the Pacific Northwest, then ride their motorcycles all the way to Alaska by way of the rugged Alcan Highway.

***

Jimmy eased his Harley onto the slick surface of the Golden Gate Bridge in a soft misty drizzle with Eddy in his wake. The height was dazzling as he caught glimpses, through gaps in the shifting fog, of the whitecaps far below. At each metal grate he felt the spin of the rear tire, losing traction as it threatened to fishtail then regained a grip on the pavement. As he glided below them, the tall orange towers seemed to disappear into the clouds while the thick cables dipped toward the middle of the bridge then soared upward toward the next tower. Jimmy had an edgy alertness as he tried to take it all in and avoid ramming into the vehicles ahead of him in the congested traffic.

Reaching the far side all too soon, Jimmy felt elated as he pulled into a turnoff and waited until Eddy pulled alongside.

"Hot damn, that was one hell of a good ride," Eddy shouted.

"Goddamn right. I aint leavin before I give it another shot. You goin?" Jimmy challenged.

"Ya bet your ass I'm goin," Eddy laughed.

"You're on," Jimmy hollered as he ripped out into traffic churning up a fantail of gravel in his wake as he headed back across the bridge.

Later that day the two travelers were winding along Highway 101 which, once they'd left the San Francisco Bay Area, had narrowed and lost both shoulders. The terrain had given way to thickly treed rolling hills, mountain passes and isolated pastoral valleys. Jimmy, who invariably ended up in the lead, was keeping an eye out for the frequent potholes, though the rhythmic thrum of the tires crossing each joint in the cement highway had a hypnotizing effect. Still, manhandling the huge motorcycle required a certain amount of alertness. Managing the heavy machine was tiring, a physical challenge that he loved.

It was late afternoon by the time they pulled into the town of Ukiah where Jimmy flagged down a local resident for directions to his aunt's place. They pulled up in front of the jury-rigged house located on a gravel road at the west end of town, smack up against the foothills of the Coast Range. Jimmy couldn't say he was really fond of his mother's older sister, Aunt Vesta, but by tradition family members expected to be welcome when they came to town.

"Jimmy! Well I'll be," Uncle Jeb said, letting the screen door slam behind him as he came out on the ramshackle front porch.

"Hey, Uncle Jeb. This here's my friend Eddy from Highway City," Jimmy said, shaking the big paw extended by the huge, gangling man.

"Howdy," he said, shaking hands. "I thought ya was up ta Alaska. Come on in, Vesta's cleanin up in the kitchen."

"I heard you boys comin up the street on them noisy motorcycles," Aunt Vesta said, wiping her hands on a dishtowel as she came out of the kitchen.

"Aunt Vesta," Jimmy said by way of greeting. "Eddy here's ridin along with me."

"When I seen you at Ida's place over Christmas seemed like you was headin back up ta Alaska."

"Yeah, me and Eddy's on our way up there now, but we decided to do some sightseein on the way."

"You ridin them motorcycles on up there?"

"Yeah."

"You can stay here on the couch. Don't be getting no ideas about smokin or drinkin here. And no swearin. This here's a Christian household. I just cleaned up after dinner, but I can find ya somethin ta eat."

"Whatever ya got. I'll go after some groceries later."

"Damn. Your aunt's a tough woman," Eddy said as they grocery shopped at the downtown Safeway. "Ya sure we should bunk there?"

"Yeah. We won't be spendin much time. Goddamn, she's always givin poor old Uncle Jeb hell. Big as he is, that asshole must a been born missin a backbone. He's gotta sneak out back just to smoke."

"Don't she ever smile?"

"Hell no. That woman's a religious wacko. Don't let her corner you or she'll feed you a load a crap. Man, once she gets to goin on that holy roller stuff, there's no shuttin her up."

"Well, I'm beat," Eddy said.

"Yeah. I'm ready to hit the sack. You take the couch and I'll sack out on the floor. Let's figure on headin out early and see the beach at Fort Bragg."

The day at Fort Bragg was crisp and clear, the fresh breeze off the Pacific exhilarating. After the rough ride winding through the Coast Range on the poorly graded and maintained Highway 20, they had arrived at the beach in the dazzling sunshine that reflected off the mild waves in Noyo

Harbor. They explored up the coastline, dodging the frigid breakers as they ran barefoot on the beach and spotted sealions lying in repose on isolated rocky islands just offshore. The deep barking of the behemoths echoed over the pounding surf. Later they scoured the beaches searching for agates among the rocks and seashells exposed by the low tide.

A full dinner under their belts, Jimmy and Eddy fired up their bikes as late afternoon brought a fast-forming wall of fog. A few miles inland they were back under clear skies as they rode into the advancing twilight. When darkness settled in an hour later, Jimmy discovered that his headlamp had burned out. Waving Eddy into the lead, Jimmy shadowed him on the winding road using his friend's taillight as a guide.

By the time they turned south onto Highway 101 in Willits, a partial moon had risen throwing soft illumination on the straight segments of road and deepening the shadows. As they entered the sharp curves on the long pull toward Ukiah, Eddy poured the coal to her, shooting farther ahead.

Jimmy smiled as the red taillight shrank into the distance. *Seems old Eddy's been eatin my dust long enough. He's givin me a taste of my own medicine,* he thought, cranking his throttle.

Jimmy was gaining fast when he saw the red beacon shimmy and slip sideways. He let up instantly on the throttle as he caught the momentary glint of Eddy's headlight reflecting off the white guardrail, then an ugly spray of sparks etching a path along the curve of the rail.

Christ! He hit the goddamn guardrail, Jimmy's mind screamed. As he raced toward the dark shadow of the motorcycle where it had careened into the center of the highway, it was all he could do to avoid running into it as he jammed on his brakes. In his maneuver, Jimmy lost control and his bike laid over as he slid and spun down the highway. He held on until his momentum had slowed and he could get his bearings. *Got to find Eddy.* Untangling himself, he sprinted up the highway toward the still-glowing taillight. *Got to find Eddy.*

Grabbing Eddy's motorcycle by the handlebars, he wrenched it off the pavement fully expecting to find his friend beneath the wreckage. But in the scanty moonlight he could tell that Eddy wasn't there. *Oh shit. He must of went over the edge. Got to move the bike out of the road,* his mind raced as he hastily dragged Eddy's cycle to the rail and peered over into a dark abyss. As he frantically tried to think of a plan, he saw that his own motorcycle had come to rest in the middle of the road some three hundred feet away. *Better move it in case a car comes along,* he thought, fighting the panic that was starting to take over as he ran back to his own bike.

With strength born of terror, Jimmy hefted his unwieldly machine and was horrified to discover his friend trapped beneath. *Fuck!* he thought, heaving the heavy motorcycle to the side of the road. *He's broke all to hell. Oh fuck! Goddamnit! He was under me the whole goddamn time I was slidin down the road.* Jimmy was trembling, dancing in impotent agony as he hovered in the maddening darkness and tried to think of what he could possibly do. The hammering of his heart nearly prevented him from hearing the ragged breathing of his friend who lay there in a broken heap.

The car that approached a few excruciating minutes later brought light to bear on the ugly scene. And it brought help. At the wheel was a nurse who was on her way to work on the night shift at Ukiah Memorial Hospital. She proved to be a true angel of mercy.

Later Jimmy would not remember most of the events once the nurse arrived, how she grabbed some flares from her car, how she worked to stabilize Eddy and flagged down a passing car to call the ambulance. What he did remember was his helpless terror and the refrain that echoed in his head: *Eddy don't you goddamn die on me.* He might have been saying it aloud. He might have been yelling it over and over. Later he wasn't sure.

Eddy made it to the hospital with Jimmy riding along in the ambulance in stunned silence. He haunted the hospital corridors pacing all night, willing his friend to live. All he had to show for the terrible accident was a deep scratch across his cheek, while Eddy lay in a coma with multiple fractures of both arms and legs. His condition was critical, and no one could offer any reassurance that he would survive. When the hospital staff insisted that he leave, Jimmy walked several miles to Aunt Vesta's and passed out the couch.

Every day he returned to the hospital, hope and fear driving him to his vigil. A helpless dread tore at his gut. He shared the lobby with Eddy's parents who sat with frozen expressions as if literally holding their breath, waiting for their short visits with their only son. The waiting was excruciating. Day after day Eddy lay unconscious, molded in plaster and all wired up as a machine pumped oxygen into his lungs.

After two unbearable weeks, the tide turned, and Eddy started getting better. Once he'd regained consciousness, he grew stronger by the day. Jimmy could taste his relief when he saw recognition in his friend's eyes.

Two weeks later, Eddy left for home in an ambulance. Jimmy knew it would be some time before his buddy would fully recover, if he ever did.

***

Jimmy was adrift. Depleted. He could hardly drum up interest in anything now that his biking expedition to Alaska had been so horribly derailed. While the wrecker had hauled his motorcycle to his aunt's house, he refused to ride it. He had taken to walking as his mode of transportation. The weeks of vigil and angst had taken their toll on his nerves and his bankroll as well. He'd started paying Aunt Vesta twenty dollars a week for room and board, though he seldom ate at the house. That payment did not buy him peace and quiet. He was getting sick to death of his aunt's whining voice and her religious prodding. Just as his uncle retreated to his own back yard, Jimmy began to hang out at the local bars drinking and smoking until it was late enough to pass out on his aunt's couch undisturbed.

When his money ran low, Jimmy found a job at the Mendocino Timber Company. He could catch the Crummy downtown bus for a ride out to the job site in the woods. Working in the outdoors was a boost for Jimmy who always felt energized by hard work. He threw himself into the dangerous job of setting choker collars around the ends of huge logs as a crane loaded them onto trucks. If the chain slipped as the log was suspended, Jimmy courted the possibility of being crushed. But then, he liked living on the edge. And somehow, he didn't give a shit.

With his second paycheck, Jimmy bought a car. The green 1940 Plymouth four-door sedan cost him two hundred bucks. Having wheels again restored some sense of freedom. But his spare time weighed heavy. He was never quite sure how he hooked up with Dell. The guy was an obnoxious little shit. One night as Jimmy made the rounds of the local bars, Dell moved in on him acting like his best friend. He never could ditch the guy after that.

Jimmy seriously thought about ditching Dell after he'd been in one fight too many. *That squirrely little runt,* he thought. Dell had deliberately stirred up another bar fight the night before, baiting a big guy who tackled Jimmy instead of beating up the sawed-off big mouth. *Damn it. I've had my fill a fightin,* he though touching his sore jaw. *That asshole's usin me. I'm gonna tell him to screw off.*

That Friday night as Jimmy played pool at Lefty's Tavern with a bunch of high-spirited loggers he worked with, he was enjoying the game for once. The group was in a good mood as they drank and made wagers on the pool game. When Dell caught up with him and started stirring, Jimmy told him to back off. By the time they closed the bar down at two in the morning, the drunken gang piled into Jimmy's car to find another place to continue the party. They were too far gone to realize that nothing was open at that hour.

"Well, goddamn!" one of the guys slurred, after they had toured the town and neighboring towns looking for a bar. "Let's go back and open up Lefty's."

"Yeah. We been givin him our money. He's got no business closin up on us."

The five guys had a hilarious time breaking into the bar and dragging tables and chairs outside for their after-hours party. The beer was flowing as they applauded their prank.

When the police arrived, Jimmy and Dell were the only ones caught. The other savvier guys had faded into the night. Jimmy was furious when he got locked up in jail and was hauled before a judge the next morning. Dell's dad was there to pay his three hundred-dollar bail. Jimmy didn't have that much. He'd spent his last funds on his car.

7

SHERIFF BULLOCK

To hell with you assholes, he thought as the marshal led him back to a cell after the bail hearing. He simmered for a week in the city jail before having his day in court. With a court-appointed lawyer at his side, Jimmy stood before the judge and pled guilty to the crime of breaking and entering. He and Dell were both sentenced to ninety days or a fine of five hundred dollars. Dell's dad paid. Jimmy went to the county jail. Finding himself locked up enraged Jimmy, who wasn't much inclined toward taking orders or conforming to rules. His anger saved him from utter despair, but it would prove a costly defense.

Ninety goddamn days! I'll do their time easy. These assholes aint about to break me, Jimmy promised himself as he lay on a dirty bare pad in his cell. For several days he retreated into sleep.

"Hey, you!" a trustee named Bud hollered. "Pick up that cigarette butt over there."

"You're the one threw it there," Jimmy said. "You want the damn thing picked up, do it yourself."

"Hey. I said pick it up!" he ordered, making a grab at Jimmy's shoulder.

"Stuff it up your ass," Jimmy hissed as he rounded a sharp punch to the trustee's snarling mouth.

"You're in a shitload a trouble," he sneered, holding his hand to his

129

rapidly swelling upper lip as he picked himself up off the floor.

"I hear you're not cooperatin," Sheriff Bullock said in an oily voice as he let himself into the cell a few minutes later.

"What do you mean?" Jimmy asked, staring him in the eye as he stood up so that he towered over the square built older man. *You're a nasty son of a bitch, aint ya.*

"When a trustee tells you ta do somethin, you do it," he said, a mean squint to his eyes.

"No sir. That asshole aint orderin me around."

"Think you're a hotshot, huh? I'm running this here jail and I make the rules. Better get that straight ya punk," he said, jabbing his finger in Jimmy's direction. "Get your ass on down there," he barked, opening the cell and pointing toward the cell at the end of the row. "You'll be coolin your heels in solitary."

That prick thinks he's Hitler. Well, screw him, Jimmy thought as he the cell door lock behind him.

Aunt Vesta showed up a week later.

"How'd ya go and get into trouble?" she whined as she sat across the table in the visiting room.

"Well, I didn't mean to. I wasn't stealin or nothin, Aunt Vesta. It was just a stupid stunt."

"Breakin the law's wrong and you know it is. I'm real embarrassed, but I could send some of the brothers from the church down ta pray with you."

"Goddamnit! Don't start that bullshit. I'm servin my time."

"No need to swear, Jimmy. I brought your paycheck from the loggin company. It come to the house."

"Can you cash it for me? I need some money and some Camels."

"You need ta sign it so I can get it cashed. I don't much cotton ta buyin tobacco."

"Well, here gimmy the pen. You can have Uncle Jeb buy the cigarettes."

"It's a shame you bein in here," she said, tucking the signed check neatly into her purse and snapping it shut.

"Yeah," Jimmy said. *Thanks for the pep talk. Don't let the jailhouse door hit ya in the ass.*

After a week Jimmy knew for sure what he'd suspected all along, he'd wouldn't be seeing either his cigarettes or his money.

Jimmy would never admit that he craved the cigarettes that he had no means of obtaining or that he was going nuts with nothing to do day after day. Anger was his only companion, churning and seething with an energy of its own. Without the release of physical activity, he had lost his one outlet. When he could, he slept the time away.

Jimmy sat up suddenly. He swore he was hearing what sounded like little kids giggling and talking in harsh whispers. *What the hell! They sound like they're here inside the jail.*

"You see, children. Good citizens obey the law," Sheriff Bullock's oily voice drifted down the hallway.

That goddamn snake's puttin us on display. That sonofabitch better not bring them down here, he thought, craning to see.

"Now this here is a jail cell where we lock up lawbreakers," the sheriff continued as he progressed down the cellblock with a flock of what seemed to be wide-eyed first graders trailing behind.

"Is that a bad man?" a boy asked, pointing into one of the cells.

"Yes, he broke the law and I had to lock him up. My job is to keep you safe from criminals," he said, advancing on toward Jimmy's cell.

Jimmy sat stock still willing the group to reverse course. But that didn't happen. As if in slow motion the gloating face of Sheriff Bullock appeared outside his cell surrounded by inquisitive little faces all staring at him. Inside, anger was ripping Jimmy apart, but he didn't have heart to scare the little kids.

"Hey sheriff," he said in an ingratiating voice, "if your showin off the monkeys in the zoo, where's the peanuts?"

As the kids looked up at the sheriff expectantly, he clenched his jaw while his eyes shot daggers at Jimmy.

"See! Them little kids are wantin their peanuts. Now why would an upstandin sheriff like you bring em in here an forget the peanuts?"

"Come along children," Sheriff Bullock said, herding them back to his office.

The next morning the sheriff shoved Jimmy's bowl of mush under the cell door without a word. Having burned all night over the indignity of being put on display, Jimmy was far from satisfied with yesterday's small victory. Grabbing the bowl, he flung it at the cell door plastering his jailer with the sticky gruel. The fury in Sheriff Bullock's eyes was unmistakable as he wiped his face with his handkerchief.

"I'll take care a your ass tonight," he said in a deadly tone.

"Yeah," Jimmy responded, staring him dead in the eye.

Late that night the sheriff made good on his threat. Jimmy had waited all day, knowing he'd pay. The hair prickled on the back of his neck as he heard the rattle of keys and saw the door to the cellblock swing in. The welcome rush of burning hot fury kicked in just as he spotted the goon lumbering behind the sheriff as they made their way to his dimly lit cell.

Goddamn! He brought fuckin Frankenstein. Yeah, that guy can take me apart. So, the chickenshit sheriff don't do his own dirty work.

The gloating expression was back on Bullock's face as he fitted the key into the cell door.

Jimmy stood tall and unflinching just inside the radius of the door as he stared into the sheriff's eyes.

Whatever Bullock started to say, he never finished. Just as he stepped inside, Jimmy exploded into action. Neither the sheriff nor the goon saw it coming as Jimmy whipped his club into an arch and smashed it into the leering officer's face. The bar of soap inside his sock acted like a Billy club taking the man down, breaking his glasses and leaving a gash over his eye. Jimmy only got one shot at the giant before the lights went out.

Jimmy had no idea how long he'd been unconscious, but from the level of pain he was feeling the thought of slipping back into oblivion seemed damned attractive. *Yeah. The oaf worked me over real good,* he thought as he tried to avoid taking inventory. *Shit, I got to take a piss.* But it would have to wait until he could get a grip on the pain, he decided once he'd tried to move.

He lay still a few minutes hoping the pain would ease off, but finally forced himself to a sitting position and tried to figure out where he was. One thing for sure. He was still being punished. He was sitting on a cement floor in a special cell that had nothing but a seatless toilet, and he was stark naked. No bed, no blanket, no clothes. Pain, that he had lots of. Despite the throbbing in his head, he slowly took inventory of his injuries. One eye swollen shut, a couple of back teeth missing, ribs kicked in. Each time he drew breath he winced. But his balls, they were the worst, that pain eclipsing all the others. He thought they might be busted. Jimmy leaned his back against the wall and willed himself not to think, not to feel. *It don't hurt. They aint gonna whip me.* It was all he had.

***

Jimmy stood before the judge accused of assault and attempted escape. His court-appointed lawyer had already entered his plea of guilty. As he forced himself to stand straight, he was a mere shadow of his former slim self. He was weak but not defeated, and he was angry as hell.

He'd spent nearly two weeks in his special purgatory cell, shivering in the cold while his body tried to heal from the severe beating. Only now and then would he eat the food that was shoved under his door. His seething fury that had nearly done him in was the same force that was keeping him going now.

Turning his head a bit to the right, he locked eyes with Sheriff Bullock who was sitting directly behind the prosecutor. *I nailed you right good, didn't I you sadistic sonofabitch. Left my mark on you, so you didn't get off Scott-free neither,* he thought with small satisfaction as he surveyed the row of stitches and old bruising that traced a line across the man's left eyebrow and down his temple.

"James Edwin Evans, do you have anything to say to the court before I pass sentence?"

"No sir." *Yeah, I got a lot to say. I been railroaded by that asshole. Locked up. The shit kicked out of me. All for a goddamn stupid prank and lack of money to pay my fine. I worked hard my whole fucking life and paid my own way. But you don't want to hear it. Fact is, you'd like as not bury my ass if I was to have my say.*

"You've pled guilty to the charges. Your sentence will be indeterminate with a maximum time of three years. You will be sent to San Quentin State Penitentiary where your sentence will be taken under consideration."

Jimmy didn't know what it all meant. He heard "three years" and "San Quentin." That's all. When his lawyer attempted to explain the rest, Jimmy's mind seemed to have gone blank. He just nodded and waited to be led away.

***

Jimmy had a fleeting look at the Golden Gate Bridge just before the deputy sheriff turned the car into a long driveway that wound down the Marin Mountains to the forbidding brick fortress of San Quentin State

Penitentiary. As he watched the panoramic view of the San Francisco Bay passing by, he struggled to drive from his mind the image of his gleeful, free-flying ride across the spectacular bridge with Eddy in his wake. *I aint takin this lyin down,* he promised himself as he had many times over the last month. *All I ever wanted was to be goddamn left alone. Now them fuckers is gonna pay.*

The two-hour ride south on Highway 101 had passed in silence coming to an end as the driver pulled up in front of the tall, spiked metal entrance gates of the notorious San Quentin Prison. *Fuck them! Jimmy thought,* steeling himself. Once the driver had identified himself and his prisoner, the gates opened, and he pulled forward into a small courtyard. The gates immediately clanging shut behind them.

While the driver handed over the paperwork, a prison guard ordered Jimmy out of the back seat. With as much dignity as he could muster, handcuffed and shackled, Jimmy hobbled to the inner gate, waited for the guard to unlock it and passed through into the prison. He shook off a sudden jolt of dread as that gate shut with a solid boom. It reverberated in his mind like a clap of thunder. *Well, here you are asshole. Time to get the lay of the place and start makin your plan,* he thought, blocking his mind against fears of what would happen to him there. *Go ahead you sonsabitches. Give it your best shot. I can take it. You aint gonna break me.*

Jimmy was led into a holding area where his personal belongings were inventoried and locked up. Once he'd gone through the delousing solution and showered, he was given his prison uniform, blue cotton work pants and work shirt, and then locked into a single cell. He gave stony replies to the intake clerk giving minimal answers in order to complete the paperwork. It was during the interview with the clerk that he caught on to how the sentencing process worked, finding out that he would soon be going before the Hearings Board. The board would decide his future, where he would ultimately be incarcerated and the actual length of his sentence based on his crime, his record and the interview. While he raged at the terrible injustice done to him, he could hardly see any possibility that telling his story would do him any good. *Why would them bastards believe me? Damn cards are stacked against me. Justice? A fair hearing? Not goddamn likely,* he thought.

He moved through the process like a sleepwalker. And sleep was all he wanted to do. Having a bunk with a mattress, sheet, pillow and blanket seemed damn luxurious compared to his last accommodations. The intake area was a busy place with some fifty new prisoners from all over the state to be processed. Jimmy, along with each of the other "new fish," had his own cell, and at mealtime guards herded the group down to a special area of the dining hall separated from the general population. During that first week, Jimmy barely spoke. Whenever he could, he slept. When he was examined by the prison physician, his injuries were still healing.

"Looks like you've been beaten up pretty bad," the doctor commented.

"Yeah. Old Sheriff Bullock up to Ukiah's a mean sonofabitch."

"You seem to be fit, but at a hundred twenty-eight pounds, you badly underweight. Have you had any stomach problems?"

"No Doc. I weighed about one sixty before that bastard threw me in his jail a month ago."

At the end of the week Jimmy appeared before the Hearings Board shaking with nerves and pent-up anger, but he gave it his best shot. *What the hell, I'm tellin them,* he decided. He told it all: the arrest, the ninety-day sentence in lieu of the five hundred dollar fine, the humiliation at being put on display in front of school kids, and the attack by the sheriff's goon. *At least them assholes listened, but I'm still in goddamn prison,* Jimmy thought while he waited for their decision.

His sentence came down two days later: eighteen months, less time off for good behavior. *It fucking figures,* he brooded, feeling trapped and wronged despite the fact that the sentence had been cut in half. The independent, willful spirit of an upstart who abhorred regimentation and authority was outraged at the sure knowledge that he would be locked up for a year and a half. It was now final. Real. The reality crashed in on him and the fulminating anger that grew to possess every fiber of his being became his only defense against utter despair. *Them sonsabitches aint out to give a guy a fair break. Screw em. I aint forgittin. I'll serve my time and I'll be gettin even.*

Once his sentence was determined, Jimmy was moved to the main prison and found himself in a special unit designated for low risk offenders. His cellmate, Carl, had been shot in the leg during a bank robbery. *Dumb fuck,* he thought as he watched the young guy hobble around trying to play basketball. *He's goddamn crippled for life,* he thought, unable to drum up much sympathy.

A consuming lethargy held Jimmy in its grip. Once in a while he played a little basketball in the exercise yard that was segregated from the regular prison population. His heart wasn't in it, though, and, in truth, he could hardly stand watching Carl struggle up and down the court on his crippled leg. Whenever he could, he stayed in his cell and slept.

His main destination outside his cell was the mess hall, which was an overwhelming place. It seemed the size of a football field and the noise was comparable. Vibrating with the buzz of thousands of men talking and clanking utensils, the huge area was punctuated by the commanding murals painted on the walls depicting scenes from California history. As the days passed, Jimmy's depleted body began to heal as he regained some weight. Wallowing in bitterness, he swallowed his impotent anger and spent the next few months withdrawn into a hostile sulk.

***

Three months later Jimmy boarded a prison bus bound for Solidad State Prison. He would serve the rest of his time in the medium-security facility. Once he had settled into his single cell, Jimmy set about taking control of his future. He tapped into the inferno of his consuming anger and planned his revenge. By day he learned to operate power sewing machines making prison blues in the clothing factory. After dinner he went out to the exercise yard but spurned the sports activities available. He put aside his love of softball, of hard physical workouts that had always served to burn off his restless energy. Instead, he concentrated on his education, learning the skills he needed to become a first-rate criminal.

In the spacious prison yard, Jimmy walked the gravel path that circumscribed the outside perimeter of the yard area where inmates were permitted to roam. As he strolled, he approached and grilled other inmates for information. A double razor-wire fence that was interrupted by guard towers every few hundred feet surrounded the whole enclosure. Just inside that fence was a twenty-foot wide strip of pristine lawn, untouched and untrampled, known as "dead-man's-land." Inmates were fully aware that stepping off the gravel and onto that lawn could bring them an immediate death sentence. The gravel walkway became Jimmy's twenty-foot wide pathway to education.

He was relentless in his single-minded quest for certain kinds of knowledge. None of them good. "Hey, what're you in for?" he'd ask in the privacy of the open yard, finding that most of the guys liked to brag about their exploits. He picked their brains carefully, eliminating out of hand anyone doing time for armed robbery. *Hell, no. Aint takin a chance on shootin no one,* he decided.

Eventually, he whittled down his inquiries, eliminating all but the safecrackers. He honed-in on those willing to divulge their secrets, plying them with cigarettes and an attentive audience. As he gathered specific information, he concluded that the "drill and punch" method of cracking a safe involved too much delicate guesswork. Instead he opted to bone up on "peeling" the door. Jimmy threw all of his energy, all of his anger into mastering the tricks of the trade.

By the time Jimmy was released a year later with time off for good behavior, he felt well versed in his new vocation.

8

RETURN TO FAIRBANKS

The twenty-year-old man who returned to Fairbanks in early spring of 1955 had the same energy and bravado of the old Jimmy. But his attitude and outlook were changed in fundamental ways. The new Jimmy was driven by an unrelenting craving for revenge that he nursed and embraced with a single-minded passion. He would get even.

Flying into Fairbanks with fifty dollars in his pocket and a nearly empty duffel bag, he felt no elation at being back to the wild west town he had once found so exciting. Now he had a cause, and he was prepared to exact the revenge that would relieve his choking fury. But he needed a plan.

Bunking at his old rooming house, he began to cruise the bar scene avoiding the places he might run into his old buddies as he drank and brainstormed his first heist. It wasn't long before he connected with Gene, an acquaintance from his former life in Fairbanks. He'd known at the time that the stocky, fit young guy was selling merchandise he'd stolen from the military base commissary.

"Look, I know a way to make some real dough," he said, as they made a bet on a game at the shooting gallery.

"Yeah, how's that?" Gene said, giving Jimmy his full attention.

"Well it's got some risk to it, but you're already puttin your ass on the line."

"Okay. Let's go back to my apartment and chew it over," Gene said.

"I'm plannin to get into safe crackin. Not goin for none of this penny-ante bullshit. The big money's all locked up in them safes around town. I learned the best way to do it, but I aint tried it out just yet," he explained as he paced the length of Gene's front room.

"Don't ya think there'll be guards or alarms or somethin?"

"Well shit, we'll have to case the places and find out first. I'm just askin are you in or out?"

"I been piss poor all my life, growin up on a goddamn farm in South Dakota. Yeah, I'm in if ya think ya know what your doin."

"What about your sis? She's livin here, right?"

"Yeah, but she don't say what I can do. Helen minds her own business."

Over the next week, Jimmy walked the streets of Fairbanks day and night looking for an easy target to burglarize while keeping an eye out lest he be spotted by one of his old buddies. He was well primed to do the deed, but his gut instincts kept warning him off and making him indecisive. *Talkin about it's one thing, doin it's another goddamn matter, asshole. What if it takes too long and you can't get the damn thing peeled the way they said? Listen, fucker, you aint backin out. Them sonsabitches has screwed you for long enough. Time to show them you can take what you want and they can stick it up their ass.*

"Well, I aint come up with a plan," Jimmy told Gene, his nerves screaming from frustration and lack of sleep.

"It's your idea. I never broke into anyplace and I don't like workin in the dark," Gene said shaking his head.

"You got a gun?" Jimmy asked, surprising himself.

"Yeah, a little .38 revolver."

"Let's see the damn thing. I got to have some money to buy my safe crackin tools. I spotted a busy little market out at the edge a town. Only one clerk in there at night. Get Helen's car. We're gonna do our first job."

"I don't know, Jimmy," Gene said, his eyes shifting nervously.

"Listen, I'm set on doin this," Jimmy said, locking himself into the decision. "You comin?"

"Yeah," Gene said, grabbing his coat.

"I'll do the stick up," Jimmy instructed, touching the pistol tucked in his waistband. "You be the lookout. Stand at the door and warn me if you see somebody comin."

"I don't know," Gene stuttered, visibly shaking as they cruised slowly past the store and parked around the corner off the main street.

Jimmy's heart was racing as he silenced all his wiser instincts that were screaming a warning. He sprang from the car with a furious energy. *I've waited long enough. I'm goin to goddamn do this.* Forcing himself to walk slowly, he entered the store and looked around trying, but not succeeding in looking calm. After a moment he could see that the store was free of customers and that Gene was in place at the door, nervous as a cat, pacing and looking as if he might bolt any second.

Locked into his plan, Jimmy steeled himself, pulled the revolver and pointed it at the clerk's chest watching as terror transformed the young man's face.

"Gimmy all the money ya got," he demanded, unable to keep the gun steady or the quaver out of his voice. *Sonofabitch! What the hell am I doin? I aint gonna shoot no one,* he thought as his gut twisted in a spasm of instant regret.

Speechless with fear, his eyes wide as if he were going to faint, the clerk opened the cash register after several tries. His hands were shaking so badly that he could barely retrieve the money. As he dropped the bills on the counter, they scattered.

Jimmy was reaching out an equally shaky hand to scoop up the money when he saw the clerk suddenly shove his hand under the counter. *Oh, shit. The bastard's goin for a gun. I'm a dead man,* he thought, knowing that he would not fire his own weapon. In one heart-stopping moment Jimmy watched as the clerk pulled out a hidden pouch of money and dropped it on the counter. Stuffing the loot inside his wool jacket, Jimmy turned and ran from the store to find Gene already in the car with the motor running.

Jimmy rode in silence back to the apartment, cursing himself all the way. *Never again. Aint holdin no gun on some poor bastard. What kinda asshole pulls a holdup with a pistol he aint gonna use?* he thought, tasting bitter regret. *Now I went and done it. Gotta lay low. That guy can point us out.*

"It aint much," Jimmy said after they'd counted the hundred and twenty-one dollar take. "No more holdups. It aint worth it. Next time we'll be getting more dough, a hell of a lot more."

"Well I aint goin ta jail for no fifty bucks," Gene said.

"Yeah. It was a mistake."

Now that he'd jump-started his crime spree, Jimmy became emboldened about attempting a safe cracking, assuming he no longer had anything to lose. And he knew just the target, had known all along. With money in his pocket, he went shopping at the hardware store for the tools he would need.

While Gene continued to work at his job on the military base and Helen kept her regular hours at her waitress job, Jimmy spent the week at the apartment preparing for their next heist. He sharpened the pry bars and wrapped each chisel handle with masking tape, placing them in a long canvas bag with the lead sledgehammers and flashlights he'd bought. Once he was satisfied with the tools, he began to case the target, walking around the building at different hours of the night to check out the best time to break in unseen. He didn't need to go inside, because he already knew the layout of the old log building that housed the Electrical Workers Union and he knew the exact location of its classic Gold Rush era safe.

Late Saturday night, Jimmy and Gene walked the three blocks to the Union Hall. As they passed by, there was lots of activity on Second and Third Avenues with all the bars going full tilt and the ever-present melee going on in the streets. Jimmy carried his black canvass tool bag as they hurried along. By the time they reached the quiet neighborhood where the building stood, both men had a raging case of nerves.

"How do ya know there aint a guard in there?" Gene whispered as he followed Jimmy around the building to the back door.

"I been checkin it out. Settle down! There aint no guard," Jimmy hissed, wishing he could get a grip on his own nerves. "Here, hold the flashlight so I can jimmy the lock."

As the door gave, Jimmy stepped right into the total darkness of the huge old meeting hall and realized that Gene wasn't behind him. *What the hell!* He stepped back to see his partner's dim outline still poised at the doorway with the flashlight turned off, looking for all the world as if he were about to flee.

"Let's go," Jimmy prodded, finally breaking through Gene's paralysis. "Safe's over here," he said, shutting the door behind them and grabbing the flashlight to lead the way.

Setting down his tool bag beside the grand old safe, he started to work on it while Gene silently focused a wavering light on the area that Jimmy was attacking with the pry bars. He broke into a cold sweat as long minutes passed while he tried to force a break in the welds. *This is goddamn gonna work,* he vowed as he struggled to pry up one comer of the door.

"What's that!" Gene hissed, dousing the flashlight and making a dash for the door.

"It's the damn buildin shiftin. Shit, Gene, the old wood's gonna moan and groan. Turn on the goddamn light and get over here," he said, a sharp edge to his voice. *What the hell's wrong with him? He's pissin his pants. The asshole's a pillar in a stand-up fight. Won't back down for nothin. Now he's squirrely as hell. All he's gotta do is hold the goddamn light. His bullshit's gettin on my nerves.*

With a sigh of relief, he finally succeeded in peeling back the face of the safe and continued on with the next steps of the well-rehearsed process for getting to the loot. He'd been a good student after all. His concentration was interrupted time and again as his partner gave him a jolt with an abrupt, "What's that?" Every noise in the creaky old building seemed to set Gene off.

"There!" Jimmy said with satisfaction as he pulled the pins and swung the door open.

"Goddamn. It's stuffed clear full a money," Gene said.

"Yeah. We been here too long. Let's go. Help me stuff it in the bag."

In minutes they were on their way back to the apartment. As it turned out, it had taken Jimmy an hour to peel his first safe.

"Look at that," Gene enthused as they poured over the contents of the tool bag back at the apartment. "I aint seen this much money in my whole life."

"Yeah, nine thousand's not bad," Jimmy grinned. "See, I told you there was big loot in them damn safes."

"What're you gonna do with it?" Helen asked in her soft voice, her eyes bright as she gazed at the stack of money on the kitchen table. A plain, stocky-built girl like her brother, she sat huddled at the table in her worn bathrobe.

"We're splittin even. For now, I wanna take three thousand," Jimmy said. "Can you put the rest away someplace?"

"Yeah. I'll hide it," Helen whispered.

***

On Sunday afternoon Jimmy took a long walk all the way to the outskirts of town. He desperately needed to work off his restless energy and nothing seemed to help. His success as a safecracker gave him precious little satisfaction and the money meant nothing. With nerves strung tight, he could barely eat or sleep.

Mama and Dan were just starting to eat a fried chicken dinner when Jimmy knocked on the door of their little rental house in town.

"Jimmy! Good to see you, son," Dan said, giving him a hearty handshake and a clap on the back. "Come on, you're in time for dinner."

"Jimmy!" Mama sobbed. "I just couldn't take it, ya bein took off ta jail. Recon I never thought ya' d get yourself in trouble, always workin so hard an all."

"It was a bad deal, Mama."

"It brung me ta tears hearin Vesta tell how they taken ya off ta San Quentin fer tryin ta break out."

"Forget it Mama," Jimmy said with a sharp edge to his voice. "How's the homestead comin along?"

"Not too good," Dan said, filling a plate for Jimmy and setting it in front of him. "It's tough to make a go of it when you have to haul the water. We're thinking about just staying in town come summer. Might have to give the place up."

"Are you already workin, Jimmy?" Mama asked.

"Oh yeah. I always can find a job," he hedged.

"Well, all my kids done run off. Not a one of em cares how I'm getting on. Billy went an joined up with the Air Force. Aint seed hide nor hair a him since last summer. Them ingrates just don't bother bout their ol Mama."

"Aint you doin alright?" Jimmy asked, jumping up to pace the room.

"Light somewheres. You're actin like a caged tiger. Why aint ya eatin your dinner, anyways?" she demanded.

"I aint listenin to all that horseshit about how everybody forgot about you, Mama. Here, I brung you some money," he said, peeling out two thousand dollars and setting it on the table beside her plate.

"Well, that's right nice a you, son," she said. "We can use it. Why don't ya settle down now and have your dinner?"

"Listen, Mama," Jimmy said, easing into the chair. "I want to go check on my steamer trunk I left out in the garage."

"Oh, ya mean that there ol trunk holdin a rifle and a fancy pistol and all them winter clothes?"

"Yeah."

"Well, we got rid a than oncet we heared you was in jail. Figured you'd have no use for no firearms being a ex-convict an all. Best just sell that stuff off."

"You sold it!" Jimmy said, low and fierce, blindsided by her casual disposal of his few personal belongings. *Mama never gave a shit*, he thought as he slammed out the door.

***

At midnight all was quiet in the alley behind the Carpenters Union Hall as Jimmy carefully pushed open the daylight basement window that had stood slightly ajar. He slipped through, landing softly and signaled Gene to come ahead. The window frame was a tighter fit for his accomplice's stocky body, but his partner was strong and able to pull himself through. Directing the flashlight a short distance ahead, Jimmy found the staircase and crept up slowly with Gene right behind him.

Jimmy had no trouble finding the large flat-door safe in a room off the main assembly hall. Closing the door, he went right to work.

"Leave the damn door open," Gene hissed, skittish at the thought of being closed off from quick escape.

"No. It keeps the noise down," Jimmy whispered with finality.

This time he manipulated the pry bars with more confidence and dexterity despite his trembling hands and racing heart. Inside half an hour he'd struck pay dirt even though his partner had startled him from time to time with warnings.

"The Culinary Worker's Union's somewhere in here, too," Jimmy whispered once they were packed up and ready to leave. "Let's have a look downstairs before we take off."

At the bottom of the stairs Jimmy froze, stopping Gene in his tracks. *Goddamn it. Now I'm hearin things,* he thought. But he was sure he'd heard a sound. He tried to listen over the drumming of his heart. There it was again, sort of like an exhaled breath. Signaling Gene to stay put, *don't you goddamn squirrel on me now*, he walked carefully toward the partially open door of a basement office. Leaning on the doorframe with his flashlight at the ready, he slowly pushed the door open. Running the beam of light across the floor inch-by-inch, he gradually revealing a building caretaker softly snoring as he slept on a cot.

Finger to lips, Jimmy signaled toward the entry window. Gene was the first one out.

"Fantastic, fantastic" Gene repeated over and over as they spread out the ten thousand dollar take, all nicely banded in thousand-dollar packets. "We can have anything we want."

"You guys are taking me out to dinner tomorrow," Helen said. "I've been worrying about you all night."

"We did good. Jimmy pealed that safe real fast. It was easy money."

"How much do you want me to put away for you?" Helen asked.

"I got enough in my pocket for now," Jimmy answered. He'd been quietly thinking while his gleeful accomplices gloried in the fat take.

I'm damn glad I wasn't carryin no gun, he thought, feeling empty rather than victorious. In his gut he knew that the course he'd chosen was taking him on a disastrous path. *Hey, I'm gettin ta be one hell of a safe cracker,* he thought, rueful in his attempt to blunt the pain of knowing how badly he was going wrong.

The next evening when the three of them went out for a night on the town, Gene brought his friend Monty. They ate and drank, and Jimmy couldn't remember what else when he woke up on the couch the next morning with a painful hangover. At least he'd finally gotten some sleep. Days and weeks were passing in a blur and most of the time he was in a state of full-blown anxiety.

Over the weeks as Monty hung around the apartment, Jimmy took a dislike to him, convinced that he was an opportunist. Gene and Helen were living in high style eating in restaurants and buying expensive personal items. Things they had never in their life been able to afford. Jimmy warned them, "Play your cards close to your vest." But Gene was bursting at the seams to talk about the suspense and intrigue he'd experienced on their capers, especially when he was drinking. Monty was an appreciative audience and started pushing to go along on the next heist. Jimmy refused flat out, but he eventually decide to make use of Monty's jeep.

As the hours of darkness lengthened deep into October, Jimmy went on the prowl once again. He had no idea how much money they still had stashed away. It didn't matter. He was bone tired and driven to climb back into the ring like a punch-drunk fighter. The Plumbers Union seemed ripe for the picking.

On a cold starlit night, Jimmy backed Monty's jeep up to the loading dock behind the union hall. As he carefully pried open the back door of the building without benefit of a flashlight, he kept an eye on the rear entrance of the police station just down the block. Gene was jumpy as hell.

"Come on," he said, stepping into the darkness as his partner hesitated.

"Think they'll get curious about the jeep?" Gene asked in a hoarse whisper.

"Naw. Hurry up. We're gettin out fast," Jimmy insisted, closing the door before turning on his flashlight.

The casters squealed as they rolled the heavy safe toward the back door.

"This aint a good idea," Gene complained, freezing in place.

"Help me move the goddamn thing so we can get the hell out of here," Jimmy growled.

Backing onto the dock after a careful look around, the two men heaved the safe over the threshold, across the dock and tipped it into the back of the jeep in a frantic effort to move fast. As Gene covered their prize with a blanket, Jimmy started the jeep and drove off without headlights until they turned onto Cushman.

They crossed the bridge in the dangerously loaded low-riding jeep and headed north out of town. Jimmy had chosen a private place to actually break into the safe, out behind his folk's now-vacant homestead. They were still living in town and would never know once the thing was buried. It was a clear, bitterly cold night when they heaved the safe onto the ground and Jimmy got to work. Without worrying about making noise, he had it peeled in fifteen minutes. Once more there was a large amount of cash, but burying the evidence was one hell of a job. Both men were dirty and exhausted when they rolled back into town as dawn broke.

Over the months Jimmy's existence had taken on a nightmarish quality with his singular focus on planning and executing his next heist. He gotten so anxious that he couldn't eat and couldn't sleep. His stomach stayed in a painful, burning knot. His only gratification came with the rush he felt when he planned for and succeeded in breaking into another safe, yet even that victory had become meaningless. He didn't care about the money. Never had. He was weary to the bone.

Goddamn Monty's bein a asshole, Jimmy thought as he sat on the couch, trying to relax. *Got a shittin splinter up his ass. He'd better shut the hell up.*

"Hey, I want ta go down to O'Riley's an play some pool. Maybe we can get some dinner later. There's nothin doin here," Monty pressed.

"Yeah, let's go," Gene said. "I'm up for a game or two."

"I can wax both your asses," Monty challenged.

"You assholes go ahead. I'm stayin," Jimmy said, giving in to exhaustion. If only he could relax.

"Here, you drive," Monty said, throwing Gene his keys. "You're going to be damned bored staring at the walls in here, Jimmy."

Don't be tellin me what I want, ya goddamn weasel, Jimmy thought. *Christ! It's only five,* he groaned, thinking of another long wakeful night ahead. "Guess I'll come."

Bullshit. That damn asshole don't ever shut up, Jimmy thought as he tried to shut out Monty's running dialogue on the ride over to the bar.

"Damn place aint even open," Jimmy groused, as Gene pulled into the nearly empty parking lot at the tavern.

"They gotta open up any minute. I'll check the sign on the front door," Monty said, as he sprang out of the back of the jeep.

"That ass---" Jimmy started to say, stopping as he saw police cars zooming in from all directions. "Don't move!" he yelled at Gene even before the officers reached the car with their weapons drawn. Jimmy had immediately shoved his hands into the air. *Goddamn, Gene, don't fucking move or they'll nail us right here.*

As he stepped out of the jeep and spread-eagled, Jimmy inhaled the first deep breath he'd taken in months. By the time he was cuffed and shoved into a police car, he was limp with relief. *It's over. It's goddamn over,* he thought sinking into the seat.

9

MCNEIL ISLAND

"Listen, Gene. I'll take on myself as much of the blame as I can," Jimmy said as soon as the cell door locked behind them and they were alone.

"Christ, all that money. It was too damn easy," Gene said, his expression stoic as he shook his head.

"I know, but you was only the lookout. The safe peelin was all my idea."

"That goddamn Monty set us up."

"No shittin doubt about that. Always thought that fucker was a snake," Jimmy said, feeling too drained to work up any outrage.

That night Jimmy and Gene were arraigned in the United States Federal Courthouse at Fairbanks in the Territory of Alaska, accused of one count of armed robbery and one count of burglary. An attorney was appointed to represent both of them.

When the detectives attempted to question them later, Jimmy insisted on waiting until his lawyer was present. Back in the cell, he crawled into his bunk, falling into his first deep sleep in months.

The lawyer who showed up the next morning seemed middle aged and savvy. He was direct and had all the finesse of a lumberjack.

"Listen guys, you're screwed. They've got you dead to rights," Mark Woolworth said, crossing his legs, ankle over knee, and rocking back in a wooden chair as he shuffled through his papers. "They've got signed

149

statements from their snitch and your tools were in the jeep."

"Okay," Jimmy said, leaning forward across the table, "but Gene here was only a lookout. I already got a record, served time. No use sendin him up for what I done."

"Then you're willing to plead 'guilty' to the charges?"

"Yeah. What kinda time do ya think I'll get?"

"I'm going to see what kind of deal I can make. What about you?" he asked, looking over at Gene.

"Yeah," Gene said with a stony shrug. "Can you help me out?"

"I'll do my best. Don't talk to the detectives. I'm going to see what I can negotiate for you."

Jimmy spent the next few days in steady rounds of sleeping while Gene paced the cell as they waited for their lawyer to return. When he did come back, he had one question.

"Where's the money?" Mark Woolworth asked.

"What we got left is hid," Jimmy said, distrust raising his hackles.

"Well, turning in the money is the only bargaining chip you have. Are you willing to do that?"

"Yeah, if you can get us a deal," Jimmy answered, looking at his partner and getting a nod.

After a few more days Mr. Woolworth came back with the proposition.

"I will need to plead you cases separately. The best I can get for you Jimmy is four years if you hand over the money. Gene, you're in line for a two-year sentence at a youth camp. I've been wearing them down, but that's the best I can negotiate. Have someone you trust bring the money to my office."

The lawyer seemed like a straight-up guy, but Jimmy had seen many a snake-oil salesmen in his time. He wasn't sure. *What the hell, he finally decided. I aint got no choice anyway. Helen must still have thousands hid.*

After he heard Gene tell his sister to deliver the money, Jimmy had another week to wait and wonder before his day in court.

He was numb as he stood before the judge with his attorney at his side listening to a reading of the charges brought against him.

"Do you understand the charges?" Judge Alcott asked.

"Yes sir."

"If you plead guilty to these charges, you may receive an immediate sentence."

"Yes sir."

"And how do you plead?"

"Guilty, sir." Jimmy said, standing straight, but feeling as if all the air had been sucked out of his lungs.

"And what is the government's recommendation," the judge asked, turning to the district attorney.

"Considering that the defendant confessed and did attempt to retrieve the stolen property we recommend four years' imprisonment."

"Mr. Woolworth, do you concur?"

"Yes, sir."

"Mr. Evans, I see that you have spent time in prison before. You were convicted on charges of assault and attempted escape. Do you have anything to say about why you got into trouble when you were, let's see, nineteen years old?"

"Yes, sir." *Goddamnit, I'm gonna tell him and have my say.* "I was drunk, and I tore up a bar. When I couldn't come up with enough to pay my fine, they threw me in jail. The sheriff paraded little kids in to look at me like I was some monkey in a zoo and then he brought in a big goon to beat the hell outa me. I got sent up for attempted escape, like I coulda got away from them two. Shipped me off to San Quentin when I'd never been in trouble with the law before. Was that justice? A man shouldn't be treated like that."

"You say you were unfairly punished?"

"Yes, sir."

"And what caused you to decide to commit more crimes once you were released from prison?"

"I was mad."

"You're now twenty-one years old. Is that right?"

"Yes, sir. I worked hard all my life. I didn't need the money. I was just mad."

"I think, Mr. Evans, that the recommendations of the government attorney are very, very lenient. Do you think that if the Court should be lenient with you and follow the recommendation of the government attorney, that you will serve you time without any vengeance towards society?"

"I think that I will, sir." *Very, very lenient? Oh shit, he's fucking gonna give me more time.*

"Do you feel you had it coming?"

"I don't understand what you mean, sir," Jimmy said, starting to smell a double-cross. He broke into a sweat thinking of the confession he'd signed without being able to read what it said and the money that had been turned over on faith.

"You say you think you were abused and mistreated before. Would you feel abused and mistreated if I should follow the recommendations of the government attorney?"

"No sir, I would not," Jimmy said, embracing a small flutter of hope.

"And do you think, after you have served your time, you can and will get out into society and go straight?"

"Yes, sir. I do."

"You won't let anything like this happen again?"

"No, sir."

"Do you have any reason now, Mr. Evans, why judgment and sentence of this Court should not be pronounced against you?"

"No, sir. I do not," Jimmy said as his heart pounded.

"Do you have anything that you wish to say in your own behalf?"

"No sir."

"Then I sentence you to the recommended four years imprisonment at McNeil Island Federal Penitentiary."

Jimmy slid down into his chair feeling weaker than he ever had in his life. He floated in a sea of relief. It was over.

***

As the plane approached the airport in Seattle, the Federal Marshall reapplied Jimmy's handcuffs for the landing. The aircraft heaved and dropped as it was buffeted by a November storm straight off the Pacific. While his guard shifted uneasily in his seat, Jimmy sat peacefully in place, his nervous system too worn out to respond to the jarring ride.

Jimmy and his guard were the last to deplane. He was taken directly to a prison transport car that was waiting on the tarmac, both he and his guard getting soaked on the short walk through the downpour. Although it was early in the evening, the storm darkened the sky and the moaning wind whipped sheets of water around the car on the silent ride south past Tacoma. Turning off toward the little town of Steilacoom, they drove on to where the road terminated at a dock reaching out into the churning waters of Puget Sound.

Leaning into the gusting curtains of rain, Jimmy and his guard hurried out onto the dock toward a boat that idled with a deep rumble, it's running lights turned on as it bobbed and rolled from side to side. As soon as they scrambled on board, the pilot gunned the engine heading into the blinding storm.

Inside the cabin Jimmy, soaked to the skin, sat hunched over on a bench. *Shit! They're takin me to the goddamn ends of the earth,* he thought trying his damnedest not to puke as the boat bucked, rolled and pitched as it roared into the maelstrom.

He was about done in by the time the boat reached the dock at McNeil Island. Although it was only seven at night, he could see nothing but the spotlights that illuminated the perimeter fence as he climbed an endless series of steps to reach the first and then the second level of the prison facility.

Jimmy was relieved to finally get inside once he reached the intake area. After showering and putting on dry prison blues, he was put in a holding cell where he ate hungrily from a tray of food that had been set aside for him. Bone weary and disconsolate, he crawled into the bunk. *The bullshit's over. I'm doin my time and I aint never gonna get locked up again,* he vowed as he drifted into a deep sleep.

What the hell! Jimmy thought, leaping out of his bunk to the shrill wail of sirens. His heart hammered in his chest, all senses alert as he tried to figure out where he was. Men were shouting and guards were running right past his cell. The sirens droned on and on as he sat back on his bunk reasoning that someone must have attempted to escape. *What kind of idiot tries to make a break for it off of this goddamn island?* he wondered, thinking of the hostile waters he'd traversed only hours before. Huddled in his bunk, Jimmy covered his ears trying to block out the nerve-wracking wail. *Shit, they sure know how to welcome a guy,* he thought ruefully. All the clamor continued most of the night until finally he saw the guards hauling an unconscious man past his cell.

After his three-week admission quarantine, Jimmy was transferred into a ten-man cell on the second tier in the main building. Keeping to himself, he set about serving his time as he settled into the prison routine.

Chuck Smith was the first man to greet Jimmy when he moved into the cell. An outgoing man in his early thirties, he was affable and full of jokes. He seemed to know his way around the place. A beefy guy at just under six feet, Chuck had sandy red hair, freckled skin and a contagious laugh that shook his whole body.

Steeling his mind for the long haul, Jimmy went to his assigned job on the lawn crew every day. While he usually liked the outdoors and growing things, he could see how mowing and maintaining lawns in the constant rain would fall to the guy at the bottom of the barrel. He didn't really care, though, and genuinely began to get interested in his job when he started working in the greenhouse setting plants.

"Hey, Jimmy," Chuck said, one night when Jimmy had been in the cell for a few days. "Where are you from?"

"Oh shit, I'm from about everywhere, but mostly California and Alaska, I guess."

"What'd you get sent up for?"

"Armed robbery and burglary. Stupid damn shit," Jimmy replied with a grimace and shrug.

"Yeah, me too. I've got a talent for writing bad checks," Chuck said with a hearty laugh. "It's always an adventure while the money lasts."

"Christ! I didn't even want the money. Aint that a hell of a thing?" Jimmy said, telling a short version of how his anger at Sheriff Bullock's abuse had burgeoned into a crime spree.

"That's too damn bad," Chuck said, shaking his head.

"Yeah, yeah. Everybody in this shittin place can tell you how they been done wrong," Jimmy said in a sardonic voice.

"True," Chuck laughed. "You should think about taking some of the classes here. They might help you make it on the outside."

"What's your job, anyway?"

"Oh, I'm the warden's secretary."

"Interestin job. Aint no wonder you got the inside scoop in here."

"Yeah. I like my job. I'm heading down to the gym to lift weights. Want to come?"

"No. I'm wore out."

"Black-eyed peas, no black-eyed peas," Chuck mumbled in the middle of the night, his voice frantic.

Jimmy raised up in his bunk to see his cellmate writhing and throwing his hands up in the air. *He must be havin a nightmare*, he thought, lying back.

It took a while for Chuck to settle down. *Damn weird thing to be dreamin about,* Jimmy thought not knowing yet that the nightmare would be a regular occurrence.

"See that guy over there in line, the one that's limping?" Chuck asked, as Jimmy and the other cellmates ate dinner in the mess hall, sitting on stools at one of the round dining tables. "He's the one who tried to escape a month ago. Poor bastard's all screwed up."

"Goddamn sirens startled the shit outa me my first night in here. Woke me out of a sound sleep. I didn't know what was happenin," Jimmy said.

"I hear he damn near froze to death in the water," Jack said. "First time I ever heard those sirens."

"Yeah. Not many inmates get the notion they can swim across that bay. It's too damn cold. He came out of the coma, but his brain's all screwed up," Chuck said.

"He had to be goddamn stupid to try jumpin in the water in that storm," Jimmy said. "Seems like he couldn't afford to lose what little brains he had."

"No shit," Chuck said, letting loose a peal of laughter. "You coming to the gym?" he asked Jimmy on the way back to the cell.

"Yeah, I guess."

Jimmy moved out onto the basketball court feeling out of shape as he worked his way up and down the court, passing the ball and taking a shot here and there. Although he tired quickly, he felt a surge of energy as his coordination and skill started to come back. It seemed like a long time since he'd felt the rhythm and release of all-out physical effort.

"Hey, you looked pretty good out on the court, Chuck said that night, looking up from the book he was reading by the light that filtered in through the bars.

"Damn, I had forgot how good it feels just to run."

"Yeah. Wish I could. Weights are about my limit and I just do them for a little exercise. I noticed you didn't read your letter," Chuck said.

"No," he answered from the darkness of his upper bunk, thinking that no one had noticed him slip the unopened letter into his locker.

"Have you got family writing to you?"

"I don't know."

"My family gave up on me. I can't blame them," Chuck said, his tone light.

"I never learned to read," Jimmy said in a hollow voice. *There, I said it. No use trying to bullshit these guys. Chuck would of figured it out sooner or later.*

"Hey, that's no problem. You came to the right place," his cellmate chuckled. "You can sign up for class tomorrow. Jack Wagner's a friend of mine. He'll have you reading in no time."

Jimmy lay silent in his bunk. *Learn to read? Is it possible? Go to class?* He wondered if he could stand the humiliation.

***

"Jack's expecting you to show up in his class tonight," Chuck informed Jimmy on the way back from dinner the next night.

Why the hell not! Jimmy thought, shrugging his shoulders at Chuck.

"Do you want me to read your letter to you?" Chuck offered.

After he thought a moment, Jimmy went over and pulled the letter from his locker. "Does it say on the outside who it come from?" he asked, handing it over.

"Yeah. Mrs. Brubaker in Porterville, California. Should I open it?"

"No. I know who it's from now," he said, taking the letter back as he fought a wave of shame. *Goddamnit. I don't want Glenda and Aunt Ida thinkin about me bein locked up. Christ Almighty, I sure as hell don't want them comin here to visit. I aint up for hearin about news from home, neither,* he thought, shoving the unopened letter back in his locker.

There were four other inmates in Jack Wagner's reading class when Jimmy walked into the classroom that night. The tall, darkhaired teacher, who looked to be in his late thirties, acknowledged his presence in a soft, pleasant voice.

"You're Evans?"

"Yeah."

"Grab a seat. We're just getting started," he said, turning to the other men to give them directions.

Jimmy watched the slim, athletic inmate engage his students with respect and patience.

"Let's get an idea where you need to start," Jack said, sitting down in the chair next to Jimmy with a workbook.

"Hey, you're a step ahead of the game," his teacher said a short time later. "You know all of your letters. Do you want to learn to read?" he asked, his expression sincere and direct.

"Yeah."

"If you're willing to put out the effort, you can learn. It will be hard work."

"Okay."

After that, Jimmy took the bit in his teeth, focusing his tenacious will on the effort. Three days a week he was in class learning to read. He was quick to catch on to the sounds of the consonants, but the varying sounds of the vowels were a tough nut to crack. Still, he persisted.

"I think the story of <u>Robinson Crusoe</u> will interest you. You're ready to start reading," Jack said one evening, handing him the book. "I know you can do it if you stick with it."

After Jimmy got his book, Chuck paid the price for his sponsorship. Every night after lockdown Jimmy would lie in his bunk reading as he painstakingly sounded out one word at a time.

"Chuck, what's this word?

"Spell it," Chuck would say time-after-time and day-after- day, his tone patient as he marked his place in his own book with his finger.

On the evenings when he wasn't in reading class, Jimmy wore off his energy on the basketball court whipping his body back into prime condition. But every night he struggled through a few halting pages of his book until he fell asleep, or Chuck did.

***

Jimmy was running full out on the basketball court when Pickens gave him a hard elbow in the gut. He'd already heard threatening comments in passing from the handsome black man, tall and lithe like Jimmy.

"Hey, cut it out," Jimmy said, catching his breath.

"Cry, pussy!" Pickens sneered, giving him a shove.

"Look, I'm just here to play the game. I'm not lookin for no trouble," Jimmy said, raising his hands palms out.

"Well, I'm gonna make you my bitch, punk," Pickens said leaning close.

"Screw off, I don't play no queer game," Jimmy said, walking away from a fight for the first time he could remember.

"I'll be waitin for ya, bitch," Pickens called after him.

"What's the story on Pickens?" Jimmy asked Chuck when he went back to the cell.

"He's a killer. In for life. A mean sonofabitch," he answered. "Is he on your case?"

"Yeah."

"Well, watch your back."

After the run-in with Pickens on the basketball court, Jimmy stopped going to the gym. A fight would cost him the time off for good behavior that he'd already earned. But he saw that backing down had been a mistake. *That asshole thinks I'm weak,* he thought, realizing that a showdown would come.

As spring unfolded Jimmy found a number of interests to occupy every moment of his day. He started into his second reading of <u>Robinson Crusoe</u> and Chuck began getting longer periods of peace for his own reading.

When Jimmy changed jobs, getting on with the laundry maintenance crew, he liked his work assignment much better. Every day he helped troubleshoot problems with the machinery in the big wooden two-story laundry building where inmates processed all the linen and uniforms for the facility. Huge washers and dryers sat on the ground level, big canvas bins holding soiled laundry scattered about in the aisles. On the upper floor there were small steam presses for the uniforms and long roller presses where sheets and towels were processed.

He liked maintaining and tinkering with the machinery and enjoyed the freedom to walk malfunctioning motors over to the machine shop for repair. In the shop, he got acquainted with Rodney who would soon become a cellmate. He was a friendly, talkative little guy who had a way with motors, and he had another more profitable sideline. He was the prison bookie. He had quite an operation going, Jimmy would learn. A young man with an exceptional memory, Rodney took bets on ball games keeping them all in his head, and he paid off or collected according to results in the daily newspaper since there were neither televisions nor radios available in the prison. The usual betting currency was cigarettes, candy bars and any other desirable item from the commissary. Prisoners earned pay for their jobs at the usual rate of three cents per hour and were allowed to spend a portion of their wages in the commissary.

***

Spring brought a break in the weather, ushering in light, drizzly mornings and some clear, crisp days. Jimmy sought outside sports activities in the big fenced area with ball diamonds and handball courts located on the lower level behind the prison building. When teams formed up for the yearly softball tournament, Jimmy was ready to bring his skills to Chuck's team. The Professors Team would need all the help they could get.

That spring Jimmy also found a new challenge in handball. Old Haley was king of the court and had been for some time, he discovered. Haley was a broad, short, muscular guy somewhere in his sixties who dominated in handball. No matter the temperature, the man reigned supreme decked out in shorts, a bare harry chest and a leather fingerless handball glove. Let a guy step out on his court and, with nary a word, he'd kick his ass.

The first time Jimmy played Old Haley, he'd been thoroughly whipped. Whereupon, he immediately took his place at the end of the line waiting to have another go. As he worked his way up to take another beating, he studied the old man's technique. Every evening when he wasn't in reading class he went back, making a few more points here and there as he was run all over the court and soundly trounced. Jimmy's old tenacity had kicked in and he was enjoying both the physical and mental challenge. And he had an ace in the hole. Beside being a natural athlete, he could hit the ball equally well with either hand. He would stick to it, studying the champ' s every move, until he could win or die trying.

On weekends Jimmy was in the thick of forming up The Professor's softball team. It came together with Chuck, Jimmy, Rodney, Jack, who lived by himself in a single cell, and a couple of guys from other cells. Jimmy's aptitude for pitching came to the forefront as well as his dead-on batting. He delighted in his ability to contribute to the team, to gain the respect of his mentors, putting aside his usual focus on expecting to win. Not with that crew. Still, he good naturedly coached and rooted for them. As they started into the preliminary games, Chuck made light of the competitive pressures with his jolly outlook. The guys laughed and cutup even when the team was losing.

As he left the game one afternoon, Jimmy felt a sharp blow to his chest and turned to see Pickens' leering face inches from his own.

"Hey, pussy. I like the way you pitch. Makes my dick hard."

"Leave me the hell alone you fucker or I'll kick your ass," Jimmy hissed, shoving the bully away from him.

"You're mine, punk," Pickens said, giving him a menacing smile before sauntering off and mixing into the crowd that milled around the baseball diamond.

***

On a stormy Saturday afternoon, Jimmy, Chuck, Rodney and another cellmate were passing the time playing pinochle. Although he always played to win, Jimmy enjoyed the atmosphere of light-hearted banter and the laughter that Chuck's bright personality created. And Rodney was a character in his own right with his bright mind in constant motion and a gawky kind of manner. Chuck, acting as gleeful as a kid at a carnival, had gotten the bid and was about to take the last trick when the guards showed up to shake down the cell.

"Okay, Rodney, we know you're taking bets," one of the guards said, sternly, as they searched the entire cell and patted down the men. "Where the hell are you hiding the books?"

"I don't know what you mean," Rodney said with a shrug.

"Look at these goddamn lockers. Every single one of them's stuffed with cartons of cigarettes."

"Heavy smokers in here," Rodney said fighting to keep a straight face.

Once the guards had left, the four men burst into laughter. "How do you do it?" Jimmy asked, the card game abandoned.

"It's a special talent," Rodney answered. "I've got an excellent memory."

"I don't know how you can keep track of hundreds of bets," Chuck said with admiration.

"What are you in for, anyway?" Rodney asked, turning to Jimmy.

"Goddamn stupidity," he answered with a laugh. "A sheriff got under my skin. First time I was ever locked up was for bein drunk and breakin into a bar with a bunch of other loaded guys. I wasn't robbin the place or nothin. Just stayed right there drinking like a dumbass. Bein under Sheriff Bullock's thumb went bad. Had his goon kick the livin shit outa me. When I finally got out after servin time for that dumbshit action, I got busy gettin even. Created a regular crime spree. Needed to kick my own ass."

"Best not to do any crime in Alabama," Chuck said. "Damn place left me with nightmares that won't quit."

"Got somethin to do with black-eyed peas?" Jimmy asked.

"Goddamn, how'd you know that?"

"Oh, you talk about it real clear in your nightmares."

"Yeah. Christ! It gives me the willies to think about that goddamn chain gang," Chuck said, in a grim voice. "Those assholes were plain damn brutal."

"Did they chain you together and make you work?" Rodney asked.

"Oh yes. They lorded it over the prisoners with their shotguns, entertaining themselves with our misery. Stuck me out on a farm, and me a city boy. Working out in the fields, we got sunburned and thirsty as hell with our water rationed. But the worst thing was the goddamn animals. I hated them. Once the guards found that out, the assholes turned sadistic. More than once they stuck me in a corral and whipped the mules to chase me until I fell, and they trampled me. Gave me nightmares," Chuck said.

"Must of fed you black-eyed peas," Jimmy said.

"God, yes. I wasn't sure I'd live through it, but once I got out of jail, I left that miserable damn state before the sun set."

"We lived in Louisiana for a while when I was a little kid. I'll never forget when we was just comin into the state," Jimmy said. We crossed over a high bridge and pulled off to eat. There was a old man down below by the river. Had his fishin gear and all. There he was beatin on a crocodile with a oar, trying to drive it out of his boat. All I was thinkin was, 'aint going swimmin in no river down here,'"

"Pretty smart for a kid," Chuck said, his usual hearty laugh returning.

"Yeah, well that place was full of critters. Me and my brothers was fishin for crawdads once with a piece a bacon rind. Got more then we bargained on. Billy pulled up on the string an there's a big ol black eel gone and swallowed the bait."

"Those rivers down there are full of water moccasins," Jack said.

"Yeah. Sorta confirmed my idea about swimmin. Saw some

cottonmouth when it flooded. The house we was rentin stood up on stilts so when it started pourin rain, Mama'd send us to bring everythin up onto the porch. Rained like a bastard and the river'd rise up and run right under the house. Once them waters started goin down, there was lots a snakes stranded."

"Weren't you afraid of the snakes?" Chuck asked.

"Some, but I already seen lots a rattle snakes in Arizona. We'd watch out for them after the floods.

***

Early one morning Jimmy started dismantling one of the big sheet-presses upstairs in the laundry building. Taking off the long presser handle to free up the rollers, he set it aside as he reached in the machine to get at the motor.

"Well, punk," Pickens sneered as he grabbed Jimmy and slammed him up against the machine, "aint no one in here to watch you become my bitch."

Shit! Your gonna have ta fuckin kill me first, you sonofabitch! His senses were reeling as a charge of rage blasted through his system. *This asshole aint never gonna give up on stalking me.* No stranger to fighting and defending himself even when taken by surprise, his mind snapped immediately to the rare weapon available. The presser handle, a four-foot chunk of steel, was lying on the machine right next to his hand. Without uttering a word, he grabbed the handle and with a wild swing, he took Pickens down with the first blow. He didn't stop. The predator had been relentless. Jimmy's fulminating anger had taken him over the edge. Later, he couldn't even remember what had happened after that.

When he came back to his senses, he was standing, his chest heaving, over Pickens' inert body at the bottom of the two flights of stairs yelling, "take that you fucker," and the first-floor guard was taking the presser handle out of his hand.

Jimmy was banished to his automatic thirty-day punishment in solitary. He'd been told that Pickens was alive and in a coma. In the dark cell, naked and cold, he played the scene over and over in his mind, stunned that he couldn't remember most of it. He guessed that he had hit the attacker more than once with his weapon and then kicked the vicious predator down both flights of stairs. *I musta been meanin to kill that asshole,* he decided. He found that realization quite disturbing, that and the fact that he had lost control in a red haze of anger.

Jimmy had the mental toughness as well as the life experience to endure the hardships of solitary confinement. But unlike the past, this episode represented a setback in the progress he'd been making toward reclaiming his life. While the lifer Pickens had had nothing to lose, Jimmy's future freedom was in jeopardy.

It wasn't long before he found the warm spot in the middle of the cell's cement floor. As he considered his punishment, he huddled over the warmth, assuming that it must be heat from a light bulb burning below the cell in some underground passage. He was sure that all his "good time" was forfeited, but would they bring him up on assault charges?

With time to reflect, Jimmy thought about learning to read and the fellow inmates who'd taken him on. *Damned if I'm not learnin to read,* he thought in amazement. *Chuck's one goddamn patient man.* While he could imagine how Chuck, so full of bullshit, could be a con man check writer, he had a harder time seeing the soft-spoken Jack committing a crime. A teacher on the outside, he had used his research skills and his flair for art to fashion an elaborate counterfeiting scheme making fake twenty-dollar gold pieces and selling them as collector's items until the government caught up with him.

Once he'd served out his time in solitary, Jimmy sat before the Prison Board newly showered and dressed. He'd told his story in a quiet, restrained manner. How he had tried to avoid Pickens' harassment and threats, and how he'd been trapped in the laundry where his attacker had no legitimate business. After a conference, the Board decided that the punishments already rendered would be sufficient. Jimmy would never know, but he suspected that Chuck might have spoken privately to the warden in his favor.

That night as he lined up in the chow line with his cellmates, Jimmy was taken aback by the sudden buzz his appearance created. All eyes seemed to be on him, men were pointing and giving him extra room as he passed. He could almost hear the comments, "watch Evans. He's a mean sonofabitch. Nearly killed Pickens." Gaining a reputation had never occurred to him. He had heard that Pickens was still recovering in the hospital.

Back in the swing of things, Jimmy took up where he'd left off. He was weakened by his month in confinement, but he was determined to regain his momentum.

It was another full month before Jimmy came face to face with Pickens again. By that time his friends were on the alert, watching his back in the dining hall lest the vengeful inmate sneak up on him and try to exact his revenge. But most of the time, Jimmy had to watch his own back.

He knew the day was bound to come when he would end up confronting Pickens again. He was always alert, but the thought didn't plague him. It happened in the rotunda, the main entryway to the prison offices and the classrooms. On his way to class, he spotted Pickens walking toward him. Jimmy faced his enemy, waiting.

Pickens stopped a few feet away and stared at Jimmy. "Punk, I'm gonna fuckin kill you," he said.

"Okay, but don't screw up, Pickens, because then it'll be my turn," Jimmy said, staring him down. "I won't screw up."

"You won't see it comin," Pickens hissed, as he shuffled away.

10

REACHING FOR A FUTURE

As summer brought days of bright sunshine to the island prison, Jimmy embraced life full speed ahead. While The Professors softball team was a competitive flop, the men had a good time playing on weekends until they were eliminated from the competition.

Jimmy continued to spend most of his evenings in class or playing handball. Over the summer, his reading improved to the point that he could finally follow the story once he started his third round of reading <u>Robinson Crusoe</u>.

Working in the library, the job he'd been assigned once he was released from solitary, proved to be another learning experience. While he checked out and shelved books, he practiced his reading skills. Once again, he could see Chuck's hand in his landing that prime job.

With Jack's prodding, Jimmy enrolled in the eighth-grade equivalency class where he began studying math, geography and English in preparation for testing for a Washington State eighth- grade diploma. Proud that Jack was confident in Jimmy's abilities, he gave his studies his all.

Working in the library gave him a job and a place to study. It also gave him another mentor, the head librarian, Mother Goddamn. The middle-aged inmate was a swarthy man of medium stature with dark, wavy hair graying at the temples, and he was an unabashed homosexual. Despite his deep, hoarse smoker's voice, all the prisoners referred to "her" in the feminine.

At first, Jimmy was wary, but he soon realized that Mother Goddamn was an unthreatening, kind person. She expected him to do his library duties and encouraged him in his studies. As he saw her in action, Jimmy was impressed with her compassionate treatment of those inmates who frequented the library and her genuine interest in hearing their stories. Although she would disappear into her office now and then with another inmate, he never saw her make a move on anyone.

"Jimmy, why didn't you learn to read in school?" Mother asked one day as she sat at the checkout counter. "The way you're reading now, there must have been some reason you didn't learn in school."

"I aint sure. Might be that we was movin all the time," he answered, welcoming the break from his studies.

"Was your dad in the military?"

"Yeah. My stepdad. We was movin from Texas to Louisiana and up to Michigan. Missed out on a lot a school."

"Was that when you were in first grade?"

"Yeah, I guess. By the time we was in Michigan, they stuck me in second grade then started actin like they thought I was stupid."

"What the hell. They didn't try putting you back in first grade?"

"N ah. By then I was mad, makin trouble in class. So they stuck me in with them retards weavin baskets."

"For Christsakes, where the hell was your mother?"

"She was busy workin just tryin to feed us. Even then we was hungry part of the time. Us kids always found us a job even when we was little. I had my first job earning money when I was about six."

"Wait a goddamn minute. Now you're shittin me. What the hell kind of work could you do at six years old?"

"Sold newspapers, shined shoes, worked in a nursery haulin compost, anythin we could find. That was down in Louisiana. Once we was in Michigan it was cold as hell. I talked the milkman into lettin me do the runnin for him, deliverin the milk up to the doors. Got up real early. Them damn Michigan kids was mean as hell. Me and my big brother had to fight them every damn day when we was comin home from school."

"Your brother didn't have any trouble learning?"

"Everett? No, he was smart as a whip. Once Mama brought home some old encyclopedias, and he'd sit and read them for hours. Made me mad as hell when he wouldn't come out and play."

"You found jobs all on your own?"

"Yeah. I liked workin. Always worked my ass off. And sometimes Mama thought of stuff. She'd come up with the damnedest schemes. When we was livin in Fresno, I was somewheres around twelve or so, she set us up sellin soda pop an candy bars to the golfers right beside the ninth hole at the fancy golf course. It's damn hot in the summer there, and them golfers would get mighty thirsty. Made the owners mad as hell, but we was on public land. Mama would drive us over there, and we'd haul a washtub full of ice from the car and set to sellin ice cold soda."

"She was damn enterprising, all right," Mother said, giving a throaty laugh.

"Yeah. We started hunting lost golf balls and sellin them, too. They was in big demand. Trouble was, the best place to get em was across the river. The golf course was sittin on a big bluff over the San Joaquin and when the rich guys was teeing off at the first hole, half the time the ball'd sail out over the river and land on a little island out there. Me and Everett and Billy would take a couple gunnysacks an go after them every couple a months."

"How in hell did you get to the island? That San Joaquin River's deep isn't it?"

"Yah, the current was too strong on our side. Us boys used to cross over on the Santa Fe Railroad trestle. From that side we could almost wade out to the island, not much swimmin involved. Over there the bridge was way high over the water, but we figured out how to work our way down to the river. Hardly took no time to fill them sacks with golf balls once we got on the island."

"One time when we was there, we had to quit collectin balls and turn tail. Somebody was takin pot shots at us with a twenty-two from over on the golf course side."

"No shit. They were shooting at you kids?"

"Yeah, them bullets was pingin off the rocks. Us boys made a run for it. Later on we figured out it must of been the golf course manager's son wantin the balls for hisself. I don't think he was amin to hit us, but it scared the shit outa us."

"I'm betting you went back."

"Yeah. When we run out of golf balls to sell."

"Weren't you afraid you'd get shot?"

"Yeah but we went anyway. The next time when we was goin back over the bridge to collect more balls, we got into another kind of situation. We was hiking along between the tracks and got about halfway across when we heard the train whistle behind us. Now, there aint no room on that long trestle for one damn thing except a train. And here come the goddamn Santa Fe Flier after our asses and the engineer's a blowin the whistle somethin fierce. Everett's out front screamin 'run, run' like we wasn't already scared shitless an runnin for our lives, and then I look back to see where Billy is an I see him stop dead. His shoe's fell off an he's goin back for it. I grab his hand screamin 'run' and we're runnin like hell again. All the time the bridge is gettin higher up over the river and the sound of the engine and the whistle's louder and louder. We aint gonna make it. I know it. When Everett jumps, I grab Billy an take him over the edge and the train passin sounds like thunder while we're fallin."

"Goddamn. Did you hit the water?" Mother asked, so absorbed in the story that she's leaning forward.

"No. That would of killed us. We all hit the side of the cliff gittin all scraped up while we was slidin and rollin down."

"Holy shit. Did your mother know you were using that trestle?"

"Nah. We didn't tell Mama."

"Did you ever go back?"

"Yeah, but we was a lot more careful. Didn't stay on that trestle no longer than we had to."

"Sounds like Everett was the leader of you three brothers."

"Yeah, he always looked out for us the best he could. He could be tough when he needed to be. There was a time when Everett and Billy decided I'd done them wrong some way and they decided that I deserved hangin. They did a pretty good job of it too. Didn't take me down till I passed out," Jimmy chuckled.

"The hell you say." Mother exploded. "Your big brother abused you?"

"Naw," Jimmy laughed. "Everett was the best brother ever. We was just rough kids."

***

While Jimmy was getting ready to take the eight-grade equivalency test, he was also getting much better at handball. The thick calluses on the palms of his hands showed the effort he'd been putting into perfecting his skills over the past six months. Sometime the skin on his hands would split as he pounded the ball relentlessly. Every week he was gaining on Old Haley. Having studied the old man's strategy, he began to capitalize on his weaknesses. Jimmy could hit the hard rubber ball equally well with either hand, and he made note of which shots were hard for his opponent to return. No longer was Jimmy run all over the court while the pro stood in one spot controlling the game. The tables were turning. In prime physical condition, Jimmy was enthralled with the challenge. In time he knew he would beat Old Haley. Men had already started betting on their games.

When Denny Akins moved into the cell, Jimmy and the rest of his cellmates tried to make it easy on the new kid. He seemed so young and vulnerable. Slightly built and smooth cheeked, Denny had a nervous tick and a soft voice that made him appear unsuited for the rigors of prison life. He and his brother had been tried in military court and been found guilty of raping a general's daughter.

Chuck was quick to include Denny and tell him how things worked around there. The kid was quiet, went to his job in the machine shop with Rodney and spent most of his evening time in the cell reading. Only a few months after Denny arrived, another inmate was transferred in from a youth authority facility. Gary Winslow was a tough-talking know-it-all who added an immediate note of tension to the cell. He came across as belligerent and dominant.

"Damnit, how the hell did I get stuck in a cell with a bunch a dumb sonsabitches?" he groused after being in the cell a few days. "Aint there no action around here?"

"You can wear off some steam down on the basketball court," Chuck suggested, unfazed by his attitude.

"Do I look like some idiot wants ta bounce a damn ball up and down some court?"

"Could be," Chuck said, drawing a laugh from the cellmates.

"Well shove it up your ass," Winslow said, storming off toward the gym.

Over the next month the arrogant newcomer strutted and challenged, creating an uneasy atmosphere in the cell. Once he learned that Chuck worked for the warden, he directed his animosity toward the other cellmates. Jimmy ignored Winslow most of the time but backed him down on several occasions when he turned aggressive. One night after lockdown Winslow went over the line.

"Cut that out," Denny whined, as Winslow punched him hard in the chest. All week he'd been taking the punches.

"Common ya little pussy, I'm gonna make you like it tonight," Winslow said, shoving him up against the bunk.

"Leave me alone."

"I'm gonna have ya."

"Please, leave me be," Denny begged.

"Quit whinin, punk. Best bend over," Winslow crooned as he delivered two punches to Billy's chest.

"Hey, back off from the kid," Jimmy said, jumping out of his bunk.

"Mind your own goddamn business, Evans."

"There's plenty of that action around this place, but it aint happenin in this cell."

"You goin ta fuckin stop me?"

"You bet your ass. It aint happenin."

"Well, fuck you," Winslow said, retreating to his own bunk.

At lunchtime the next day, Rodney warned Jimmy, "Watch out. I heard Winslow bragging that he was planning to cut you. Goddamn, I was glad you stuck up for the kid. I can't believe that asshole."

"Yeah, thanks. I'll be ready for him."

That night right after dinner, Jimmy confronted Winslow who was sitting on his bunk. "Have you got it straight now about what kind of action goes on in this cell?"

Without a word, Winslow shoved his right hand into his pants pocket as he rocked forward to get up and come face to face. With that confirmation, Jimmy turned loose a lethal ball-busting kick that the aggressive bastard never saw coming. He collapsed with an agonized squeal. Rolling him on his back, Jimmy quickly pulled a makeshift knife, a sharpened piece of metal wrapped with tape on the handle end, from Winslow's pocket. He was indeed planning to cut Jimmy. Without a weapon being found there would be fewer questions on the part of the guards. Grabbing the incapacitated, moaning hoodlum, Jimmy and Chuck hauled him out onto the landing. Once they'd placed his bedroll and the contents of his locker beside him, they called the guards.

"That guy wants to move," Chuck said when the guards arrived. "He doesn't like this cell."

"What happened to him?"

"He seems to have hurt himself. Maybe he should go to the infirmary."

"Yeah. Looks like it," a guard said, displaying a total lack of curiosity.

When Winslow got out of the infirmary three weeks later, he avoided Jimmy entirely. He never threatened revenge. The cellmates thought that by then he'd been wised up about Jimmy's tough reputation. Later Denny would opt to move out of the cell where he had found protection and move into a cell where he would become another inmate's bitch. Neither Jimmy nor Chuck understood it, but in prison acceptance came with the territory.

∗∗∗

In September representatives from the Washington State Board of Education tested Jimmy along with six other men. He succeeded in passing the eighth-grade exams, later receiving his diploma. That victory was something Jimmy had never thought possible.

After a full summer of playing handball in the evenings, Jimmy started holding his own on the court. His first win had been sweet, but Old Haley had redoubled the attack shots that had made him legend. Now, with total concentration, Jimmy could beat the old man nearly every other game. They drew crowds and wagering on the winner became a hot item of interest in the prison. As summer faded into fall, Jimmy got even better at running Old Haley all over the court, reversing rolls. The old man still had tricky shots in his arsenal, but daily Jimmy was learning to counter them.

Nearly a year had passed since his despairing arrival on the island. Now he was making progress in his life, achieving milestones, and he began to feel confident. Despite the fact that he still stayed alert watching his back, Pickens hadn't made good on his threats. In the mess hall, Jimmy's cellmates kept an eye on the man as he went from table to table as a server, but so far, he'd never approached their table.

∗∗∗

"There's a new class starting. You should sign up for it," Chuck urged early that fall.

"You're full of shit, Chuck," Jimmy said with a smile. "What're you tryin to wring me into now?"

"It's something you already know a little about," he said with a mischievous grin.

"Come on, you bastard. Tell."

"It's called 'The Power of Positive Thinking.'" The idea is to learn the skills you'll need to get ahead in the outside world.

"What makes you think I know anything about that shit?"

"You're one of the most positive thinkers I've ever met."

"Bullshit!"

"No. Look how you decided to beat Old Haley at handball. You just made up your mind and thought positive. And you backed it up with hard work. When you take a notion to do something, you never quit."

"Yeah. I'm listenin," Jimmy said, boosted by the affirmation. "The class is designed to help you direct that kind of positive thinking to improve your life. Just sign up. What have you got to lose?"

"Damn, Chuck. You're some smooth talker."

At first, Jimmy was sorry he'd signed up for the class when he found out after the second meeting that he would have to do some public speaking. *Goddamn that Chuck. Blowin smoke up my ass so now I can't just go and quit,* he thought as he prepared for his first informal talk. Luckily, he had many interesting stories about Alaska to draw from.

"Can you listen to the talk I've gotta give in class tomorrow?" Jimmy asked Mother Goddamn during a quiet time in the library.

"Sure. Is it for the Dale Carnegie course?"

"Yeah. That damn con-man Chuck roped me in."

Once Mother had listened and made suggestions, she asked Jimmy about some of the adventures he'd had in Alaska.

"From hearing your talk, it sounds as though you really enjoyed your life in Alaska."

"Yeah. It was great. I guy could work hard and live free. It was a real wild place and the people was interestin."

"You went back, didn't you, when you got out of prison?"

"Yeah."

"I was wondering why you got into crime. You'd never done that kind of thing before, had you?"

"No. I was fuckin crazy. I was so angry and tired of bein screwed. But it didn't make no sense."

"Couldn't you just go home?"

"Home? No. I didn't have no home. By then I'd been on my own for a long time."

"What about your older brother? Weren't you close to him?"

"Everett? No, I didn't have him neither. He was fucking murdered in Korea."

"I can see that'd be enough to make you angry."

"Yeah. It did."

Jimmy couldn't help but like Mother Goddamn. She was always setting aside books for him and the latest National Geographic Magazine. He had discovered the true pleasure and distraction of reading. His speed was picking up as he read himself to sleep each night and filled any idle time with stories. Over time he had seen that Mother was a good listener not only for him, but for any inmate who needed to talk. She never gossiped. He guessed that's why they called her "Mother." He also noticed that she never talked about herself.

***

As fall turned into winter, McNeil Island endured constant storms that brought torrents of rain. While the days were short, wet and dark, the hours became long and monotonous for the inmates. Missing the outlet of playing handball, Jimmy, along with most of the other prisoners, became increasingly restless.

"Hey, Jimmy," Chuck said in his best sales-pitch voice. "I've found you the chance of a lifetime, but you've got to jump on it fast."

"What the hell're you sellin me now?"

"Have you ever thought of being a barber?"

"No. But I got pretty damn good at cuttin my nephews' hair."

"There a new barbering class starting next week. You should sign up, so you'll have a sure job when you get out."

"Goddamnit, Chuck, I'm sick of classes."

"Hey, you can get a Washington State Barber's License once you finish the course. It takes eighteen months and there's lots of guys wanting to sign up. You'll have time to finish before you walk."

"Yeah. I'll have time and then some. But, you know, I aint never had no trouble gettin a job. I'm strong and I'm a damn hard worker."

"It'll be good for you, Jimmy. And it'll make the time pass easier. You need a challenge and a little change of pace."

"Yeah. I'm getting a little cooped up in here now that I got finished with all that public speakin you talked me into," Jimmy laughed, shaking his head even as he knew that Chuck was looking out for him.

"It did you good," Chuck said, turning loose a peal of irresistible laughter.

***

"Goddamnit, Chuck," Jimmy said, slamming his new study manual down on the table in the center of the cell. "Look at this. I've got to learn all this bullshit."

"It looks harder than it really is, Jimmy. Come on I'll help you get started."

"Wait a minute. I thought I was learnin to cut hair. I wasn't bargainin for learnin no anatomy, goddamn names in Latin, for christsake."

"You're not letting a few Latin names scare you off, are you?"

"Looks to me like a lot more studyin than doin."

"Yeah. That's why you get a barber's license. They'll be testing you on this shit. Now are you going to tell me you can't do it?"

"Hell no. Not when you put it that way," Jimmy said, laughing despite his irritation.

"Hey. You can count on my help. And Jack will pitch in, too."

Once he became committed Jimmy jumped into his studies, hell-bent as usual. The going was tough but learning to read had been harder. Within the month he was cutting hair in the prison barbershop every day. Jimmy discovered he had a natural knack for giving a nice even cut. Before shaving any of the general population, the student barbers practiced on each other with a straight razor, stropping the blade to a razor-sharp edge and shaving clean all the angles of the face and throat without nicking the skin. There was a certain element of trust involved in the process, an element hard to fully embrace in a fellow prisoner, but the final hot towel treatment was as close to pure pleasure as any could find in that island prison.

"Gave my first shave today," Jimmy said over dinner with his cellmates.

"Yeah. How' d it go?" Chuck asked, his eyes twinkling as he waited for Jimmy to drop the rest of the story on them.

"Well, great. My hands was shakin, me bein kinda nervous and all. Took me the longest goddamn time, but I shaved him clean as a whistle. Never come close to nickin him."

"Good. It's nice to get the first one out of the way," Chuck said. "I like the hot towel treatment best. It makes me so relaxed I sometimes fall asleep."

"Well, the guy got kinda restless. He didn't say nothin, but he wouldn't let me do the hot pack afterwards."

"Goddamn, he missed the best part."

"I guess he decided he'd sat there long enough. Didn't say a goddamn word the whole time, but he seemed kinda shaky when he was gettin up. That's when I seen all a his clothes was drenched in sweat. I figured the poor bastard must a been thinkin I might slip with them shaky hands and slit his throat."

"It sounds like you might have lost your first customer," Chuck snickered as all the cellmates broke into laughter.

Through the long winter and into spring Jimmy worked in the barbershop by day and studied by night. He worked long hours boning up on the anatomy of the head, hands and feet, learning the nearly unpronounceable names and functions of muscles, nerves and blood vessels. He studied diseases of the skin, proper handling and sterilization of equipment. Digging into each class, he frequently called on Chuck to drill him and help him prepare for tests. Periodically, he faced official testing by examiners who came from Washington State. He was always prepared and amazed to pass with flying colors.

***

Summer was in the air; Jimmy was back out on the handball court and poor Old Haley had finally met his match. Jimmy, redoubling his effort after the long winter, took the old man to the cleaners step by step. He wasn't a particularly generous winner nor was the deposed champ a very good loser.

"Take that old man," Jimmy grunted, whacking the handball so that it spun and dropped dead to the old guy's left.

Old Haley never talked. He was used to slaughtering his opponent from one set position, while the other guy was reduced to a panting klutz. In all the months he'd played Jimmy, he'd given no quarter.

"You skinned through on the last game. But now I'm takin you out," Jimmy said, challenging his opponent's mental game as he slammed the ball home once again. When Old Haley began to lose on a regular basis, he simply quit coming, leaving Jimmy as the reigning champ and a major void for the betting crowd who had relished the competition. There were many new challengers, but Jimmy continued to reign supreme.

Softball teams formed up again for the summer league, some twenty of them. On weekends, Chuck, Jack, Rodney, Jimmy and a few other guys, The Professors Team, warmed up for the season by winning a couple of games. Jimmy enjoyed the spirited sense of teamwork, the easy joking around.

The barbering classes were still hard work but going well. When Jimmy was assigned to cover the Monday evening hours that the barbershop stayed open to accommodate the outside trustees, he ran into a hitch. One night, covered in hair, the barbers closed up shop and made a dash for the showers. They arrived just as Three-Fingered-Jack, a particularly spiteful guard, was locking the place up.

"Sir, we need five minutes just to get the hair off," Jimmy said.

"You're too late."

"They always let us shower when we stay late to cut hair," he insisted.

"No. You're too late. Get on to your cells."

Jimmy was thoroughly pissed when he slammed into the cell. "What a asshole," he growled. "Now I gotta hit the damn bunk wearin everybody's goddamn hair. That prick!"

On the next Monday, the hostile guard who had a couple of missing digits, let the men shower after work glaring at Jimmy the whole time. It wasn't hard for Jimmy to put together the fact that the warden had called the little tyrant on the carpet, no doubt Chuck's doing. But there would be repercussions.

Soon Jimmy experienced the guard's retribution.

"Hey you, Evans!" Three-Fingered-Jack barked. "Spread em," he ordered, pulling Jimmy out of the chow line and patting him down for contraband.

"Goddamnit, Chuck. Now I got Three-Fingered-Jack on my ass. Shit, I'm gettin my showers, but he's out to screw me. He's pullin me out a line an pattin me down every time he sets eyes on me. It's only a matter of time before he finds somethin or plants it and I lose my good time."

"I think you've got to outsmart him," Chuck said, after a few minutes of contemplation.

"Well, he's makin my life hell."

"Yeah. What about playing his game? Maybe going right up to him every time you see him and being really solicitous."

"Like what?"

"You know, like 'how are you today?' and that kind of thing."

"Shit, kissin his ass? Huh. I guess it's worth a try. He can't exactly throw me in solitary for bein extra nice," Jimmy said, grinding his jaw.

The next day as soon as he saw the aggressive guard, Jimmy sprang into action.

"Good morning, sir!" he gushed. "Are you having a good day?"

"Get back in line," Three-Fingered-Jack mumbled, turning his back and walking rapidly away.

For the better part of a week, Jimmy kept up the pressure.

Whenever he saw the man, he turned on the gratuitous charm and put him on the run. The revenge shakedowns were over, but Jimmy would keep his guard up.

***

The mid-summer carnival was a welcome break that the inmates looked forward to every year. This year, Jimmy had one goal in mind. He wanted to win the greased-log contest. The previous summer he'd washed out in the first round but, always geared to winning, he'd had a whole year to think through his strategy.

Carnival day arrived with a clear sky and a gentle ocean breeze. Chuck, with his ebullient personality, always made these occasions more fun. While the big, beefy man laughed all the way across the yard, Jimmy ran the three-legged race with him. They stumbled along all off kilter, finally collapsing over the finish line dead last.

When Jimmy climbed astride the greased log, though, he was intent on winning. Holding his sawdust-filled gunnysack at the ready, he waited for his opponent to take the first swing, took the blow and used the guy's own momentum to nudge him right over the side. Employing his inherent grasp of basic physics, Jimmy's plan worked as he took on all comers. Taking a clue from last years' experience, the consummate competitor had adopted an added strategy to give himself an edge on traction. A quick trip to the sidelines between rounds and a brief plop of his butt in the dirt provided a nice coat of grit on his greased-up pants. Even as his energy flagged, Jimmy determinedly defended his log as each fresh contestant tried to unseat him. Jimmy was in his element. The big blue ribbon was just the icing on the cake.

In the softball league, The Professors, amazing themselves, were cruising toward the top of the standings as the playoffs commenced at the end of the season. Jimmy was consistently pitching no-hitters and his teammates at bat were, more often than not, connecting with the ball. It was an exciting series for the team considering that Jimmy and Jack were the only two who bore any resemblance to an athlete.

In the final playoff game, the score was tied at one-all when The Professors came to bat. Jimmy was kicking himself for giving up that run. In turn, he had hit the only homer so far for his team. Now he was rooting for Chuck who was at bat, knowing that even a base hit would make his friend's day. And there it was, a hard swing and a resounding thunk as he lambasted the ball. As it sailed into the outfield, Chuck took off in his chugging sprint determined to make it a home run. Jimmy could see the glee in his friend's proud posture. As Chuck pushed himself, concentrating on the distance to the base, he lost track of the ball, which had bounced and continued to skip across the outfield. The Professors were up on their feet cheering for all they were worth as he approached second base, and he finally glanced up to check on the ball. Pounding into second base, Chuck went down suddenly like a fallen tree. And there he lay writhing in pain.

"Goddamnit, Chuck!" Jimmy goaded, once his cellmate came back from the hospital with a big leg cast. "You're the only asshole I know could break his damn leg jumpin on second base."

"Did I ever say I was a goddamn athlete?"

"No, you sure as hell didn't. You aint no liar," Jimmy laughed.

"Well, we almost won."

"You made one damn sweet hit there."

"Yeah. I did, didn't I," Chuck said, proudly as his body shook with his good-natured laugh.

***

Winter set in again and Jimmy could seldom get out to play handball with the pouring rain. He was busy with his classes and his barbering job. Now that he was doing more skilled labor, his pay had increases from the standard three cents per hour all the way up to thirty cents. He was already thinking about having at least a couple hundred dollars saved by the time he was released. With "good time" he had less than a year left to serve.

While Chuck was recovering, Jimmy sought out Jack's help with his studies. The tall, quiet teacher was generous with his time and interested in seeing Jimmy succeed.

As spring approached, Jimmy began to dread taking the state board examinations. Not only would he be tested on all the material covered in the eighteen-month course, but he would have to pass the practical examination where he would be observed giving a haircut, a shave and a manicure.

For several months both Chuck, who was getting around better, and Jack helped Jimmy review all of his workbooks. On the late June day that the Washington State Licensing Examiners arrived, Jimmy was nearly in a state of nervous collapse. *Goddamnit, I passed all the tests before. Now I gotta show them assholes I know this stuff. All that time I spent studyin. Christ Almighty, I gotta pass.* And pass he did after waiting excruciating weeks for testing results toward the end of October. By that time, Jimmy had his eyes turned toward the mainland and the freedom that was moving within his reach.

***

Jimmy had his discharge date set for late spring in 1958. His last week at McNeil Island went slow and fast. Sometimes, especially at night, the minutes crawled by at a maddening pace while Jimmy lay awake. One moment he was charged up with anticipation and confidence and the next he'd be fighting a jolt of dread. At times it felt more like waiting for his execution rather that marking time until his release.

With Jack's oversight he had written a letter, a remarkable first, to his Aunt Ida asking if he could stay at her place for a while once he was released. He was greatly relieved by her warm response. He had kept her unread letter and felt no desire to read it even then. He was done with the past.

Two weeks before his scheduled release, he'd spent several hours down in the clothing room picking out his discharge outfit. After trying on a number of suits, he'd decided on a tweed sports jacket, dark brown slacks, a casual blue short-sleeved shirt and a pair of brown leather shoes. Accustomed to wearing prison blue, Jimmy had felt strangely lost as he handed the new clothes over to the clerk. They would be pressed and ready for him on his day of discharge.

Once the word was out about his upcoming release, Jimmy and his cellmates began to be more vigilant about watching his back. He'd heard of inmates settling grudges just before a guy got out. If Pickens was going to make his move it would be coming any time.

His last day of incarceration dawned bright and clear. Jimmy's nerves crackled with tension as he quietly emptied his locker, bestowing his stash of cigarettes and candy bars on his cellmates before accompanying them to breakfast in the dining hall one last time. Jimmy adopted Chuck's forced cheeriness, acting casual to mask his impending sense of loss.

"Go get em, tiger," Chuck said, reaching out to shake hands as they were leaving the dining area. "You've got the balls to make a life for yourself, Jimmy. It's been a real education knowing you."

"Thanks," Jimmy said, gripping his friend's hand.

Both men turned away abruptly, Chuck going on to his job in the warden's office and Jimmy back to his cell to pack up. Returning alone to the cell where he'd lived for the past three years, he gathered his few remaining belongings from his locker and rolled his thin mattress into a compact bundle with his bedding inside. He hastily turned away from the exposed springs on the bare bunk and rushed through the cell door knowing he'd erased all signs of his presence.

The clerk in the discharge area was expecting him, but in the end, it took a couple of hours to take care of all the details. After turning in his bedding, Jimmy dressed in his new clothes and began signing all the paperwork. His two hundred and twenty-three dollars of savings that he'd put aside from his barbering was given to him in cash with a leather wallet.

While his new duffel bag came with a change of boxer shorts and a pair of socks, he carefully added the evidence of his hard work and achievement: his eighth-grade diploma, his Carnegie Certificate and his Washington State Barber's License. He also threw in his "King of the Log" blue ribbon.

Finally, he was ready, and Jimmy just sat there for another hour waiting for the transport boat. As his apprehension grew by the minute, that hour turned into hard time.

Jimmy took long strides nearly outpacing the guard to reach the yard gate in the prison perimeter fence. His heart hammered as he waited for it to swing open, feeling almost as though he were making an escape. As he descended the series of cement steps leading to the boat dock, he never looked back. As surely as the rain would continue to fall on McNeil Island, he was putting prison life behind him. And with it, the world he'd known for the past three years.

He boarded the transport boat mid-morning on a bright, clear day. On the short run to the mainland, the brilliant sunshine reflecting off the waters of Puget Sound was a welcome contrast to the dismal howling storm that had raged on the evening when he'd been brought to the island in the supply boat. That trip was still sharp in his memory.

Once he'd alighted on the mainland, he climbed the ramp leading up from the dock and got in the waiting prison car. The driver was talkative, but Jimmy felt too overwhelmed to carry on a conversation. He had to contain an explosive energy that he knew was caused by a bad case of nerves. His stomach was in knots. It had all come down to this day. Now it was on him to make good.

The driver wished him good luck when he dropped him off at the Tacoma Greyhound Bus Station. Jimmy nodded and, grabbing his duffel bag, sprinted into the station. Using the prison coupon, he bought a ticket on the last bus leaving for Porterville, California that night, stuffing it in his wallet with his two hundred dollars. He had needed a destination and being with his cousin Glenda and Aunt Ida had seemed the best choice.

Moments later, he burst out through the station doors, feeling so anxious that the building seemed too small a space. He walked for hours, up and down the main street, going as far as he wanted in one direction then turning back to pass the bus station and charge toward the opposite end of town. All afternoon and into the evening he walked, carrying his duffel bag, breathing in the fresh air, and soaking up the sunshine. Darkness fell and still he walked, stopping only long enough to buy a Coke. While his explosive energy started to burn off as he became exhausted, the thought of riding in a closed bus still brought a sense of dread.

It was nearly midnight when he boarded the bus to Porterville. As he took a seat in the rear of the Greyhound, he braced his trembling hands on his knees and closed his eyes. *Damnit, I'm ready,* he told himself. *I aint never been without a job for long. I can take care of myself like I always done.* And now he had a trade. He could read. And he'd spent three years with men who believed in him. At twenty-four Jimmy would start again. Live his life. He was free.

ACKNOWLEDGMENTS

Writing this story and getting it into print took a team of friends and family to whom I am most grateful. It has been a trip. My thanks to Barbara Hunter who suggested and encouraged; to my readers Anne Tolliver and Stacey Evans who brought insights and managed proof reading; to my friends Brenda Gregory and Stacey McGurk for their support: and to my granddaughter, Courtney Evans, for her beautiful cover art.

ABOUT THE AUTHOR

This author loves stories. My life has come in stages, many seeming dramatic, at least to me. That realization hits home while I reminisce as I watch age eighty rushing toward me. Raising a family, working as an RN, helping with family businesses, have all kept me on the move. Still, over the years, I managed to explore my artistic side creating scenic oil paintings. Now seems my time for words. In retirement, with a lifetime of experiences to explore, I thought my husband tales quite remarkable. So, here's to Jimmy!

Carol C. Evans